Once
We
Were
Friends

a novel
by

Bryan Mooney

Books by Bryan Mooney

~

Once We Were Friends
Indie-Murder in the City
The POTUS Papers
Eye of the Tiger
Love Letters
A Second Chance
A Box of Chocolates
Christmas in Vermont

These books are available wherever fine books are sold.

Acknowledgments-

I would be remiss if I did not thank all of my wonderful and faithful readers at Aberdeen. I appreciate your support and encouragement. Thank you, thank you, and thank you! I would also like to thank my editor, Erica Orloff, and my muse Judith Hanses for their help. Finally, I would like to thank my friend and cohort, Dr. Robert Johnston for all his technical help and assistance. Thanks, "Dr. Bob."

Dedicated to
My Bonnie

Once We Were Friends

Summer 1959. It was a different time, a quieter and gentler time. America was at peace or rather it was a time between wars. For Davey Malloy it was the start of summertime in Saint Louis, a week after Memorial Day and days after his twelfth birthday. He now had his freedom and the entire summer to do whatever he wanted. He and his best friends Timmy and Sunny were free to go hiking, fishing, play ball, biking, swimming, and exploring. They would have a grand old time that year, but that summer would turn out different than they ever would have expected. It was a summer Davey would never forget, a summer that changed his life forever.

Years later, one became a cop and one landed on death row—but life always returned to the summer of '59. If only...

Chapter One

Midnight –

Nathaniel Hutchinson had settled into bed for some long-needed rest; he was tired and worn-out. The seventy-eight-year-old attorney soon began to drift off, dreaming of fishing with his friends, laughing, some beer drinking, and card playing, as his eyes finally closed. The farm outside was peaceful and quiet with only the sounds of crickets and the patient hoot of the white barn owl drifting through the open bedroom window. It was a cool Florida night providing welcome relief from the warm sunny September days.

The phone on the old wooden bedside table rang and yanked him from his peace and quiet. The time on the alarm clock clicked over to read 12:03 A.M. He lifted the receiver. "Hello?" he said.

"Hello? Mr. Hutchinson?" the voice on the other end queried.

"Yes?" said his shallow voice, still craving sleep; his eyes remained closed.

"Sir, this is Gladys Turner at the Circuit Clerk's office. I know it's after midnight, sir, and my husband would shoot me if he knew I was working this late, but I thought y'all would want to know," Nate heard her say with her distinctive South Georgian accent. "I just received an email and… well, sir, your appeal was denied. I'm so sorry; I wish I had better news for you."

He sucked in a deep breath before saying, "Thank ya, Gladys." He rubbed his eyes as he sat up and swung his feet over the side of the bed, running his hand over his balding head. Long, thin strands of gray tresses now replaced his once-healthy head of jet-black hair.

"Good luck to you, sir. I'm sorry I didn't have better news for you. And I'm sorry to wake you and the missus. Good night."

"Good night, Gladys." He hung up the phone and bent over in sad disappointment glancing at the alarm clock again. It read 12:07 A.M. Timothy Elroy Walker's execution would take place in less than eighteen hours. At six P.M. Walker would receive a lethal injection at the Florida state prison in Starke, Florida.

Nate knew the drill and knew the amount of work that now had to be done in order to prepare for Walker's final appeal. He did not have a lot of time. His next step was to file a writ with the emergency applications department at the United States Supreme Court.

Rubbing his eyes, he knew the appeals office opened at nine A.M. He glanced at his pillow. He breathed in deep. *Best get started,* he said to himself.

He knew his client was guilty; Walker had told him so at their first meeting and even confessed to it in court at his trials. Now he had been on death row for twenty-six years. Nate was Walker's fourth lawyer and had been for the past ten years. Walker had fired him so many times that it had become a running joke. *How do you fire a pro-bono attorney?* Now, it had come down to this, and this was no laughing matter. He took in a deep breath and began to cough.

"You okay, Nate?" asked Agnes, his wife of forty-nine years. He felt her kind and gentle hand stroke his back and touch his neck, calling him back to a tempting sleep.

"It was denied." He sighed. "God damn it, they denied our appeal. All that work, gone. I had hopes for that appeal."

"Oh, Nate. I'm so sorry but you gave it your best, darlin'. Come back to sleep, you need your rest. You been looking real tired here lately."

"No... I got things to do." He said with a labored sigh.

"Nathaniel, I know you were counting on that appeal to give him some more time. However, it's over now, dear. Let the law take its own course. Come back to bed, please?"

He believed in the concept of the death penalty. He felt it was a deterrent to crime, but he always thought it should never be quick or easy. That's just the way it should be.

Two months earlier, the aging attorney had filed a last-minute appeal with the State Supreme Court. He filed his writ after the U.S. Supreme Court ruled in another case that intellectual capacity should not be determined solely by a score on an I.Q. test. The State of Florida ruled someone had to have an IQ of at least 70 before an execution could take place, Walker's IQ was officially listed at 71, but

Nate always questioned whether Walker somehow rigged the tests. He was smart, real smart. Nevertheless, legally, it was still grounds for an appeal, he thought to himself. Now that appeal had been denied. The next step was to ask the highest court in the land to spare his client's life. The court of last resort, the United States Supreme Court.

"I have other things that must be done," he murmured.

"For Walker?" Agnes asked leaning closer. "That ungrateful ingrate... ummmhf?" Her voice trailed off, and she stopped short of finishing what she was saying. "Nate, he never appreciates anything you do for him; he never did. And not once did he say thank you for all you've done." His body tensed next to her.

He turned to look at her and solemnly told her, "Agnes, dear heart, I took a vow when I became an attorney that I would fight for my clients to the very best of my ability. Guilty or innocent, that's what I swore to do. Nothing should be left undone, especially when someone's life is on the line—regardless of whose life it is. I take the vows I make very serious... just like the vow I took when we got married. And have I ever let you down?"

Ashamed, she whispered, "No, dear. I love you. I'm just worried for you, that's all, your heart, and all." Changing the subject she asked, "What's next?"

"Time for me to get up and get my final appeal paperwork ready and I don't have a lot of time. They open at nine o'clock. You stay here in bed and get some rest. I'll try to be quiet. Go back to sleep."

When he stood, Agnes felt the bed lift up and saw his outline standing there in the dark. She reached out and touched his leg, "I'll be down in a little bit to make some coffee and then some breakfast. I love you."

"Love ya too, sweetheart." He kissed her forehead and grabbed his wristwatch from the bedside table. He looked at the time, *eighteen hours to go before the execution. Not a lot of time.* He headed for the bathroom and closed the door so as not disturb her. He slowly shaved the grey stubble from his weathered face and began to plot his next filing. *This may be Walker's last chance at a reprieve.* He knew he would have to talk to his client this morning. *But what would he say to him? What could he say? The truth always worked before...but now?*

The black-and-white tile floor was cold on his feet. Swinging open the broken door to the old medicine cabinet, the one he promised Agnes he would fix years ago, he looked for his heart medication. He searched among the multitude of amber bottles with various white labels until he found the right one. *Bottle's empty. Shit.* He forgot, he had meant to get a refill when he was in town Saturday, but with the deadline approaching and all... well...*Don't tell Agnes; she'll only worry. I'll pick some up later at the pharmacy when I go into town.*

He washed his face, combed his thinning hair, then brushed his teeth and since he was working from home, he put on his worn but comfortable khakis, the ones with the rip in the back pocket. He slipped on his tattered sneakers and an old blue chambray work shirt that was hanging from the back of the closet door. After pulling up his red suspenders over his shoulders, snapping them to his chest for good measure, he walked down the creaking wooden back steps and could smell the aroma of fresh coffee emanating from the kitchen. He smiled. *Agnes.*

"Agnes sweetheart, I told you to sleep some more. I won't be long doing this stuff. Hell, I've done so many of them for all the other courts. They all ask for the same thing, mountains of paperwork and old files."

She turned from her stovetop and gave him a gentle smile. As he walked past the old coffeemaker, she glanced at her knight in shining armor. He kissed her neck, gave her a loving tap on her behind, and then took a sip from her coffee mug sitting on the small kitchen table. She poured him a fresh cup of coffee and handed it to him, flavored just the way he liked it, with a hint of cinnamon. His cup was an old mug his father had given him years ago, right before he died. The golden emblem was fading, Elks Lodge #57, Jacksonville, Florida. An imprint on the side read *Judge Theodore "Hutch" Hutchinson—Retired.* His father had served on the bench for over thirty-seven years before he died, one year after his retirement.

Nate stood, looked at her in her housecoat, gave her a peck on the cheek, and headed for his office. "Thank ya, darlin'."

"Breakfast in an hour," she said from the kitchen as he walked away. He waved his hand in acknowledgement without turning around then shut the door to his office behind him so Hero, his aging golden retriever, would not disturb him.

Nate's wood-paneled office workplace grew smaller every year as the boxes, filled with paperwork, files, interviews, writs, and court hearings for Walker, continued to grow and crowd him out of his prized real estate. His office was in stark contrast to the rest of the small farmhouse, which was kept neat and proper by his well-organized wife. In her domain, there was a place for everything and everything was in its place, but in his office, files and boxes were scattered everywhere. Only he knew how it was organized.

She hated to come inside his office, and when she did, she had to resist the temptation to clean it up and organize it for him. This was his domain. There were over sixteen boxes on the floor, lining the wall, and when she would ask if he needed to keep everything forever. "No," he would always say, "Just until it's over."

Twenty minutes later, she tapped on his office door and handed him another cup of coffee.

He looked at his watch, 1:15 am. *Time is running out.*

3:39 A.M.

She couldn't sleep she was so excited. Or rather sad and excited at the same time as she grabbed her t-shirt from the chair and slipped on her sandals and headed for the kitchen to make herself some tea. The cottage seemed especially cold that morning as she walked downstairs. An empty bed was always cold. She saw her Irish setter, Kelly sleeping in the corner. Must be dreaming, as her mouth continued to move while she slept.

Today was a going to be a different kind of day for Sari Novak. Today was her last day at the company she started and ran for the last ten years. Today, she was selling her company and turning over control to the world's largest purveyor of coffee, The Seattle Coffee Company. She had met and far exceeded the goal she had originally set for herself when she started the company. Her goal was to raise and donate two million dollars to the Anna Novak Research Fund. She managed to raise over three and one half million over that period. She was proud of what she had done.

Six years earlier, she had moved her company headquarters from Ohio to Miami to be closer to her overseas shipping connections. It was a long and tedious relocation, but it was already showing positive results. Selling the company now was the right thing for her to do. Her time would be her own, to do with what she wanted. Time … all she needed was time.

She walked down the steps of the beach cottage, making her way around the piles of boxes, which lined the wall and then accompanied her down the steps. She had put everything else in storage from her South Beach condominium but brought the boxes containing her most precious things with her. She had many memories in those boxes. Good memories.

Her condo was far bigger than the cottage, too big, with five bedrooms, six baths, three wrap around balconies and pool, but here at the beach cottage it felt like home. Probably because of him. She didn't miss South Beach and was glad she had moved here, she only wished he was here. She poured a cup of tea, looked out the window, and watched the moon still shining over the ocean as the waves rolled in. This was the same ocean she had seen so many times from her balcony in Miami, but here it seemed more personal, more intimate, as if it was hers, all hers... and his. The pain in her side had returned and had migrated to her back. It hurt. Time to sit down.

Maybe now she could finish the book she had started. But she never had the time. She glanced at her laptop on the desk, and with grim determination set down her teacup and began to write, and write. No time like the present. Once again, time, precious time.

Chapter Two

7:57 A.M.

She knew they were going to be late. Why would today be any different? But it was. Today was the day.

"Mitchell...come on...get up!" she muttered aloud after entering his dark hotel room. "You have to be at your book reading in an hour." There was no activity from the bed. "I thought you'd be up by now. It's nearly eight o'clock." Still no movement.

Finally, she heard a voice speak from beneath the covers, "Carol?" he groaned; it sounded more like an accusation than a question. She often wished she could have seen him in action back when he was a homicide cop. From all she'd heard about him he was ...

"Carol?" he repeated.

"Yes, who else would it be?"

Carol Ann Litchard, Cal to her friends, thrust open the drapes. In one sweeping motion, the twenty-nine-year-old literary agent invoked brightness to the darkened room, allowing the early-morning summer sunlight to stream inside and chase away the shadows.

He pulled the sheets higher over his head to cover his eyes to keep out the start of the day.

She looked over at her client as his leg moved slightly, falling out from beneath the covers. "Come on my friend, time to get up," she said shaking the bed in an effort to wake him.

No movement until a long groan greeted her. "Oh no... I need coffee," he mumbled like a dead man, sounding more like the tough homicide cop he used to be.

"Here, have a sip of this" she volunteered, handing him her latte in a foam cup, "then take a shower and get dressed. Hurry up. We don't have a lot of time."

Fingers appeared from underneath the sheets, searching for the coffee cup.

She saw the long scar across the back of his hand, which extended up his arm. She guided the cup to his clutching fingers and watched it disappear under the sheets.

"Ugh God, Cal," he said ... "that's just milk. There's no coffee in that. Order me some real coffee will you?" he muttered in disgust.

"Hey, I'm your literary agent, not your servant, remember?" she said with a grunt to her star client.

She had met him three years earlier while working at the Gardner Agency when her boss, Gayle Gardner, was still alive. Carol had been working for Gayle since leaving college seven years earlier, then last year Gayle assigned her to work with him. His first book was good, got rave reviews, and it sold well. She had a great planning meeting with him in anticipation of his book being completed. He and the stories he wrote intrigued her; he put his heart and soul into his writing- but also had the true skills of a writer to back up his ideas.

Over a year ago, the three of them had dinner one night when he visited New York to talk about his latest book. The next evening just the two of them met again and had a great meal, a bottle of wine, and then another, followed by dessert and coffee. They talked for hours upon hours. She could listen to him talk forever. Her life had not been the same since. He drew her in closer and closer with his outlook on life and his writing. He was a complicated man. When Gayle died two months later in an auto accident and the agency disbanded, Carol opened her own shop and approached him about representing him. She was not hopeful since the other New York powerhouse literary agencies were also courting him. She had no job, no clients, no money and no prospects. She was surprised but grateful when he called and said yes. She needed him for her fledgling agency and so wanted to work closely with him. But it came with a price.

Carol had learned a lot over the years from Gayle, but now over the last few months she had broken her own number-one cardinal rule— never fall for a client. She knew he had met someone recently while in Florida, but she still felt drawn to him and his writing, compelled to read every word. She could not explain it, she wanted to know everything about him.

She heard the sheets rustle again.

"Please?" he murmured. His leg moved.

She could never say no to him; that was always part of the problem, and today they were running late.

"Okay Mitch, but you see, if you were up and ready, I could order your usual—two eggs over-easy, side of ham, and a toasted English muffin with some marmalade."

Finally, picking up the room phone, she ordered a pot of coffee and a bagel for breakfast.

Still no further movement from underneath the sheets.

She repeated her wakeup call to him again; by now, it was something she was accustomed to doing. "Late night?" she asked, already knowing the answer. "I should have known. Come on, time to get up, time to pay the piper."

The smell of spilt whiskey, burnt cigarettes, and stale cologne filled the air. She made her way to the nearby armchair and sat down while she finished perusing yet another manuscript given to her by someone in her apartment building. Everybody had a "friend" who just finished writing what they felt was the next great American novel. Most of it was crap. She sipped her lukewarm coffee. She saw two half-empty whiskey glasses on the floor next to a nearby ashtray filled with cigarettes. The rank smoky odor was disgusting as she shoved the ashtray away from her across the floor with a push from the toe of one of her high-heeled shoes.

She stretched out her long limbs, crossing her legs at her ankles causing her skirt to tighten across her thighs and rise slightly. Sometimes she would catch Mitch casting an admiring glance when she sat that way. Was it sexy? No…comfortable. She sat up in the chair and uncrossed her legs.

Forcing her way through yet another manuscript she complained to no one in particular, "I can't believe the crap people write. I've heard other agents say they can tell a manuscript is crap just by reading the first page. Hell, I can tell by reading the opening sentence." She tossed the blue-covered, three-inch thick manuscript into a nearby metal trashcan, making a resounding noise in the silent room. She looked over and watched his bed—still no movement.

They were going to be late, and she could not afford to anger anyone at this point in their book tour. Today was going to be a busy day. The last day of the tour. She was home, New York, the capital of the world.

Only one more day, Carol. Then he would return home to the beach ... to her... and be out of my daily life. Remember Cal, he's so much older and ... he's taken.

She looked up, "Mitch, come on... get up, you got a big day ahead of you," she said as she removed *The New York Times* from the black linen bag she had taken off the doorknob to his room.

"Where are we?" came the question from underneath the sheets.

"New York."

The downtown hotel room was large and expensive, but it was close to the mega-bookstore and near all the uptown publishing offices. She knew if he stayed here, he would not be late for his meetings that morning. *Yeah, fat chance*, she thought to herself.

Carol heard the sheets rustle and saw him stand; wearing only his blue boxer shorts, then watched him stagger towards the bathroom. She saw him run his fingers through his rumpled sandy grey and blonde hair while she admired his well-sculpted but slightly aged physique. He looked at least ten years younger than the age on his driver's license. He closed the bathroom door, and she soon heard the sound of running water from the shower.

Empty liquor bottles from the mini-bar littered the floor. *It must have been some night last night* she thought to herself before returning to her newspaper. Then she thought to herself, *Today was going to be a tough day...a very tough day.*

When he reappeared, he had already shaved, combed his hair, and stood in front of her wearing only a smile with a white towel strategically wrapped around his waist. He looked good, real good.

"What's on the schedule for today?" he asked toweling off his face before he turned and dropped the towel to get dressed. He began to pull his clothes from his suitcase lying on the luggage rack. She watched his every move before looking at her cell phone to view their calendar of events for their last day together.

"Well," she stuttered, "we grab a quick bite to eat for breakfast when our room service is here, and then you do your book reading at the Megastore followed by a couple of hours of book signing, then you can schmooze with the manager for a while. They sell a lot of your books, so talking with him certainly can't hurt book sales. Then off to mid-town to have lunch at *Velliggios*. After that, on to your next reading at Brighton's, then another one at Reed's Bookstore and then end up the day with a short press interview here back at the hotel, then drinks with Dan Eliot, Senior Editor of Windham Press. Then maybe dinner here, just you and me."

"Yeah, tell me again, why are we meeting with Windham? We already have a publisher."

"He's responding to some inquiry, a manuscript, you sent him." She gave him a look... her displeased look.

"Right... I forgot about that," he said absentmindedly.

"Yeah... well, I had to clear it with Fosters and Riggs, our current publisher to make sure they didn't have a problem with us meeting with them. Apparently, you had already talked with the top brass there. Remember Mitch, that's my job, and hey, you're lucky they said it was okay. You could have really screwed up some things, Mitch. You can't be shopping manuscripts around, Mitch; we have a contract with Fosters & Riggs, and we could both get in a lot of trouble, expensive trouble. Understand?"

"Sorry, I understand."

"Okay, just don't do it again." She could not get too angry with him. He had stood up for her when she needed him the most. He went to their publisher after Gayle died and said he wanted Carol's new agency to represent him. They wanted to change the contract, eliminating movie royalties paid to Carol for any potential movie deal for the new book. He said no and had them give Carol the same contract they had with Gayle. That alone would make Carol in excess of $250,000 dollars in commission. She respected that kind of loyalty and she admired him for sticking up for her.

"Now, getting back to Windham, this is just an exploratory meeting with Dan Eliot who handles new book acquisitions. His boss, female, the CEO at Windham is named Kincaid, well, she liked the book you sent her, and wanted a meet. Besides, they're one of the big ten in the publishing business. It can't hurt to talk to them. He mentioned she might join us later, so I need you to keep your wits about you. Okay?"

"Okay. Got it."

"Want a cigarette?" she asked.

"No," he muttered.

She paused and asked quietly, "Do you need a drink?"

"No... no thanks..., I found out, it doesn't help," he said as he pulled on his socks then his shoes and looked at her with his trademark half smile.

The jagged scar on his hand had healed, but the scar to his heart had not. She saw it in his eyes and wanted to go to him, wrap her arms around him and hold him, do anything to help ease the pain. *Cal, he's taken.*

He now stood before her in what had become his standard traveling uniform for the last six weeks: white t-shirt, khakis, sneakers, and a well-traveled navy blazer.

"What else?" he asked as he tucked in his shirt, pushing a wild strand of hair away from his face with his fingers.

She looked at him with a smile. As always, he cleaned up nice... real nice.

"Tomorrow, you have a flight back to Delray Beach, and you can go back to your little beach house in beautiful sunny Florida.

She stopped for minute before continuing. "But today will be a hectic day."

He grunted. She was keeping him extra busy today, he thought to himself. *Today of all days.* He thought to himself, *I've waited years for this day. Today it will be over—finally.*

A knock on the door echoed throughout the room. She was up before it even registered with him and his dimmed senses. The bellhop set down the tray with a pot of coffee and a bagel with some cream cheese. She signed the receipt and sent him on his way.

"Black." It was more of a statement then a request.

She gave him a dirty look.

"Please."

He looked at her cutting the bagel in half as she began to eat.

"The other half is yours," she told him, handing him the plate.

"A half of a bagel? Carol, I'm starvin'."

"We're having an early lunch at *Velliggios*, so this is just to hold you over until then." Just what she needed, another Italian lunch, but it was Mitch's favorite restaurant when they were in New York.

She saw his disappointment. "But on the bright side you got a great review in the *Times* today, which should help boost sales. She rustled through the paper. "Ah here it is ...and I quote, *Mitch Patterson continues his great story telling with his latest book, the hard-hitting story,* The Search for Timothy Walker. *The ex-cop documents the relentless months' long nationwide manhunt for Timothy Walker, founder and leader of The Boston Brotherhood. It is a spellbinding tale, and his latest effort is already climbing the Times bestselling sales charts.*"

"Damn good if you ask me. Right, Mitch?"

"Yeah." He chuckled. "You know, I still remember what Raymond Chandler said about critics and publishers, something like—*It's wrong to be harsh with the New York critics, unless one admits in the same breath that it is a condition of their existence that they should write entertainingly about something which is rarely worth writing about at all."* He chuckled. "Where's the damn coffee?" he muttered to himself changing the subject. He did not like discussing reviews. They were just somebody else's opinion of his work. Mitch preferred to write the stories and leave everything else to Carol.

"Here you go." She looked up at him, "Tell me about this new manuscript. I don't know anything about it. When I checked in at my office and then returned a call to Dan Eliot at Windham, well he had called and mentioned an interest in a manuscript you sent him and his boss. Mitch, that's my job, you know, to know everything going on with your career. Remember me, Carol Litchard? Principal Agent of Litchard and Associates, literary agents? The agency that represents you." She saw his head droop.

"He also said the manuscript you sent didn't even have your name on it. It had the name of somebody named Roger, Roger Winston? Don't you think people can tell it's your writing? Come on now?"

"It's just something I wrote—short, something very different from what I usually write. One of my first books. I figured I'd just send it off to a few people in the business. Since it was unlike anything I've done in the past and... well, I didn't want you to waste your time on it. It was the first book I ever wrote many, many years ago. Honest, Carol... I'm sorry."

Oh boy, a first book. And a novella. She hated it already. Smile, be pleasant, Carol.

She wanted to hold him, but then wanted to smack him—what with those lost blue eyes, drooping head, and that heartfelt remorse written on his face she just stood there helpless, just looking at him.

"Let me be the judge of that, will you?" she finally said. "Hell, I haven't even seen the damn manuscript. I have no goddamn idea what it's even about and we're meeting with some of the most powerful people in the publishing industry tonight, and over drinks he or his boss might casually ask me, 'Well Carol what did you think of his latest effort?' Duh? I'll feel like a real jerk... Come on, Mitch."

"Sorry, Carol... I guess I just didn't think it all the way through...that's all."

She reached out and gently moved the wild strand of graying blonde hair from his forehead, placing it back into its rightful place. "Okay, okay, what's the title, and what's it about?"

He smiled that Robert Redford smile of his and said, "It's called *Summertime,* and it's a coming-of-age story. Short, it's a novella." He stopped before continuing; "I can email it to you or put it on a flash drive for you. I think I even have a hard copy of the manuscript if you want to see it," he said. His eyes came alive talking about his latest project.

Surprised at his emotion she told him, "Give me the hardcopy, and I'll breeze through it today while I'm waiting for you. I'm a fast reader. At least this way I'll be able to speak halfway intelligently about it when we meet with him tonight for drinks."

He reached into his worn, brown-leather courier bag, retrieved a tattered manila envelope, and handed it to her.

She looked inside at the cover title, *Summertime* and shoved it inside her briefcase with the admonishment, "Come on now, we gotta go, just don't ever do that again. Okay?"

He nodded.

She took in a deep breath, kissed him on the cheek and walked out the door with her briefcase in one hand and her large leather purse slung over her shoulder.

Chapter Three

Nate completed the Supreme Court appeal forms he retrieved from his office filing cabinet and from the Internet. As he prepared the final paperwork for the appeal, Linda, his legal assistant at his office in Jacksonville, was feverishly researching and organizing everything else he needed. Agnes was busy proofreading the final copy to get it ready to send off. Time was running out.

He could reach the clerk at nine o'clock. *Five minutes to go.* Impulsively, he dialed the number early, and a young voice answered. "Good morning this is Chuck Thurman, Liaison Office of Emergency Applications, can I help you?"

"Yes, I hope so. I know that I am supposed to have this paperwork in ten days in advance of the scheduled execution, but my stay was just denied by the appeals court."

"When is the DOE?"

"Excuse me?"

"I'm sorry, when is the Date of Execution."

He paused before saying, "Oh… that would be… today, at six P.M. In the State of Florida."

"Whoa. We don't have a lot of time then, do we?"

"No, sir. I just finished filling out the thirty-page OSCA-15 appeal form. I have one in my file, but they changed the form last month so I got the latest one off the Internet."

"Fine, that's the most current copy. That's a good start. I'll walk you through the rest of the process. I'll need copies of all your rulings, the trial transcripts, copies of all previous writs starting with the local ones first, then I'll need…" his voice rambled on.

Nate was quiet as he wrote down on his yellow legal pad everything the young man was saying. He felt overwhelmed, and his small wood-paneled office felt like it was closing in on him as the voice on the other end of the line droned on with everything he would need for his last appeal. His heartbeat quickened. The veteran attorney had spent the last eight hours collecting most of the things he was asking for, but he would need much more. He would have to call Linda at his office in town and get more help. Time was running out.

"Then when you have all of that, you just submit it to me, and I will direct it to the appropriate justice. If you have any questions, do not hesitate to call me. Good luck, sir. Oh, and I will need all of this no later than one o'clock since the execution is set for today. And don't be late."

"You'll have it. Believe me. Thanks for all your help."

Chapter Four

9:01 A.M.

It was late for her. Usually she was up early, but today was not like any other day. Today was…

Sari poured herself a fresh cup of *Teanna* peach tea. As she opened the front door, a flash of red ran past her, Kelly her Irish setter. The cottage looked out onto the ocean. She took in a deep breath. Then took another sip of tea. The fresh salt air was invigorating. The sound of the crashing waves brought renewed energy to her. Surfers were already out attacking the breakers. The beach was beginning to fill with people carrying their umbrellas, towels and coolers down to the waves. Just another wonderful day at the Florida beach. The warmth filled her body and eased her soul.

She covered her eyes and looked to the sky, as a flock of ten or so majestic pelicans glided by overhead. Marauding seagull were already hunting for a handout from the beachgoers. She could tell it was going to be a hot day, but it was always cooler by the water.

She checked her phone, no calls or messages. Nothing. Today was going to be a trying day for the two of them. But both of them had agreed, no calls today until everything was done, then it was time for them to move on with their lives. It seemed like a good idea at the time. *Damn him.* She wasn't going to call him. *Let him call me first,* she thought. He would be home soon.

She closed the door behind her and began her daily jog on the beach. Her run would help keep her mind occupied.

Just jog, girl, don't think about it. Or anything else.

"Come on, boy," she hollered to Kelly, her aging Irish setter. Well, actually his setter that he had when she moved into his beach house two years earlier. Now she had adopted him as her own since he had been gone for what seemed like forever. "Let's go for a run."

She took off down to the shoreline and began her morning jaunt. The sand felt cool to her feet and the soft sea breeze comforted her. It was a crisp clear chamber of commerce kind of day in south Florida. She missed him.

When she was finished her daily jog, she ate a half of a grapefruit and poured the last of the tea. *Enough of this*, she thought, time to get dressed and get to work. *I'm sure he'll call later.*

9:05 A.M.

The Megastore was only six blocks from the hotel, and by the time they arrived, the manager had the room and the podium ready and waiting for him. Arrayed in front of the platform were rows of chairs with a lone seat for Carol set off to the side and out of sight. They were five minutes late, having been caught in a torrential downpour. She kept looking nervously at her watch, as always. It was her Catholic upbringing, if she wasn't fifteen minutes early then she considered herself late.

Shortly after they arrived, the double doors of the reading room opened. Soon it was standing room only. Carol and Mitch slipped in behind the curtain. He smiled that nervous smile of his before every reading and went to the waiting stool. He glanced at his cellphone for messages, then at Carol as he picked up the book, cleared his throat, took a drink of water, and began to read.

The
Search
For
Timothy Walker
by
Mitchell Patterson

I remember, over twenty years ago, when I first read about Timothy Walker killing five people and being sentenced to death. I stopped in the middle of an intersection to finish reading the newspaper account and saw his picture for the first time in years. He had changed. He looked angry and fearsome with his shaved head and multiple tattoos. Later, I had followed the trials, his convictions, and appeals with great interest. Then I read that he was on death row in Starke, Florida. When I heard his appeals were denied, I was truly moved and conflicted. Then five years ago, he escaped from death row and went on a killing rampage across the country for three months. He killed my wife Sandy and my son Derek. The ones I held most dear in the world. That's when I joined the hunt for personal reasons.

It took months, and I had been closing in on my long search for him after his escape. We chased him to a small town outside of Wichita, but he had slipped through our police dragnet yet again. He was running out of places to hide. After months of being hunted, Walker knew the end was near and was tired of running. Even though he said he would never go back to death row alive and would die before giving himself up, he surrendered peacefully at a local Kansas state police roadside checkpoint. He was driving a stolen pickup truck from an elderly couple he murdered on Drury Lane. The reason he gave up? He was out of bullets.

The Florida Legislature passed a bill titled the Timely Justice Act requiring the governor to sign a death warrant within thirty days of a capital conviction by the State Supreme Court and the state would be required to execute the defendant within 180 days of the warrant. The governor promptly signed the bill and three days later Timothy Elroy Walker was placed on the immediate To Be Executed list. Now his time had run out after waiting on death row for over twenty-five years.

They all said he was a bad seed, a bad influence, something evil, but at one time many, many years ago, I knew him as a friend, a good friend… no… he was my best friend. Timothy Walker was… Mitch's voice quivered slightly as he continued, but he soon began to read his mystical words and draw his audience in then he held them, captive in his spell.

Carol had heard him read the same opening aloud many times over the last few weeks at their many stops on their nationwide tour. His words were captivating and soon his voice drifted away into white noise. Unseen from behind the podium curtain she retrieved the blue-covered manuscript from her purse. Just what she needed, a coming-of-age story. She leaned back in her molded plastic chair, and began to read.

Summertime
by
Roger Winston

JUNE 1959

It was a different time, a quieter and gentler time. America was at peace or rather it was a time between wars. For me it was summertime, a week after Memorial Day but days after my twelfth birthday. It was a bright sunny morning in suburban Saint Louis, school was out, and I now had my freedom! I had the whole summer to do whatever I wanted, to play with my friends, go hiking, exploring, biking, fishing, and most of all to watch TV.

My best friend Timmy and I would explore the complex of caves on the bluffs by the river as we had done every summer for years. The caves were old Indian burial grounds, and Timmy always said sometimes he heard the ghosts talking as we walked deep inside the tall caves. He made spooky noises. It gave me chills, but he only laughed and made more strange sounds to scare me. Sometimes we walked down the railroad tracks for miles and miles until we came to the old quarry where we watched hunters practice shooting light bulbs floating in the murky green water. You could hear the bulbs pop and explode, leaving a trail of white powder in the air. One time some hunters brought an old television picture tube and threw it into the pond. When a rifle bullet hit, the sound was so loud, then another one hit until it exploded. Timmy loved it. I still remember the awful sulfur smell that filled the air afterwards.

Other times we would go to Ortman's funeral home down the street on Lackland and use the curved *Jai alai* mitts that Timmy's brother "Dutch" brought back from Miami. We tossed a hard red rubber ball against the tall brick wall at the back of the building. It must have been real loud inside. Later Timmy always joked, put his head down, his hands together as if giving a eulogy, "Dearly beloved," he mocked with a smile "BOOM. We are gathered here together, BOOM! BOOM!"

Old Mr. Ortman would hobble outside and yell at us to stop, before throwing up his hands in disgust. Timmy and I would just laugh, but after a couple of weeks, he started paying us a quarter each to open the car doors for people as they drove up for a funeral. It got so sad watching everybody cry all the time, we stopped going there. Then we would have water balloon fights, mud ball and sling shot wars with the other kids in the neighborhood— and we always won.

Every summer, we built something in Timmy's backyard behind his pool house or on one of the vacant lots in the neighborhood. Over the previous summers, we constructed a doghouse, a tree house, a tunnel to our fort on a nearby lot, and last summer we made a cool clubhouse, we called our "castle," We made it from old wood and stuff from nearby constructions sites. Timmy loved planning and building so much, he said he wanted to be an architect when he grew up, just like my dad. His dad was a doctor but was hardly ever home. Timmy loved the clubhouse, and I knew I could always find him there, hiding in our "castle." He seemed at peace there. Me, I loved watching television.

You see the year was 1959, I was twelve years old, and I wanted to be a cowboy. I wanted to be like Roy Rogers, Wild Bill Hickok, The Lone Ranger, the Cisco Kid, and all the other cowboys I saw on TV every day. I wanted to ride like the wind, slung over the side of my charging steed, the wind blowing though my long and flowing hair as I rode through the rocky gorges out in the wild, Wild West.

I had just two tough decisions left to make; the first was what kind of cowboy hat I wanted to wear. Should I choose the big wide black sombrero like the Cisco Kid, or settle for the off-white rustic one, wearing it cocked to one side on my head like Wild Bill or the dressy white one favored by the Lone Ranger?

And the second decision was—of course—I had to choose my horse. My trusty mount that would be my daily companion, my friend, my advisor, and many times my rescuer when I would get trapped in quicksand like in the TV shows. Like them, I would throw my lasso over the saddle of my faithful companion and he would pull me out and save me. I liked the palomino of Roy Rogers but I loved the white horse of the Ranger. However, on black and white TV, they all pretty much looked the same.

Then I decided, why choose just one? I would have all my favorite horses at my disposal and ride whichever one suited me that day. I would ride like the wind when I needed to be somewhere in a hurry. I would ride like the Ranger! The Lone Ranger. He was so brave, so proud. He helped everyone and never waited around for people to thank him or give him any tips or money or a cold Coke or anything. What a hero!

Yes, for as long as I remembered I always wanted to be a cowboy. Yes, that's what I wanted to be.

Chapter Five

I loved living in Saint Louis. We lived in what they called the suburbs; areas outside major cities like most post World War II American cities. Millions of "after the war" boomer babies were being born and growing up all across the country, and Saint Louis was growing just like every other big city. The war was over, and now everyone was relieved that the Korean Conflict was settled once and for all. Many Korean refugees came and settled in the United States after being displaced from their war-torn country and had nowhere else to go.

Affluent suburbs began appearing all around the city as retired executives and professionals, managers, and business owners moved their families from the cities out to the suburbs. In these neighborhoods, you knew everyone and everybody knew you, which was both good and bad. If you got into trouble, everyone knew where you lived and they knew your parents. This was not always good because your parents knew every bad thing that you did by the time you reached home. They were standing at the door waiting for you. But growing up in the suburbs of Saint Louis was great in the 1950s, especially where I lived.

When I was very young, our family moved from the city to a small, sleepy suburb called Overland. We lived on a street called Lackland named after some Confederate Colonel, Cornelius J. Lackland. The two-lane road had huge sycamore trees on both sides stretching the entire length of the street for as far as the eye could see. The trees were so tall they touched together at the very top. It kept our house so cool all day long during the hot summer.

Nearby neighbors included the mayor of Overland, the chief of police, a retired judge, two doctors, a banker, and us, the Malloys. The Malloy household consisted of me and my five brothers and sisters (Josh was the oldest, then Jane—named after my mom, then Jack, me, my younger sister Joanie, and of course, baby Janet) and my mom and dad, eight in all—and nine if you counted our border collie Dizzy.

Everybody had names that began with a "J," except for me. Mom said she almost lost me to the fever and wanted to make sure she never forgot about it.

My dad was an architect and worked for an engineering firm; he was always really busy at work. He worked hard and liked to read the daily newspaper and have dinner waiting for him when he got home. I always walked up to the corner store and got him his paper at Clarks Pharmacy.

Across the street lived one of our neighbors; I called him "Stinky" Sammy Murdoch. Sammy owned the local Chevrolet dealership. When his wife would go visit her mother in California, he always had lots of pretty, young female visitors wearing short shorts or swim tops walking around his house. You could see them through their front picture window wearing their swimsuits. Funny thing was he didn't have a pool. I guessed they were just practicing or it was just hot inside his house.

When he backed his white Chevy convertible out of his driveway, I always heard him singing, with his pretty blonde friends, "See the USA, in a Chevrolet, America is asking you to buy," then he would wave to me and drive off. I never liked him much. He stunk of stinky old English Leather aftershave.

My dad was very busy, and most days he was working. I never got to see him much, and my sisters and my mom would take off and go shopping just about every day and my mom would buy my sisters clothes. They were always saying they never had anything to wear.

I could care less about clothes. I had a couple of pairs of jeans, the ones from the prior summer, which I would cut off above the knees and then mom always bought me a few new pairs for my birthday. She said I was growing like a weed. I also had my Sunday dress pants for church. Every day I usually wore my jean cutoffs, my Keds or PF Flyer sneakers, and my favorite—a red t-shirt with yellow USMC initials across the front. My brother Josh sent it to me from his Marine boot camp two years before, and even though it was old, it was my favorite shirt. I wore it nearly every day.

I always had my old army surplus bag strapped to my back where I kept my canteen, a comic book, and any empty soda bottles I would find along the way. They were worth two cents each at Weis food market.

Summertime for me was always great. Every day felt like a Saturday, and I checked the icebox door, where a magnetic pink flamingo that my aunt brought back from Florida held up a list of my daily chores. When I was finished with my chores, I was free for the whole day. The list was usually things like, cut the lawn, take out the trash, wipe up the kitchen floor, take Dizzy for a walk, or clean up the dog poop in the backyard. My younger sister Joanie and my older sister Janey's list was always the same, do her nails, and wash her hair and other girl stuff. My sisters never really had lists.

Once I was done with my chores for the day, I was free! I could be an explorer, a cowboy, an adventurer, a police officer, or whatever else I wanted to be that day. Or I could go fishing at Lake Sherwood where the big mansions were or go swimming at the Legion pool. I never went into the deep water since I didn't know how to swim. Sometimes Timmy and I went fishing at the Catholic seminary on Midland Avenue. That's where my brother Jack went to school. He was studying to become a priest.

When my youngest sister Janet was a tiny baby, sometimes I would sneak off early to go exploring and get away from the baby's crying and screaming. She never seemed to stop for a long time. But that's just the way she was.

I loved summertime. It was the best time of the year. I counted the days until Memorial Day when school would be out for the summer or at least until after Labor Day. Timmy and I would go exploring, and we always had plenty to eat for blocks and blocks around our house. We ran through the long, treed backyards of all our neighbors. Every yard had something different to eat growing in their backyard or their side-yard.

Our next-door neighbors, the Vitts, had delicious cherries and grapes and then two houses away lived retired Judge Matthews who had huge apple trees. Other yards had peach trees, persimmons, crabapples, pear trees, and anything else you could think of to eat.

Every year Timmy's mom grew a huge tomato garden with over fifty tomato plants behind her pool house. There was nothing better than to pick a ripe tomato, sprinkle some salt over the top, and take a big bite from it. So fresh and sweet. It was better than candy and almost as good as a Twinkie or Susie-Q. Boy, it was the best.

On Thursday nights, my mom and dad would go to the A&P grocery store and shop for groceries for the week. When they got home, my dad would honk the horn and everybody would run outside and help unload the car and carry the bags of groceries inside the house. Then we all helped to put away all the food. I liked to help put food on the shelves because then I could see if there were any special treats or cookies or anything else like that in the grocery bags. The only problem was Thursday nights were when my favorite show, *My Little Margie* came on TV and the car horn always seemed to honk just as Margie was getting into trouble, again. If my mom needed anything before her weekly Thursday night shopping trips, it was my job to go to the local store and get what she needed. Either Weis Brothers Market or Schnucks grocery store.

There were numerous side streets off Lackland and many other homes, some like ours, built before the war and before the big developments began to be built. The new brick houses around the neighborhood were owned by our retired wealthy neighbors, many of whom had maids or cleaning ladies who helped in their homes. Both neighbors on either side of our house were stately brick homes, and they always had help constantly coming and going. Our next-door neighbor, Mrs. Jost, was always hiring and firing her help because she said they stole things from her kitchen. I heard her tell my mother one day. "You just can't trust them. You have to watch 'em like a hawk."

Our other neighbors, Mr. and Mrs. Vitt, had a friendly maid named Cora who came to visit them three days a week. I liked Cora. She was a nice Negro lady and when she smiled her round black face lit up the whole world. She always had a smile on her face, and she told me funny stories about when she lived in Mississippi as a little girl. I could tell just what kind of day it was going to be when I would stop by the basement window and kneel down to say hello to Cora. I loved talking to her.

Cora was so nice and had worked for the Vitts for so long she was considered a member of the family, at least that's what they always told everybody. She would be downstairs in the basement standing by the open window, near our driveway, ironing clothes and usually wore a red bandana wrapped around her head. It had to be hot in that basement because she always had the fan on, blowing in her face and hair to keep herself cool.

She smiled all the time, while the perspiration dripped off her forehead, but she never stopped ironing clothes. Sometimes, she would be singing until she saw me and then stopped and smiled at me and would say with a huge smile, "Hi ya there, young Mr. Malloy. How y'all doin' today, Davey Malloy?"

"Ffffine, Miss Cora. Hhhhow are yyyyou?" I would sit in the dirt outside the window and watch her iron while we talked.

My mom would yell from the kitchen window to stop bothering her and leave her be, but Cora would always just smile and say, "Tell your momma, it's all right with me chil'. I don't mind; I can use the company. You're a good boy."

We talked for hours or rather I talked and she ironed and nodded her head to show me she was listening. I told her of my dreams, of my friends, and my world. I told her about Sunny and she would just smile, a smile like a warm apple pie, it was so nice and sweet.

"You like that pretty young lady now, don't you, Davey boy? Come on now, you can tell Miss Cora."

"Yes, Miss Cora I gggguess I really do. She's my bbbbest friend." I could talk real easy with Cora.

But it seemed that whenever I would mention Timmy's name she would stop what she was doing, whether it was ironing, folding, or starching clothes, and look right at me pointing her finger and say, "You best stay away from him, young Davey, you a good boy, but that Timmy... well, he's a bad lot. You hear me? You best stay away."

"Yes, mmmma'am," I would say and then excuse myself to run an errand. It was not good to argue with an adult, you could never win, but nobody knew the Timmy I knew. He was my best friend. Nobody knew him the way that I knew him.

Two summers before, at the American Legion pool three big bullies from Saint Ignatius, the Catholic school I went to, came up to me and started making fun of the way I talked and ... my stutter. Timmy jumped up from his chair next to me and stood between them and me, towering over them with his fists clenched and his eyes flaring. He looked like a wild man.

Tim was tall and thin with long, strong muscles and went to a different school, a public school. He looked them right in the eye and in a low voice, almost like a growl said to their leader, the biggest one in the group, "You'd better leave my friend alone, or you'll answer to me. Do you understand me, punk?"

It was scary to listen to him. His voice was filled with danger and anger. They soon walked away, muttering about him being a crazy person, but he was the only one in the whole wide world who ever stood up for me. I never forgot what he did that day. Never. From that day on he was my best friend and always would be my best friend.

Chapter Six

I love watching television, but one Saturday morning I turned on the TV and sat with a bowl of Wheaties, waiting for the TV set to warm up. Nothing happened. Then the screen came on, but it was all fuzzy and swirly.

I turned the TV around and took off the rear panel. The inside of the TV was alive with bright lights. I looked at each one. Then one blinking light went out, then another. There were the culprits, two different tubes were dark and needed to be replaced. After unplugging the TV, I plucked both tubes from its innards.

I went to the kitchen and got down the old coffee can that contained money to pay for replacing worn-out television tubes. The TV had worked fine the night before when my dad and I watched the Friday Night fights. Saturday morning was just not a good time for the TV to go blank on me. All of my best shows were coming on, My Friend Flicka, Hopalong Cassidy, Lassie, Cisco Kid, Fury, and best of all, Wild Bill Hickok. After taking the TV tubes from the television, I ran down the street to Irv's Liquor store, which was located next to Weis Market.

Weis Brothers Market was a small neighborhood grocery store. It had an entrance door on the left and an exit door on the right. You left through the exit door, after you paid for everything. It had three short aisles with the meat counter in the rear, run by the butcher, Billy Weis, the owner's nephew. The owner's wife operated the register at the front of the store, and his daughter Louise made sure the shelves were stocked. Just two blocks away, it was the closest grocery store to our house. I always waved at Louise as I walked by and into Irv's Liquor store.

"Hi, Irv," I said walking inside and immediately went to the testing display panel for TV tubes.

"Hi ya, Davey," said Irv, the owner, who lived down the street from us on Charlack.

"Hi ya, kid," said his son, Barry with a big grin and laughing at something only he thought was funny.

"Since I'm the ccccustomer, the name is Ddddavid or Mr. Malloy to you, Bbbbarry," I said puffing out my chest.

His eyes glared at me. He would have jumped over the counter and punched me into oblivion if his father had not been there. I wasn't afraid of him because I was a really fast runner, and he was at least forty pounds overweight and would never be able to catch me. He was a bully, and nobody liked him. He went to school at Ritenour where Timmy went to school.

"Okay, Barry," said his father. "Don't you have a truck out back or something to unload?"

"Yeah, Pop," he responded, mad that he had to go back to work. I returned my attention to the tube tester. The tubes were dead all right. I bought replacements and rushed home. I wanted to watch the Lone Ranger then the Sky King show about him and his daughter and sidekick Penny. I unplugged the TV, situated the new tubes tight into their socket, plugged it back in, turned it on, and soon the TV was humming along again.

"Davey?" a voice echoed from the kitchen shattering the illusion from the small black-and-white nine-inch Magnavox television view of paradise. That was the voice my mom used when she wanted something. I slouched my shoulders lower to hide my presence. Silence from the kitchen.

"Davey? David, are you in front of that TV again? You need to go outside and play."

I didn't answer.

"David? David Matthew Malloy! Will you answer me?"

Whenever she used my full name like that, I knew I was in some terrible trouble.

"Whhhhat, Mom?"

"Why don't you go outside and play?"

"Okay," I said, defeat obvious in my voice as the ranger rode into view.

"Wait a minute. Before you go, Davey, I want to talk to you."

Uh-oh, those were not good words to hear. *What* did I do wrong now? "Yeah Mmmom, I'm cccomin." I looked back lovingly at the Lone Ranger then I heard a loud poof noise coming from the rear of the TV and saw white smoke rising from the back of the small screen. It was dead. I would have to wait until dad came home that night to fix it. I quickly turned off the television and unplugged it from the electrical socket.

My mom sat me down in our living room; she sat in her favorite chair while I sat on the golden-colored sofa. "Sit here, beside me," my mom said. She gave me her stern look, and then softened when she told me. "Mrs. Hammacher, your English teacher, called me last week on your last day of school. She said you were a good kid and everybody liked you, but you daydreamed a lot and she couldn't get you to focus in class. She said soon you'll be starting high school and you need to do really well if you want to get into a good college. Otherwise you'll never amount to anything… according to her."

College? Ughh, I thought to myself.

My mom sat in her chair and rubbed her swollen belly. In a few months, another member of the Malloy family would soon be joining me and the rest of the family.

"She was concerned about your reading level. She said you were very smart but strongly suggested you read more books."

"Mommmm,I hate to read all thhhhat readin' junk. It's boring,"

"I know Davey, but you have a very active imagination, and it takes a lot to hold your attention. However, I have a book I think you'll like—and starting right now, I'm going to sit down with you, in a comfortable chair, pour a glass of iced tea, and ask you to read a chapter for me. Okay? Just one chapter a day. Will you do that for me?"

I could never say no to my mom.

"Sure, Mom." She was due to have the baby later in the fall, and she joked to the neighbors she was looking forward to spending ten days of peace and quiet in the hospital, a "vacation" she called it.

The house was nearly empty. My oldest brother Josh was overseas in the Marine Corps. My brother Jack was going to summer school at the seminary. He was studying to be a priest, but he still was working delivering newspapers and as a part-time lifeguard at the American Legion pool. My dad was at work, and Janie, my oldest sister was working at Barclay Bakery. The baby was sleeping and my other sister was down the street playing with her Barbie dolls and her friends and their dolls. *Ugh!*

Our living room was cool and bright even with the lights out, though it was really hot outside. I sat on the sofa, and my mom showed me a book:

The Three Musketeers
by
Alexandre Dumas

"I've hhhheard of that one, Mmmom." I excitedly leafed through the pages.

My mom sat back, propped up her feet, and let out a loud sigh. She looked uncomfortable. She sipped her glass of iced tea. She smiled, still trying to get comfortable.

"Davey," she started, "The Three Musketeers is a book written by a French writer named Alexandre Dumas. The story takes place a long time ago. It tells about the adventures of a young man named d'Artagnan after he leaves home to travel to Paris, to join the brotherhood called the Musketeers of the Guard. D'Artagnan is not one of the musketeers of the title; those are his friends Athos, Porthos, and Aramis, inseparable friends who live by the motto *all for one and one for all*. They are good friends who take the young d'Artagnan into their group and under their wing. Okay, now you can start reading." She handed me the heavy book.

I felt like I was starting a new adventure. I felt the cover gently with my fingertips, as if I was asking permission to open the door to their adventure. The book lay in my lap as I turned the cover and opened it.

The Three Musketeers
On the first Monday of the month of April, 1625, the market town of Meung, in which the author of the Romance of the Rose was born, appeared to be in as perfect a state of revolution as if the Huguenots had made a second La Rochelle of it. Many citizens, seeing the women flying toward...

I began to read about a young man who wanted to travel, a young adventurer. He told of his life story. He told of his desire to be free, to be a Musketeer, to travel the world. This was not a reading assignment like in school; this was a journey, an adventure. I devoured the story in great gulps and was disappointed when the first chapter ended. I began to turn the page, eager to press on.

"No Davey, one chapter a day? Remember? That's all. That's our rule. Read every day but only a chapter a day; that way it will become a habit for you. Now go out and play, and get some fresh air. But first, can you bring me another glass of iced tea? Please, Davey?"

"Sure, Mom," I said only half-listening still thinking of adventures I just read about on the high seas.

I picked up the phone to call Timmy, but somebody was already on the telephone's party line, "I'll be done in just a little while, Davey," she said. It was Mrs. Davis, the old widow from down the street. She always lied; I knew she would be on the phone forever. When I finally got through Timmy's mom said he was gone, out playing and she didn't know where he was.

The next day, I was sitting in the living room, waiting for my mom. I got a cushion for my mom's back, a stool for her feet, and a cold glass of iced tea on a coaster sitting on the table all set for her.

I was ready to read the next chapter. No, the truth is, I couldn't wait to read more.

My mom smiled her pretty smile as she came in and saw the stool and tea waiting for her. She sat down and handed me the book.

I opened to my bookmark where I had left off the day before. Soon, I was lost inside the story of the three comrades who let young d'Artagnan join their group. They were a band of brothers, they fought together, they traveled together, and they got drunk together... they were Musketeers.

As my mother dozed in her chair, I could not put the book down and read more and more chapters turning page after page, eager to begin the next page, anxious to see d'Artagnan's travels through his eyes.

My mother woke up and said. "Okay Davey, that's enough reading for today."

I read four chapters that day, the next day, and another four the day after that, as my mother slept. I yearned to see what new adventures my new friend would have, who he would meet, and where he would go. I loved this new book and was soon more than halfway through it, and could not wait to read on. Maybe I'd be a musketeer someday.

When I was reading a few days later, my mother awoke with a start by the loud backfire sound of a motorcycle rushing by on Lackland. She rubbed her eyes and said, "That's all the reading for today. You are doing really well. Mrs. Hammacher would be proud of you and your reading. But for now, I have some things I need you to get for me from the store."

I pretended I didn't hear what she had to say. "Mom, this is a great book!" I told her. "That's us, Timmy, Sun Lei, and I are just like the three musketeers! All for one and one for all."

Timmy and Sun Lei (I always called her Sunny) were my best friends. Timmy I had known my whole life, but Sunny just moved in to the neighborhood last year. The three of us did everything together, except when Sunny had to take care for her grandmother who was always sick. Or when she went away for school to Chicago.

We loved to explore and go on hiking trips by the lake and the railroad tracks. We had our own private "territory" of five square blocks and our own treehouse we built in Tim's backyard.

My mother gave me her stern look. "Sun Lei is very nice, and she is always very polite, but she's at least a year or so older than you and Timmy. And… well…Davey, I really wish you wouldn't play with Timmy. He plays too rough, and there's just something about him I'm not sure I like."

"But Mom, Timmy and Sunny are my best friends. We're the three musketeers!"

She hugged me and whispered, "Just be careful, will you? Promise me?"

"Sure, Mom, I promise. Timmy's a good guy, just a little wild."

"What do you mean wild?" I had alerted her motherly instincts, and that meant trouble. *Shut up, dummy*, I said to myself. I liked hanging around with Tim. It was fun.

"You know, Mom… he does some crazy stuff, that's all—but he's okay. Do you have your grocery list," I asked her, while changing the subject. She smiled and slowly got up from her chair, holding her belly. I didn't want to tell her that Tim and his mom went out of town for a while to visit Timmy's older brother in the Ozarks. "Dutch" Walker was being held in the Ozarks at the Southern Missouri Regional Correctional Facility prison south of Malden Missouri serving time for…

A thunderous round of applause jarred her. Carol was jolted from the story. Where was she? New York. Megabookstore. Mitch. Ah yes, Mitch. The applause beyond the curtain caused her to look up from what she was reading, and she reluctantly set the manuscript down on a nearby chair.

"Carol?" she heard the voice say somewhere in the distance. She applauded for him as she stood and then walked to him.

"Great job, as usual," she whispered to him.

"Thanks," said Mitch, hugging her and giving her a slight peck on her cheek.

Her body shook. She wished he wouldn't do that, but he didn't have a clue and she wasn't about to say anything.

"It was a good reading. They were really into the new book," he said.

"Done?"

"No, I just needed a bathroom break and wanted to stretch my legs."

"Now it's time for you to autograph and sell some books," she said aloud moving away from him.

"Sounds good to me," he said with his casual boyish smile, leaning in close enough for her to catch a scent of his spiced after-shave. She didn't know if she was seeing a different side of him in his new book that caught her eye or rekindled her feelings for him or the aftershave ... or all three. All she wanted to do now was to read more of his personal story that he was sharing in his latest book. *Focus Carol.*

Chapter Seven

He was busy doing his pushups when Shiminek, the senior guard on Cell Block D walked to his cell door, "Walker, you got a phone call. Turnaround, you know the drill." All the guards hated Walker for what he done when he broke out of the "The Green Block."

Everything was painted a dark desolate green in an effort to keep the inmates calm. Walker was kept at the very end of Cell Block D, isolated from all the others and from the guards. But since he had a scheduled execution date, he was on "the watch." The guards joked that was to ensure he didn't cheat the grim reaper or the fine citizens of the great state of Florida.

"Hand me your meal sheet."

Walker slid his last meal request under the cell door and took two steps back away from the door. Shiminek laughed as he read it aloud, "Fifty-ounce steak, a pound of French fries, grits and lots of fresh asparagus along with three scoops of raspberry ice cream."

He laughed before turning serious, "Okay, Walker fun's over, turn around and put your hands behind you through the bars." Then he hollered, "Man comin' out!" He said aloud, waiting for the required backup and witness. Darrell Jones joined him, a big man from Louisiana, former football player who didn't take kindly to Walker either, but he just did his job and shut up.

When the cuffs and leg irons were on and tested to make sure they were secure, the electronic door slid open, and Timothy Walker shuffled towards the phone at the desk in the middle of the room. It was on a small wooden desk, with only a phone and notepad but no pen. A large red button was affixed prominently on the wall. On the face of the switch was one word, LOCKDOWN. It was to be used only in the event of a breakdown in security. Closed-circuit cameras monitored every move in every cell. Since Shiminek brought Walker from his cell, he was the one responsible for him until he returned there. The Czech guard sat him down and picked up the phone, holding it close to his ear.

"Hello?"

"Tim, this is Nate. Our appeal was denied. Sorry."

There was silence on the other end of the line. Walker was quiet for once.

"Shit. Should've figured. Didn't those boneheads read the documents? Did you send them everything you were supposed to send them? All the doctors' IQ tests and everything?"

"Yeah. They got everything, but they still said no. I don't think they believed you had an IQ of 70."

"Hmmph. So, what's next counselor? You're the hotshot lawyer, what's the next step? Huh?"

"I'm putting together an appeal to the Supreme Court. Has to be in by one o'clock today." Nate knew deep down inside that Walker had somehow rigged the IQ tests; he was no dummy, as a matter of fact he was one of the smartest inmates he had ever dealt with on death row.

"Well, you better get crackin' counselor. Call me if you need me. You know where to find me. So long."

He shuffled back towards the cell. *That steak was going to taste mighty good tonight*, he thought. *And they better not forget the raspberry ice cream.*

Chapter Eight

Mitch walked with her to the other room where a table had been set up for him to sign a stack of his books. He turned to her and asked, "What'd you think of the new book?"

His agent smiled before responding, "It's very interesting, and you were right—it's very different from the other books you've written. But I'll give you my complete verdict later, I want to read some more."

The line inside the bookstore for the signing was already forming with a group of impatient fans holding copies of his latest book.

"You okay?" she whispered making her way behind him.

"Yeah … I am now. Thanks for caring." He smiled again, and she left him to his admiring fans. *Was the room was beginning to feel warm? Yes, that must be it.*

He pulled out his phone and went to check for messages. Nothing. Disappointment showed on his face. He shrugged his shoulders in resignation. "Showtime," he proclaimed as he sat down to sign his first book.

Carol waited to make sure he had everything he needed to work his magic before she retreated to find an easy chair located in the lounge outside the cookbook section of the bookstore. She quickly opened her briefcase and eagerly returned to her reading…

"Dutch" Walker was being held in the Southern Missouri Regional Correctional Facility prison outside of Malden, Missouri. He was serving time for armed robbery. Police investigators never found the gun used in the crime so the courts could only sentence him to serve an eight-year term in prison. He would be out in three years with good behavior. His mother swore he was innocent and that he was at home with her the night the crime occurred. Unfortunately, the police found out she was in Los Angeles with her physician husband attending one of his many medical conventions. They would have charged her with perjury if they could have proved it.

I always liked Dutch. He was the same age as my older brother Josh, and he always kidded with me and roughed up my hair every time he saw me. He made me laugh. He was a body builder and had huge muscles on his arms, and I couldn't believe it...he had tattoos on his biceps. A skull and crossbones on one and the name Mary tattooed on the other! Just like a pirate. When he was living at home, he would lift weights in the Walkers' front yard every day, causing traffic to slow and girls to honk their car horns at him as they went by their house.

Dutch, with his ever-present cigar hanging from his mouth, rode his motorcycle from Saint Louis to Las Vegas then to Memphis where he went to work as a bodyguard for Elvis Presley. He always sent pictures to Timmy showing him and Elvis and a bunch of other guys they called the "gang." He sent pictures of them playing football on Elvis's front lawn and standing guard at his concerts. Wow! I wished I could meet "The King" someday.

Timmy and his mom had been visiting Dutch in southern Missouri for weeks. The prison was in the "boot-heel" of the state about a six-hour drive from Saint Louis, deep into the Ozark Mountains. I heard it was not a nice place. My mom would have gone crazy if she knew Timmy was visiting a prison. She didn't like Dutch much either.

"Davey? Stop daydreaming. Here's the list of things I need from Schnucks market," my mother said as she handed me her list.

"Sssssschnucks?" I moaned. The nearest grocery store was Weis Brothers Market, and it was only two blocks, but Schnucks was a much longer walk, more than fifteen blocks away. It was a long walk on a hot day with bags of groceries.

"And come right home, and don't you dare stop anywhere. Do you hear me, David Malloy?"

When my mother used my full name that was her way of saying I better listen to her and do what I was told.

"Yyyes, ma'am. I'll cccome right hhome."

"You're a good boy, Davey. Has anyone ever told you that before?

"You have, Mom. All the ttime."

She wrapped her arms around me, hugged me and kissed the top of my head. "Hurry now; go on, your father'll be home soon. And dinner will be on the table."

It was a long walk to Schnucks, both there and back. When I had to carry two bags, the groceries were so heavy that I always had to stop at different places to rest and get some air conditioning to cool off. Sometimes I would rest at Overland City Hall, sometimes at the

YMCA, and sometimes at the new post office. When I went into the post office, so it didn't look like I was just hanging around, I liked to study the FBI wanted posters.

I loved to look at the pictures, just in case I ever saw a wanted criminal on the street that I needed to arrest or report to Chief of Police "Johnny" Gestridge. Looking through all the wanted posters I thought, maybe I'd be a cop one day, track down all of these criminals and receive a big reward. Or maybe I could just find one and they would give me a cold Coke and a Banana Flip, my favorite with all that oozy white cream on the inside and soft Twinkie-like stuff on the outside. I liked it even better than Twinkies.

A block in Saint Louis was a loosely defined unit of measurement used in the Midwest, which defined distance. If you were giving directions to a stranger, you counted each intersecting street as a block, regardless of how long it actually happened to be. From our house to Weis Market was one block, but a long block so I always figured it was two blocks.

I started the long walk to Schnucks, over fifteen blocks away and it was hot. It was going to be a long, hot summer. I had to walk to Schnucks since the list had too much on it to carry on my bike.

It was stifling, and I could not breathe for a minute. The air was very still. There was no breeze at all.

I walked past the big brick house of Mr. and Mrs. Jost, our longtime next-door neighbors. They didn't have any kids and were not sure what to make of me and the big Malloy clan living next door.

They always sounded so formal or maybe they were annoyed at me for something I had done. I was never sure. They were nice, but when Mrs. Jost offered candy from her clear-cut glass crystal candy bowl, she would always say, "Have one, won't you, David?" And she meant just that, have one, not two or three or more, just one. *How could I take just one when she was showing me what seemed to be a bushel basket full of chocolate Hershey candy kisses?*

Mrs. Jost waved to me as I walked by. She walked towards me and away from her brand new Edsel parked in the driveway saying, "Hello, Davey. How are you today?"

"I'm fine, Mrs. Jost. How are you?" I answered politely but continued to walk. It was too hot to stand still.

"Very fine, thank you. Tell your parents I asked about them."

I stopped walking. "What did you want to ask them, Mrs. Jost?"

"It's just a manner of speaking, David. Tell them I wish them well, okay?"

"They aren't sick that I know of, Mrs. Jost."

"David, don't be so annoying. Just tell them I said hello, okay?" said a now thoroughly annoyed Mrs. Jost. *Why is she always so mad at me? I guess I'll never know.*

"Oh Davey," she called after me, "Charles wants to talk with you. Can you wait a minute, please?" Charles was her longtime husband. She had showed me their wedding pictures once when he had hair, and he looked like a totally different man, young even.

"Sure, Mrs. Jost."

"Charles?" she called to inside the house. "Young Davey Malloy is out here. You wanted to talk to him, didn't you, dear?"

"Yes, I'll be right out," came a deep voice from inside. He came out dressed in his usual khakis, and an old blue and silver Air Force t-shirt he loved to wear. It was stretched tight across his chest.

"Hi, Davey. Having a good summer so far?" he asked drying off his hands with a red work towel. *Must be working on his car again, as always.*

"Hi, Mr. Jost. Yes sir, it's going to be a great summer." It was hot standing there on the sidewalk. I moved from one foot to the other.

"Good. You remember my ham radio set that we used a couple times in the basement, don't you?"

"Sure do, Mr. Jost. That was swell, talking with people from all over the world." I wasn't hot any longer.

"Would you like to have it?"

My heart leapt. "Are you kidding? You bet." *This was great!* One day we had talked with people from all over the globe, from Germany to South Africa to Japan to California, and although we could not always tell what they were saying, they did speak enough English for us to find out where they were located. I put a pin on a map to show their location.

"Stop by later, and I'll give it to you."

"Thanks Mr. Jost." *Wow! My very own ham radio!* My mind was reeling with the adventures I could have with my newfound BlauBruin International IR-2600-K radio. *I could be an international Musketeer.*

"Now Davey, the only thing is—it's very expensive."

"I'll be real careful with it Mr. Jost, I promise."

He paused, appearing slightly annoyed at being interrupted, "I know you will be, Davey. What I started to say was...it's a very expensive radio but since you being a neighbor and all, I would only ask you to pay, say…twenty dollars?"

I swallowed hard. "Wow! Mr. Jost, I don't have that kind of money."

I could see the wheels moving behind his eyes as he said, "Well, tell you what, you just wash my car twenty times, and we can call it even. What do you say?"

I would rather drink battery acid than agree to that, but I really loved that radio so I agreed.

"Sure Mr. Jost, but if I can come up with the money on my own, I'll just pay you. Okay?"

He made a frown but agreed by saying, "You got a deal, Davey. Shake."

We shook hands on the blood deal, and I started to think of ways to make money that summer to pay for my new beloved radio. I had washed his car a couple of times the previous summer in his drive-in-basement-garage, and I promised myself I would never do it again.

The last time I washed his car, it took him twenty minutes to show me how he wanted the car washed and dried. He always began by saying, "Take your belt off so you don't scratch the car, and then put a towel over your jean zipper so you don't scratch it. Then water the car down completely with this special hose attachment, including the wheels, then wash it with a big sponge and some soapy water, then dry it with a goat skin towel called a chamois, making sure you turn the chamois over every time you use it." And that was just the outside of the car. It took him another twenty minutes to show me how he wanted me to do the inside and then an additional fifteen minutes on how he wanted me to clean his tires.

I had to find another way to make the twenty bucks. I had to. Not easy, but I knew I could do it. I continued to make my way towards Schnucks to do my mom's shopping. Only another ten blocks, I thought to myself. The heat had returned only it was hotter.

As I neared the City Hall building, the chief of police's car was just pulling out of the police station onto the side street near me. I waved at Chief Johnny Gestridge, and he just smiled at me, touching the rim of his gold braided police cap, our kind of secret salute. He lived down the street from us on Charlack Avenue, across from Sun Lei's house. The sheriff had a daughter who was Joanie's age and two sons, both in the Marine Corps.

I had signed up last summer to be an honorary Overland police cadet for the summer and scoured the neighborhood searching for criminals and lawbreakers. I wanted to be a police officer so bad. When I turned in my substantial list of grievous crimes and offenses, the police officer at the front desk took one a look at the long list and promptly threw it in the trashcan. Then he told me to leave and not come back. It was then I decided I wanted to be a cowboy instead. I kept walking towards the supermarket; with the sidewalk so hot, it felt like the bottoms of my PF Flyers were on fire.

Chapter Nine

Schnucks was the best supermarket around. It had lots of comic books, real tall ceilings like at church, wide clean aisles, bright white-tile floors, cool almost cold air conditioning, lots of free food samples, and women in pink and white uniforms asking if they could help you find anything or if you wanted a free sample. For a grocery store, it wasn't that bad. I asked if they had any Twinkie samples, and the old lady at the food counter shooed me away.

I checked everything off my mother's list including two tubes of Ipana toothpaste, Kool-Aid, two large bottles of Vess Cream Soda, two dozen eggs, a gallon of milk, Velveeta cheese, Grape Nuts cereal for Jack, a loaf of Wonder bread, and two cartons of Camel cigarettes for my mom and dad.

Also on the list were three cans of Carnation evaporated milk. *What the hell was evaporated milk, and why would anyone want to buy it if it was evaporating? My mom also always asked for a bottle of Karo syrup, something for the baby. But what was it?* I knew this was definitely going to be a two-bag trip, I could tell just by looking at the shopping cart, which was filling up quickly.

I only needed one more item. I tried to find it on my own but finally had to resort to asking a store clerk for some help. I walked up to a woman by the pharmacy who was busy stocking shelves in the soda aisle and showed her my list.

"Can I help you young man?"

I whispered in a low voice to the uniformed sales clerk in aisle four. "Excuse me."

"Yes? How can I help you young man?" she asked, sounding impatient.

"Excuse me." I said under my breath, lowering my voice so no one else could hear me. I moved closer to her and showed her my mother's list. I pointed to the item on my list that I was looking for in their store. "Where can I find this for my mom and sister?" I asked.

She lowered her glasses from her nose, took the list in her hand, and proclaimed in a loud tone, "Kotex? Feminine pads are in aisle seven, young man," she said it so loud that I knew the whole world could hear her, even the people in China who were probably just waking up.

"Thank you," I told her, now more interested in looking for a place to hide than in finishing my mother's shopping. I retrieved the last item on my mom's list and made my way out of the store as quick as I could. I did not look around, but I am sure everyone in the supermarket was standing there talking and laughing at me, wagging their fingers in my direction, pointing at me.

Once outside the store I walked as fast as I could, carrying the two heavy brown paper grocery bags. Rivers of perspiration ran down the center of my back, and the heat had now become unbearable. I looked up at the summer Missouri sky and saw no relief coming from a passing cloud. The sky was a beautiful shade of blue but a hot blue. Steaming blue.

I tried to walk in the shade using the shadow of the trees that lined Lackland, but they offered little relief from the scorching sun. Near Schnucks they didn't have the big old cool sycamore shade trees like we had in front of our house. It was hot.

Making slower progress than I usually made I saw an oasis up ahead—the City Hall building. It was always so cool there and at the post office down the street. They had air conditioning, cool air conditioning. The library was in the same building as City Hall but on the second floor.

I walked inside, went downstairs to the Coke machine just outside the permit office. I set the bags down and reached inside my jeans, searching, and found a hidden nickel, leftover from yesterday's grocery trip. I put the nickel into the machine. A small bottle of ice-cold Coca-Cola came sliding out making a lot of noise. The cold bottle cooled my hand. The rewarding taste was moments away.

I was not supposed to be using their Coke machine because it was so cheap and only for use by city employees. But I would see salesmen go inside the permit office all the time and buy Cokes for the clerks there and everybody looked so happy. If a salesman could use it, I sure could, I thought. I lived there in Overland, my dad paid taxes, so I just sat on the downstairs steps and slowly drank the cold Coke, all by myself. At home, I always had to share my soda with everybody else. That was the rule at home, but not here. It was all mine.

I knew where all of the cheap soda and candy machines were located in our small town. The best penny candy was sold at Nielsen's Delicatessen, which was across from Barclay Bakery. I kept drinking my cold soda.

The door to the permit office opened and a big man, wearing a plaid shirt and yellow tie walked out and began yelling at me.

"You're not supposed to be in here, son! You know that. This soda machine is for city employees only. You best git now, boy! Git while the gittin's good," he roared. "I have a good mind to call Sheriff Gestridge right now and have you arrested," he glared at me like I had just killed somebody or something terrible like that. "As a matter of fact I am going to go inside right now and tell him we have a trespasser here. Yes indeed, that's exactly what I am going to do!"

Without saying a word, I grabbed the two grocery bags, my cold Coke and ran up the steps as fast as I could. I heard laughter coming from the basement, as the door closed behind him. I didn't want to be arrested, so I ran upstairs and set down my bags. I saw on one side of the hallway the big white double doors with a gold sign over the top— Office of the Mayor of Overland. I took a big sip of my ice-cold Coke. *Still good and cold! Ahhh!*

Turning to the right, I saw the library. Somebody came out, and as the door closed, I felt its cool air rush over me. I saw the library was empty. It was small, smaller than our basement, but it was the perfect size for me. I went inside and wandered around, looking to see what books the library had, still carrying my grocery bags. I looked in wonder at all the great books. Wow!

"Ummm, young man!" came a disapproving voice from behind me. "You can't come in here with that drink."

I looked at my now nearly empty soda bottle, took one last big swig, and handed the librarian the empty bottle. She held it as if it were contaminated with an infectious disease before she deposited it in the trashcan. It hit the bottom of the metal can with a loud thud. She looked at me with those sharp eyes; these were eyes that said *behave.* My mom looked at me with those same telling eyes any time we had company come visit us.

I walked around and soon stopped in front of a different set of bookshelves marked murder mysteries, travel, biographies, and history. As I reached for a book, the woman appeared behind me and said, "Are your hands clean young man? Do you need to wash up?"

"No ma'am," I said in the most polite Irish Catholic response I could muster. "My hhhhhands are clean, but ttttthhhhank you so much for asking." Smother them with kindness is what I learned in my many years of parochial school training.

She seemed impressed with my polite manners but kept watching me nonetheless.

I walked around the library, now seeing it for the very first time as a neat place to hang out rather than as just a cool oasis from the hot sun.

"Is there anything special you are looking for, young man?"

I started to say no but then politely asked her, "Do you have the book *The Three Musketeers?*"

Her smile broadened. "Why of course, by Alexandre Dumas! That is a great book for a young man like yourself."

She walked me to the other end of the library, pulled the book from the shelf, and began talking about it. My eyes did not leave the book she held in her hands. I could not wait to rejoin my new friend *d'Artagnan* in his latest adventures.

"Thank you," I told her and gently took the book from her hand.

I put the bags of groceries on a chair and sat down at one of the long mahogany tables in the reading section, and opened the book. I found the place where I had left off and began to read. Soon I was transported back to another time and another place, a wonderful land of adventures with my friends, the three musketeers. It was breathtaking. The pages ran together. I read and read some more trying to consume the words on the page as my imagination soared and then after what seemed like an eternity I came back to earth. I read the words as they sprang from the page then I devoured the final words:

… M. Bonacieux, having left his house at seven o'clock in the evening to go to the Louvre, never appeared again in the Rue des Fossoyeurs; the opinion of those to be best informed was that he was fed and lodged in the same royal castle, at the expense of generous Eminence.—**The End**

No, no, it can't be! It's over? My adventures and my journeys were finished. I heard the rustling of papers by the front desk.

"What did you think? Did you like it young man?"

"Oh, yes. Yes, ma'am. I liked it very much, Miss…"

"Mrs. Corcoran, but everyone here in the library calls me Meg."

"Do you have anything else like this here? Meg?"

"Why yes I do," she said her eyes open wide in delight. "Follow me.

"I think I have just the book for you. And maybe a few more," now she sounded excited to help me.

She handed me, *Sea-Hawk* by Rafael Sabatini, *Hardy Boys Mystery Search* by Franklin Dixon, and *The Adventures of Tom Sawyer* by Mark Twain. "Mark Twain is from right here in Missouri. You may also enjoy these biographies. They are about famous and very talented people. They are wonderful to read for a boy like you."

She handed me the biographies of Robert Fulton, George Washington Carver, and Thomas Edison. Mr. Fulton invented the steam engine, and young Thomas Edison discovered electricity. She was opening a completely new world to me. I could not believe the treasures I held in my hands.

"I always say once you read about the lives of great men and women, your own life will never be the same,' she smiled for the first time. She had a pretty smile. I measured people by their smile. She had a good-person smile. She was very tall and thin. A slight bit of grey hair hung over the sides of her reading glasses. She wore a beautiful gold dragonfly brooch on her blouse. Certain ways you looked at her, she was beautiful, especially when she smiled.

I quickly looked through each book as she stood there proud and smiling. When I was done she asked, "So which ones would you like to take home?"

"Home?" I asked as my eyes grew wide.

"Yes, this is a library after all."

"Oh, I forgot. But I don't have a library card."

"No?"

"No ma'am, I don't," I told her.

"If you don't have a library card, I'll need you fill out this information for me and I'll make one up for you. In the meantime, did you want to call home to your folks so they don't worry about you?"

"No, thank you. I'll be fine. I just live down the street and besides…" I shot a glance to the clock above the entrance door. It was almost nine o'clock. Looking out the library's front window, I could see it was dark outside. *Home? Five o'clock dinner? No! Oh shit! Boy was I going to be in for it!*

I quickly put the books into my ever-present army surplus shoulder bag on my back and ran home, the heavy bags bouncing from side to side. There was a black-and-white police car and Chief Gestridge's police sedan parked out front of our house. Neighbors stood outside across the street with their hands to their mouths whispering to one another and pointing at me. They waved for me to join them, but I shook my head. I scrambled around to the back of the house, opened the rear screen door and made my way inside. I was real quiet. It was then I heard my mother crying. She was sobbing.

"He's such a good boy. I'm sure he's lying in a ditch somewhere, bleeding, or dying. He loves to explore with that Timmy who lives down the street. I told him to stay away from him. He's such a bad influence on my Davey. My Davey is a good boy." She continued to sob.

While I hated to hear her cry, I was touched by the loving tone in her voice. And it was all for me. Just me!

"I understand, Mrs. Malloy," came the deep baritone voice of Chief Gestridge. He should have been a politician.

"Do you have a recent picture or can you describe him for our missing persons report? Please?" asked the other inquiring voice of the young investigator who accompanied the chief.

"He is tall... about this high... say four or five feet tall and skinny, you can almost see his ribs through his t-shirt. He never eats enough, but he's still growing like a weed. He has blond hair that sticks out everywhere. Even as a baby, he always had this colic at the back of his head. And he was just twelve... next year thirteen... if he ...." She started to sob. "He would have been a teenager. Oh my God where does the time go?" More sobbing from the living room filled the house.

"Mrs. Malloy, ma'am, please. Does your son have any distinguishing marks on him ma'am?" I heard the younger sounding voice ask my mother.

"What do you mean?"

"Like a tattoo or birthmark?"

"A tattoo? Heavens no. Officer, this is a young Catholic boy not a member of some California motorcycle gang like, like..." She paused to catch her breath. "Wait, he does have a strawberry birth mark on his neck. It's in the shape of a heart. It gets bright red when he gets excited or angry, which he sometimes does. Both he and his older brother Josh have one on their neck. But a tattoo? Well I never. If only he would walk through that door, I would hug him, kiss him, and never let him go. I miss him so much. That Davey is such a good boy." Her sobbing became louder.

I took that as my cue to make my entrance. "Hi, Mom! I'm home. What's with all the police cars out front?" I asked triumphantly. *I was sure she would want to hug me and that they would all lift me on their shoulders and shout my name, maybe even sing my name in a special tune or something. Maybe now she would bake me that special...*

"Davey!" she screamed at the top of her lungs. "Where have you been? I've been worried sick about you."

I swallowed deep. "I stopped at the library to cool down and..."

"You were where? David Matthew Malloy your father is out looking for you as we speak, and when he finds out..."

The front door opened, and in walked my father. He ran to me and squeezed me so hard I thought he was going to break one of my ribs or something. "Oh my God," he whispered in my ear. "Davey, I thought I lost you."

"He was at the library all this time," my mother said standing behind him with her arms folded in front of her now that she knew that I was alive and home safe and sound.

My father stood and looked at me with those disappointed eyes. "Is that true, Davey?"

I was suddenly ashamed that I had let them down. I had not called them and caused them to worry about me. I bowed my head and said, "Yes. I'm sorry, Dad. I was reading and lost track of time. I didn't mean to make you and Mom worry." My brother and sisters were now hiding behind the living room chairs, eyes peering over the top, waiting to see what my father would say.

"Go to your room. No dinner tonight, and you're grounded."

"Grounded? For how long?"

"Forever. Go to your room, but first apologize to you mother. She was worried sick."

"I'm sorry, Mom. Really I am."

"Go to your room," whispered my mother. "We'll talk about this later. Your father and I were worried out of our minds. We thought you were dead."

"Dad, I just stopped there for a minute to..."

"David Malloy, go to your room, now. You are old enough to know better."

"I guess we don't need this report anymore do we, Mrs. Malloy?" interrupted the Chief who had been standing nearby as the scene unfolded before him. The other officer ripped the sheet in half and stuck it in his pants pocket.

"No Chief, I think not," said my father. "Thank you both so very much for coming. Sorry to put you through so much trouble."

"No trouble at all. Just glad he's home safe and sound," said Chief Gestridge looking at me as I scurried to my room.

"Goodnight, officers," Mom said and walked them to the door. She then turned to face me, raising her finger, pointing at me. "Go."

I went to my room, which was now my prison. *This can't be happening; this is summertime. What the hell was I going to do now? I was grounded. What was I going to do?* The stack of books from the library beckoned me. I opened one, and began to read. It was *The Sea-Hawk* a swashbuckling adventure tale written by Rafael Sabatini. *Maybe this was not going to be as bad as I thought it was going to be.* I began to read, but I was hungry, real hungry. My stomach growled.

My mom came in about an hour later with a tray of food for me. "Shhh, quiet," she whispered putting her finger to her lips. She tousled my hair. "Eat this, and then go to bed. Don't tell your father, and don't you ever, ever do that again. Do you hear me, David Matthew Malloy?"

"Yes, ma'am. I'm sorry, Mom. Really."

She kissed my forehead and whispered, "I know you are, Davey. I love you. Now eat. You're as skinny as a bone."

My father was calmer than I thought he would be, but he still grounded me for two weeks, with no TV, no fishing, no bikes, no exploring, nothing except for church and loads of chores.

I cut the lawn, edged and weeded, cleaned the garage, moved the patio and porch furniture, vacuumed the house, mopped the kitchen floor, painted the front porch, washed the screens on the whole house all under the watchful eye of my sister Joanie.

My oldest sister Jane worked at Barclay Bakery down the street. She always brought home the best desserts and cookies. She smiled when she heard what had happened to me and whispered to me, "No cake for you, you're being punished." I love their cake. But later that same night she saved me a piece and sneaked it to me after dinner.

Mr. Jost was out of town on vacation but said I could pick up the radio when he got back. Timmy was out of town visiting his brother again. Sunny was in Chicago living at her older sister's house to help out after her sister had a baby. I missed both my friends, especially Sunny, she was so smart… and cute, but I was at home, by myself with no friends, alone. Grounded.

I settled into a routine over those two weeks of solitary confinement, I would get up, eat, do my chores from the list, and then read. Later, I would have lunch with a sandwich and Kool-Aid and then went back to my reading. I would lie on my bed and feel the cool summer breeze come through my window facing Mr. Jost's backyard. It was heaven. I finished book after book. I would read at night with my flashlight hidden underneath the sheets. I could hear the of haunting howl of the night freight train far off in the distance, its loud whistle piercing the clear night air and the echoing sound of the grey owls flying in the dark searching for food.

My suspension was over in two weeks, but I continued to read. I loved the library books Mrs. Corcoran had given me to read.

When I returned them to the library, Mrs. Corcoran had an odd look on her face.

"Is everything okay? I hadn't seen you in a couple of weeks and thought maybe I scared you away."

"No, I was grounded for coming home late that day."

She smiled at me. "I see," she said with a knowing smile. "Did you like the books I gave you?"

"They were the greatest, Mrs. Corcoran," I said as I placed them on the return rack. "Do you have any others?"

"Of course, Davey—we're a library, remember? Now, follow me." She grabbed her glasses from her desk and walked with a determined gait. She stopped just past the counter and turned to me, "The library is arranged by areas of interests and the biographies and autobiographies are here. Now, let me see, let me see," she repeated again looking through the shelves for some special books. "Ah, here are some I'm sure you'll like." She looked through the shelves talking to herself until she found what she was looking for, ones she was sure I would like.

"Here we go. I have biographies on Eli Whitney, Louis Pasteur, Michelangelo, and of course Benjamin Franklin." She put them in my hands as we walked back to her desk. I treasured them like gold. "So I take it you like to read?"

"Not until my mom had me start to read *The Three Musketeers* when school was out for the summer. My English teacher said I needed to read more, so my mom has me read a chapter every day."

"She sounds like a very smart lady."

I smiled. "Yes, she is. The smartest." She began walking and searching the shelves as I followed behind her. "She helped me write a story for school last year. I really liked it doing that," I whispered. For some unknown reason I was sharing this with her, something I had not shared with anyone else before. *Why did I tell her that?*

She stopped and looked at me strangely before sitting down at her desk and stamped the books with the date when they were due back to the Overland library.

"Really?" she said sounding amazed. She handed the books to me and said, "Would you mind doing something for me?"

"No, Mrs. Corcoran. What?"

"I have a test I would like you to take for me."

"A test? Gee, I don't know... this is summertime, and I'm not crazy about tests. Besides I always do so poorly in..."

"No, it's not really a test. It's a writing exercise. You see I used it years ago to evaluate creative-writing students at the university where I taught and I thought maybe... well..." she paused and looked at me. "Trust me. Can you write me a short story?"

"Sure. I can do that. I like to write." My enthusiasm must have been evident because she smiled at me.

"Good. Sit here with this pencil and paper. It's simple really. You have ten minutes. I'll give you three words and you think about a story using those words and then write it down. But you only have ten minutes. Okay?"

"That's it?"

"That's it. Ready?"

"Sure."

"These are three words that I usually use—woman, ring, and moon. Now, take your time, and just write a story. But remember, you only have ten minutes. Starting...now." She looked at her watch and walked away from the table. She returned to her desk, and began sorting through her books, putting them back in their proper place on the shelves.

I thought about the words: woman, ring, and moon. I thought about them again and again for a couple of minutes and then closed my eyes. Soon a story began to form in my mind and then I began to write:

I could see the outline of the woman in the light of the moon, as she appeared to be walking straight towards the center of the bridge. She stopped a couple of times, leaned over the bridge railing as if she were in pain. I became concerned that she might be a jumper, because we've had many of those sorts come out at night with the full moon. My job was to make sure that on my shift, they did not succeed.

I grabbed my coat and slowly walked towards her, but I could hardly make out her face in the early evening fog. She appeared to be in her late forties wearing a long, red coat, and I saw that she clutched something tightly in her hand. It was cold at the top, near the center span of the bridge, but I had gotten used to it over the past twenty-two years that I had been working here.

"Evening, ma'am"—I said gently. But even with my most compassionate voice I startled her. "I'm Frank Adams with bridge security." She looked at me, then laid the wedding ring down on the bridge railing... and started sobbing. "I just wanted to..."

"Time's up," said Mrs. Corcoran from her desk. "Now, let me see what you've you written."

I handed her the paper then I watched her lips move as she read what I wrote. She looked up from my story once and gave me a strange look. When she was finished reading, she set the paper down and didn't say anything at first. Then she looked at me, smiled and said, "This is good, Davey. Very good. It's okay if I call you Davey, isn't it? "

"Sure. That's my name. That's what everybody calls me except when my mom gets real mad at me then she calls me David."

"How old are you?"

"I just turned twelve... but I'll be thirteen soon," I said proudly.

"That's nice. Davey, would you like to practice your writing this summer? Not a test, just between you and me... and your mom if you like. What do you say?"

"Well, I'd love to try... but what would I have to write about?"

"You can write about anything you please, but the thing is you have to write something every day even if it's just to write to say hello or goodbye or the sun is hot. Okay? Deal?"

"Deal. Sounds like fun."

She went to her desk and began searching in the bottom drawer until she found what she was looking for, and handed it to me. It was a black leather-bound book with the word JOURNAL printed on the front. "Here you go. Write whatever you want in here and just bring it in with you when you come here to the library. No rush, no pressure."

"Okay." The journal had lines on the inside and was about the size of large paperback book. *This should be fun.* I walked home thinking of different stories I could tell.

Chapter Ten

As soon as I walked inside our house, the phone rang. Both of my sisters ran to answer it, but my oldest sister Janey was taller and faster and grabbed it from the wall. I heard her mumble something and turn away. She must be expecting her new boyfriend to call. She was always on the phone with him. His name was Rodney or something like that. He seemed nice.

"Davey… it's for you, it's that Walker boy," hollered Janey with a disgusted look on her face. She pointed her finger at me, "Don't be on the phone long, you understand? I'm expecting a very important phone call."

"From Rodney?" I mocked as I picked up the phone and made a face at her.

"Hey whatcha doin'?" Timmy said.

"Getting ready for dinner. My dad'll be home soon. "When d'you get back from…?"

"Earlier today. I called you, but your mom answered, so I hung up. I don't think she's too crazy about me."

"Don't do that, man. You'll worry her. She'll think you're some gambler or something calling."

We were always getting phone calls from guys with deep voices wanting to place bets. Apparently, there was somebody else with the same name as my dad, by the name of James Malloy who was a bookie. One day I got three phone calls in a row, and on the last one, I took his bet on some baseball team or something. I'm sure somebody was really mad after they couldn't collect from the real bookie. When I told my father about it, he said not to do it again. "Just hang up," he told me.

"You going to get a paper for your dad tonight?" Timmy asked.

"Yeah, usually I do, but I don't know when. Soon I guess."

As if on cue, my mother hollered from the kitchen. "Davey, hurry now and go get your father's newspaper."

I whispered into the phone, "I'm leaving now for Clarks to get the paper."

"Stop by the castle for a minute. I have something cool to show you."

The castle was our secret meeting place. Last summer, they built a new church on one of the vacant lots we played games on just down the street from Timmy's house. We played war in those huge overgrown fields. We used water guns, peashooters, and slingshots. But then they cut the grass and tore down all our forts, bulldozed all our hills and tunnels.

Tim talked to the night security guard, and he said we could have all kinds of stuff from their junk pile. We hauled home some building stuff, plywood, two by fours, roof tile, everything we needed to build a cool clubhouse we called it our castle. "Just don't take the new lumber," the guard told us, but Timmy took it anyway. That's just the way he was. Timmy also took some electrical tools from the builder in order to get it done fast. He said it was okay to steal from them he said, since they stole our land from our territory.

"See you in five minutes," I said.

My mom hollered from the kitchen, "Davey, go get your father's paper now and don't stop anywhere. You come right home, do you hear me?"

"Yes, ma'am."

The pharmacist Ralph Clark and his partner Bob Roman ran Clarks Pharmacy where I got my dad's paper. Mr. Clark owned the building and rented medical offices upstairs, and Lackland Office Supply shared space with him on the ground floor.

In the pharmacy, they had a soda fountain where I could get a cherry or a chocolate Coke from the teenage girl who worked there. She was pretty. Her name was Charlotte.

I usually read some comic books before getting my dad's paper, the *Saint Louis Post Dispatch,* but I knew he was on his way home and I didn't want to be late for dinner. I handed the boy behind the cigar counter a nickel for the paper and he kept holding his hand out. "It's seven cents now," said Jimmy Clark, Mr. Clark's oldest son.

"What? When did that happen?"

"Yesterday. That'll be seven cents, Davey Malloy," he said with a sneer.

"I don't have any more money."

"Well, go home and get it." He spit the words as if it were some dreaded disease.

I ought to pop him in the nose, I thought as I searched my pockets for some hidden change. Then I found it, another nickel. "Here, now you owe me three cents." His smile vanished as he rang up my sale and gave me change from the register. I took my newspaper and change and left the store. I thought to myself, *I really do hate that kid and his smug smile.*

I walked past Timmy's front yard, past Raggedy, their mean, longhaired dog that was tied to a tree beside their house. He growled and lunged at me, but his rope was too short as it jerked him back off his feet, but he continued to growl and snap at me. Timmy was always teasing him, poking him with a stick and it made him mad. And crazy-like.

The padlock on the castle door was off, so I knew he was inside. I stood in front of the door to our clubhouse and knocked our secret knock. Knock, knock, knock... knock, knock... knock. I waited.

Soon I heard the door unlatch from inside and watched it swing open. Timmy walked outside the clubhouse, and I could smell cigarette smoke through the open door. I hated that smell. He stood there and stuck out his hand. We shook hands using our secret handshake.

His hair was shorter than the last time I saw him. He usually had real short brown hair on the sides of his head and kept it long on the top. It was always flopping in front of his eyes. He would snap his head back to move it away. That day it was short everywhere but with streaks of yellow sprinkled throughout. He was tall and lean, his muscles showed under his t-shirt. Lifting his brother's weights, I imagined. He was strong and always won any arm-wrestling contests in the neighborhood. As a matter of fact he never lost at anything.

"New hhhaircut?" I asked.

"Yeah, I saw a magazine and this is the way they wear it in California now. The sun gave me the yellow streaks. I also used some Sun-In to help it color it. Cool huh?"

"Yeah, mmman. Hey, I can't stay lllong. I gotta get hhhome for dinner."

"Hell, you can never stay long," he said then lit a cigarette and blew out a puff of smoke. "Wanna drag?" He was always smoking. I shook my head no.

"Hey man, wait 'til you see this."

"Timmy! Are you smoking?" A shout came from his house as the door opened and his mother walked outside onto the porch overlooking their pool. She was very pretty.

"Is that you, Davey?"

"Yes, mmma'am."

"How are you?" she shouted from the porch wearing a white top and short shorts while holding a cocktail glass in her hand.

"I'm fffine, Mrs. Walker. I jjjust stopped by on my way hhhome from the drugstore to get my father's pppaper."

"Good seeing you again, Davey. Don't be such a stranger now. It's so hot, come by anytime and use our pool," she smiled and waved at me before she disappeared back inside the house to get another drink.

They had built a swimming pool and small changing cabana off to the side. I loved watching her walk around in her two-piece swimsuit, and I had dreams about her sometimes at night, some very real dreams. But that was one thing I never told Timmy. He would kill me. One day I was so hot, I stopped by after mowing some lawns to make some money. I cooled my feet in the cool water of their pool, she made me some lemonade, and hot dogs and we talked for a long time and… but I never told Timmy. Never. Or anyone else.

Timmy waved at her and said under his breath, "She thinks you're a saint. Always telling me, 'Timmy, you should be like that young Davey Malloy.' On top of that, she thinks you're cute. Come on, follow me."

We went inside our castle, and he walked to one of the mattresses on the wooden floor and lifted it up and reached underneath. He pulled out an old dirty rag wrapped around something, but I couldn't see what it was. Then he stood before me and slowly unwrapped his new prized possession. I could see the pride and excitement in his eyes. When he was done, he held it in his hands—it was a blue-gray handgun. I had seen enough cop shows to know what it was and know what was used for—it was used for no good. My legs started to shake watching the way he held it and spun it around. Trying to be like a cowboy on TV… or a gangster. It seemed so natural for him.

"Here, it's a .38 caliber special," he said, shoving into my hand.

It was scary at first, but its warm wooden handle made it felt cool to the touch. The steel barrel made it feel heavy and, for some strange reason, powerful. I could not take my eyes off it as I wrapped my fingers around the butt and held it tight in my hand before I handed it back to him. I took in a deep breath of air. It was exhilarating and scary at the same time.

"Thanks."

"They call it a suicide special. Don't ask me why," Timmy said without looking at the handle with a splotch of red at the bottom.

Blood?

A wicked smile covered his face. He pointed it at the floor as he loaded it with three shiny silver- and gold-colored bullets and spun the chamber around and around. He lifted the weapon higher and pointed it towards my stomach. I heard it click as he pulled the hammer back with his thumb. My stomach churned sour and for the first time in my life… I was afraid. Really afraid. He had that look of evil in his eyes.

"Whhhere dddid you get thhat?" I asked backing away from him. The gun barrel remained focused on my midsection. Dead on. He didn't say anything at first. His eyes were glassed over. He pulled the trigger. It made a loud metallic click. I nearly threw up.

"It's my brother's. He asked me to keep it for him while he's away in the joint, but he said I could use it anytime I wanted. Wanna hold it again?"

"Nnno."

"Are you sure? Afraid? Are you a chickenshit?" he asked with a sneer. That was the worst thing in the world to be called by somebody—chickenshit, coward, wuss, it all meant the same.

He pointed the pistol at me again, moving it from side to side in a slow random motion, and pulled the hammer back again, ready to pull the trigger. Then I heard it—knock, knock knock… knock, knock… knock. I waited. He didn't move he just stood there with the pistol in his hand. Like he was in a trance.

Again I heard it—knock, knock, knock… knock, knock… knock. It was our secret knock. Only one other person knew our secret knock call sign—Sunny.

"Come on in, Sunny," I shouted. Tim awoke from his stupor, shoved the pistol into the back of his jeans, and pulled his t-shirt down to cover it.

"Hey guys, can anybody join the party?" she asked with a smile stolen from the heavens. It was so good to see her again. I had not seen her in a while since she was away at school then left for Chicago to be with her sisters. I didn't realize how much I missed seeing her, but she looked different, very different. The braces were gone.

"Hi guys," she beamed to both of us as we did our secret handshake.

Sunny had such big, beautiful, round dark eyes, and tan skin. Her eyes glistened like evening stars. Her hair was shorter now, but she still wore the same white Elvis t-shirt, jean cutoffs, and sandals, however, she no longer looked like the tomboy we knew from last summer. Her t-shirt seemed snugger than I remembered it.

Timmy kept looking at her.

"Hi, Timmy," she said to him, then looked at me with her eyes lowered and whispered, "Hi, Davey. Good to see you again."

"Hi, Sunny," I said with a smile.

Tim and I hugged her hello, but she stepped back and looked at us. Timmy could not take his eyes off the front of her t-shirt. "What?" she asked him. He didn't say anything.

"What are you looking at?" she finally asked.

"You grew boobs over the winter, that's what," he blurted out. Her face turned red and for the first time since I met her she did not have a snappy retort for him. Finally, she changed the subject. "So what's going on lately? What'd I miss?" she turned and asked me.

Timmy jumped between us and said, "Well, Davey and I were just talking about going to the Legion pool next weekend for the Fourth of July. Wanna go?"

"Sure. Are you going, Davey?" Both Sunny and I didn't know how to swim, but we loved to go in the shallow water and goof off, splashing water on each other with some of the other kids.

My brother Jack was a part-time lifeguard at the Legion pool. He gave swimming lessons and tried to teach me to swim many times, but I never got past the "guppy" stage. It was the same with Sunny.

Timmy was a strong swimmer; he even tried to save Neil Jacobs from drowning in the quarry last summer. It was late in the day, and it was just the two of them. He said he tried his best, but the little kid died anyway. Shame, he was a nice kid. But I never wanted to learn to swim after that for some reason.

"I'm nnnot sure. I ttthink so."

"Try to make it won't you, Davey? It won't be the same if you don't go." She touched my cheek before leaving in a whirl. "Gotta go," she said walking out the door.

I turned around just in time to see a dark scowl on Timmy's face. I had not seen that look before. "Oh my God, I gggotta get hhhome with my dad's paper. He'll bbbe furious if I'm late for sssupper. Gotta go. See ya later, Tttim."

As I closed the clubhouse door behind me, I heard Timmy say in a low sweet mocking voice, uttering, "Try to make it won't you, Davey? It won't be the same if you don't go. Shit on that!" A chill went down my spine as I heard him spin the chamber of the gun, once, then again.

Time to get home with the paper. What's going on with him? I thought to myself. *Spooky. I have to talk to him, and sooner rather than later. He was not going to be …*

"Hi ya, Carol," she heard the voice say and looked up from her reading. Mitch stood there with his usual smile as she shoved the manuscript back into her briefcase. She had been lost in the compelling story of Mitch or rather Davey and his childhood. It also was helping to explain many things. She wanted to read more. She felt his hand on her shoulder. It was warm and enticing.

"Like it?" he asked like a school kid.

"Love it," she said.

"It's a good book, isn't it?" he asked giving her a strange look.

Her mind caught up with reality, "Yes," she told him and turned to him to ask, "Are you done already?"

"No, I'm just taking a break. They're setting up some more books for me to sign, but I thought I'd come back here and see how you're doing."

"I'm good," she said with a smile. She felt closer to him than she ever had in the past. And she didn't know if that was a good thing.

He discreetly checked his phone for messages, and then quickly shoved it back in his pocket.

"Anything?"

"No." He tried again.

A store clerk came by, "Mr. Patterson, we're ready for you, sir. Anytime now," he said.

"Be right there, Jerry," he said shoving the phone back inside his pocket, kissing her on the cheek. "Enjoy the book, Carol. It will keep you company while I make us both some money."

"Talk to you later," she said and turned back to continue her reading.

Chapter Eleven

When I walked in the door, my mom said my dad got bogged down at the office and would be a little late and for me to go wash up for dinner.

"They charge seven cents now for a paper," I told her. "Can you believe that? Seven cents."

"Your father will be furious. Whew! That...that's a forty percent increase. Umph! Go wash up."

The phone rang, and the race was on to see who was calling. "Davey, it's for you. It's Sunny," hollered my sister Jane. "Don't be on long. I'm expecting an important..." her voice trailed off in the distance.

"Hey, Sunny."

"Hi ya," came her sweet reply. "Everything okay?"

"Yeah, sure. Why?"

"I don't know you just seemed different and Timmy... well, he was just plain weird as usual."

"No, I'm okay." I decided not to tell her about the gun. She would just be upset. I knew Timmy would show it to her sooner or later just to impress her. I would warn her in my own way.

"I hope you can make it to the pool on Saturday. They're unveiling the new flag at the Legion. Imagine that, Alaska will make it forty-nine stars and Hawaii will be fifty states. Soon, they're going to run out of room on the flag. They're going to have a big celebration at the Legion. Should be a lot of fun. Please come, Davey. I haven't seen you in ages, and we have a lot to catch up on together. And I have a belated birthday gift for you. Try to make it okay?"

"Okay, sure. I'll be there."

"Oh and Davey, I almost forgot. My grandmother still wants to have you come to our house for that dinner we promised you last summer. She keeps asking me about it."

"Sure. Just let me know when you want to do it. And I'll ask my mom if it's okay."

"Okay. See'ya Saturday."

After I hung up the phone, I could not get Sun Lei out of my mind. My thoughts drifted back to the previous summer when I first met her and her grandmother.

Chapter Twelve

I remember, it was the previous summer, and I was walking back from a trip to Schnucks grocery store for my mother. It was hot. The weatherman said it was hottest day of the year. The hottest day in ten years they said that night on the news. *Just my luck to be walking back fifteen blocks from the store, again.* As soon as I walked outside from the store, I felt the hot air slap me in the face. It was brutal. Mom said it was okay to stop and get a Coke and she even gave me money for the soda machine.

Halfway home I stopped at Overland City Hall and went downstairs for a Coke. I got two. One for then and one for later. I drank one down almost completely then shoved the second one into my rucksack and started walking home again.

Only four more blocks to go, I thought to myself. Up ahead on the sidewalk I could see in front of me the unmistakable outline of an old Korean lady dressed in black all hunched over. It was Mrs. Moran. She was pulling her overloaded grocery cart. The heat must be really getting to an old woman like that, I thought. She was barely moving. My Uncle Frank, the cop, told me Koreans could work outside in the rice fields all day without so much as breaking a sweat. He used to say, "They are different from us; they can work outside in the hot sun forever." I don't care what he said; it was hot and she was barely moving.

As I came up behind her, she was resting against one of the huge sycamore trees, which lined our street. My house was only two blocks away.

"Afternoon, Mrs. Moran," I said, as I walked around her. She mumbled something in reply. I kept walking, but something inside me made me stop and turn around. I looked at her. Her face was bright red, and her eyes looked glassy.

I stopped and walked back towards her. It was a step, which would change my life forever. My father always used to say, "Life has many paths," and looking back I could see that my life changed on that day.

"Are you okay, Mrs. Moran?" I asked her as I approached. She didn't know who I was, but everybody knew the old lady in black who pulled the shopping cart home every day. Her name was Moran, and she moved in down the street with her granddaughter and two grandsons.

She seemed startled. Her eyes were even more glazed now as if she was going to collapse. I set down my bags on the hot sidewalk and pulled the still-cold soda from my bag and handed it to her. She glanced at it as though it were poison. She stepped backwards. *Did she understand English?* I thought to myself. I opened the bottle with the P-38 can opener that Josh had given me and hung around my neck.

"Here have some. It's okay," I told her. "It's cold, and I haven't drunk out of it at all, honest." I don't know if she understood what I was saying, judging from the look on her face. I took her hand and gently touched it to the cold bottle. She smiled.

She looked at me then looked at the bottle before her; she began licking her lips. She took the bottle and drank a sip. She took another, and her lips once again took in the cold refreshing liquid. Her face was not as red.

"Go ahead, have another sip," I urged her. This time she took a big drink and kept on drinking. Soon I watched my nickel investment disappear, with one last resounding bubble at the bottom of the bottle. But I didn't mind; it was worth it to see the look on her face.

When she was finished, she burped then managed a little embarrassed grin. She then bent over in what appeared to be a slight bow of thank you from her crooked little frame. I felt better in that moment than I had ever felt in my whole life. I wanted my life to be frozen just at that second, so I could die with that feeling. I was so glad I stopped to help her.

I swung both my grocery bags onto my hip and then grabbed her cart and starting walking with her. It was heavy. It was hot. She looked at me, bewildered. Two blocks away, when we reached my house, I stopped and told her, holding up my hand, "Wait here, please." I ran inside and set the groceries and my mother's change on the table.

"Mom, I'm back," I yelled to her and my sisters, who were downstairs in the basement watching my mom do the ironing.

"Okay. Did you get everything?"

"Yes ma'am, I did. I'll be right back in a little bit."

"Don't be late for supper, Davey."

"Okay, Mom."

I grabbed a Howdy Doody glass we got when my Mom bought some Welch's jelly and I filled it with ice and cold water.

Mrs. Moran was still standing right where I had left her. She looked at the glass of ice-filled of water, and for the first time her eyes grew wide and she managed a small smile. She drank the water and took a deep breath and started to grab the cart.

"Let me help you?" I asked. "Please? It's only a couple of blocks."

She smiled, nodded her agreement and handed me the handle to the cart but said nothing.

We did not say anything the whole time we walked to her house. I don't think she spoke much, if any English. We walked down Lackland and then turned onto Charlack and walked down the sidewalk of the steep hill to her house at the end of the street a few blocks away. She grabbed my belt from behind me to steady herself. Her tiny little steps had a hard time keeping up with my large strides as we gained momentum down the hill. I slowed down, and she managed a weak grin at the bottom.

Hers was the last house on street, but next to it were three large vacant lots where we played baseball the summer before until it became overgrown with tall grasses and weeds. It was perfect place to play and was now part of our "territory" where Timmy and I played.

Her big, dark red brick house had a large porch on the front with a swing hanging from the ceiling and two metal rocking chairs. Many times, I saw her on the porch sweeping the leaves and dust from the big porch. I never saw anyone using the porch. I would occasionally see her grandsons coming home from high school, but then they would disappear inside the house. They never joined us on the ball-field, I guess because they were never asked.

Mrs. Moran took her overloaded grocery cart from me at the base of the steps, but she was too weak to pull the cart up the steep set of stairs. I pulled it up the steps and then stopped at the door and for some reason I went to say goodbye with a slight bow. She shook her head as she unlocked the glass door and invited me within, with a slight motion of her hand. I hesitated but she waved again with a small smile motioning for me to come inside.

The interior of the house was dark but cool. The smell of unfamiliar foods and spices filled the air. A variety of red and yellow colors showed through the multitude of curtains that covered the windows. There was a small altar with candles on a table off to the side in the living room, next to her sofa. I could barely see the kitchen at the back of the house.

My feet were frozen in place, my eyes trying to take in my strange new surroundings. I took in all of the wonders of what I dreamed the Orient would be like, including the bust of a large smiling Buddha on a table in the next room, which appeared to be the dining room. I surveyed the living room and dining room with its large cherry table with lace placemats set for four along with ornate ivory chopsticks positioned on the side of the plates. There were family portraits lining the mantel of a fake fireplace leaning up against the living room wall. Stairs on the left lead upstairs with more family pictures on the wall, but I could see nothing more. Pictures of the snow-covered mountains in Korea were everywhere. Everything was very clean, neat, and orderly, and nothing seemed to be out of place. It was so quiet, like a church.

I saw a shadow move quickly in the other room by the stairs and then heard raised voices in the kitchen. Two darkened figures approached me from the back room; one was Mrs. Moran but the other person I could not see until she was out of the shadows and standing in front of me.

Mrs. Moran was accompanied by a young girl, about my age, perhaps slightly older, but about the same height as me; she was beautiful. A slightly built girl with long black hair that looked so soft I wanted to reach out and touch it and feel it between my fingers. She was the most beautiful girl I had ever seen in my life. My chin dropped, and my mouth opened wide. Her large almond eyes and calm, bewitching smile immediately put me at ease.

She held out a red apple to me. I looked down at it, but my gaze quickly returned to her. I could not take my eyes off her. It was then that I heard her angelic voice whisper, "My grandmother told me what you did." To me it sounded like a prayer. "That was very kind of you. I thank you, and my granny would like to thank you." She extended the apple once more, this time with a slight smile. "For you, please."

I didn't know what to say and just stood there staring at her, an apple in my hand. Finally, I took the apple and heard my mouth, which was now operating independently of my brain, say, "Thank you. Thank you very much. Will you marry me?"

She laughed and said something in a different language to her grandmother, but I was not deterred. "I'm serious," I told her.

Mrs. Moran said something, and the hopefully future Mrs. Malloy, responded in the same language. Her grandmother laughed a hearty laugh while covering her mouth with her hand, chuckling. I guess it was somewhat funny.

"Perhaps later, when you are ready," the young girl said coyly, once again captivating me with her wondrous smile. "In Korea," she told me, "tradition has it that a girl must be asked three times before she consents to being married. It is to ensure that the suitor is serious and honorable in his intentions. And I have only just met you."

"Okay. Then will you…"

She placed her fingertip on my lips. "Shhh." Her touch was like that of an angel or the beating of a butterfly's wings.

Regaining my senses, I told her, "I'm sorry, I didn't mean to embarrass you." Then pointing to her grandmother, I said, "Please tell Mrs. Moran I was happy to be able to help her today and please thank her for the wonderful apple."

"Mai Ran."

"Excuse me," I said, turning to face my future bride.

"Our family name is Mai Ran… not Moran. We are Korean not Irish," she giggled, without the hint of a correcting tone, the sound of which I heard constantly in school. Twice in one day, I was embarrassed. A red flush started from my neck and traveled to my face. My embarrassment must have shown, because she took my hand and told me, "It is a common mistake here in America. My grandmother is honored to have you as a friend. A true friend is someone who does such a grand thing with no thought of payment. But I don't even know your name and… if we are going to be married I think I at least need to know what people call you."

"I'm sorry. My name is David Malloy," I said still holding her soft, warm hand and looking for any excuse to continue holding it. "If you won't marry me today, will you at least tell me your name?"

Again, a small smile crept onto her lips as she shook my hand. "My name is Sun Lei. My mother's family is from Korea, and my father is from China. You are welcome in our house at any time, Mr. David Malloy. My grandmother has asked that perhaps you would honor us with your presence one evening and join us for dinner?"

"I would love to, but please, my friends call me Davey. I would like you to call me Davey… if that's okay?"

"Of course," she said, slowly withdrawing her hands from mine, under the watchful eyes of her vigilant grandmother.

"Thanks again for the apple," and I turned to walk out the door, still lost in thoughts about my wonderful Sun Lei. *Sun Malloy, it has a nice ring to it.*

I reached the porch outside and was greeted by two large figures who lifted me off the ground, leaving my feet dangling in mid-air, one of my tennis shoes slipped off my feet and dropped to the ground below. They began yelling at me in a strange twisted language. *Korean?*

"Who are you?" they both yelled finally in English. "What are you doing at our house? Why are you stealing apples from our home? Where's my *halmoni?*"

"Yes," said the other one who was as big as a mountain. "What did you do with our grandmother?" I looked at each one, left then right, as they each pummeled me with questions, their eyes ablaze with impending fury.

"You think you can just walk right in and steal from us just because we are Korean? We will teach you!" said the bigger one.

The unseen blow landed in my stomach. The punch hurt my stomach and deflated my lungs, I could not breathe. I gasped louder and louder. My world began to spin. The voices were interspersed with words I could not understand, similar to what Sun Lei had spoken.

The door behind us opened wide and the little old lady dressed in black came out swinging and yelling both in English and what I took for Korean, "You dum' boys! Leave him 'lone! He David. He good boy. You no touch, ever. You hear me, you dum' boys! Let him down!" The world went black as I passed out on their front porch. I floated in darkness with an aching pain in my stomach.

I don't know how long I was out, but when I awoke, I could hear her voice asking me, sounding a million miles away. "David? Davey are you okay?" a distant voice asked.

Her face was fuzzy, but soon I could make out her smile, then I saw the beautiful face of Sun Lei in front of me, applying a cool washcloth to my forehead. Her *halmoni* was leaning over her shoulder behind her whispering something in her ear.

"Are you all right?" she repeated.

"Yes, I'll be all right," I said coughing "… if you marry me," I responded, figuring maybe I would catch her with her defenses down. *Maybe she would take pity on me.*

"He's fine," she said aloud in both English and Korean to everybody, before helping me stand up. Sun Lei brushed up against me, and I felt her small chest touch my arm. Our eyes met for a brief moment. I could smell the sweet subtle scent of her jasmine perfume when she leaned close to me, and then she placed a soft kiss on my cheek.

She kissed me! My heart soared, but before I could say anything else, my attention was diverted to her brothers who moments before had me dangling in mid-air. They were watching everything that was happening.

"These are my two dumb brothers, Mang and Trac," said Sun Lei in a disgusted tone.

"We're so sorry," said the two contrite oversized boys. "We didn't know who you were." They were both as large as a house, with their heads hanging down, being cowed by a tiny, old, Korean woman. They extended their hands to me in remorse all under the watchful eye of the stern looking Mrs. Mai Ran. I shook their hands vigorously. I would rather have these two as friends than as enemies, I thought.

"No hard feelings?" they asked, both looking nervously at their grandmother.

"No," I said. "You did what I would have done," I told them, not really knowing exactly what I would have done. "But I have to go now, it is time for dinner, and my mom doesn't like me to be late. Goodbye," I told them, and for some unknown reason I bowed before I left, as a way of saying goodbye and out of respect. The two huge brothers and Sun Lei giggled but bowed in return.

I walked away as they returned inside. I looked back waiting, wishing, hoping she would turn to watch me, and then I saw her, she turned to look back at me, smiling.

What a day! I thought to myself as I ran home for dinner. I didn't know it then, but I had found the one person in the world that I truly loved.

After that day, Timmy and I played in the fields next to her house regularly, and she began to join us. She turned out to be a real tomboy and said she just wanted to be with friends with us. I smiled to myself thinking back to that day last summer. We played together every day. That summer we became best friends until she went off to school. She was the best.

Now she was still on my mind, but this Saturday I would see her again at the American Legion pool. I could hardly wait. I was sure Timmy would be there.

My mom hollered from the kitchen. "Oh Davey, I nearly forgot. Mr. Jost dropped by earlier and left something for you. I put it on your bed."

I ran to my room. On my bed was my new radio, the Blau-Bruin International IR-2600K! This was great, I could now talk to the world. I loved it. My thoughts drifted to Sun Lei and Timmy's Smith & Wesson snub nose .38 pistol. But for now I had to figure out a way to pay for my newfound treasure. I knew just what I would do. I would...

"Carol?" Her reading was interrupted by the sound of a familiar voice, pulling her away, "Carol? Carol; are you ready for some lunch? I'm all done with the book signings, and I'm starvin'."

Carol looked up from the manuscript she was reading; the book signing took longer than expected but was finally over, and she saw him standing there in front of her, watching, waiting. Mitch's eyes seemed much bluer than she had remembered them just an hour or so earlier. Trusting blue, she thought. Warm and tender blue.

"Ready for lunch?" he repeated.

"Yeah, sure," she said reluctantly putting the manuscript back inside her travel bag. "Interesting book. Let's go eat." She couldn't wait to get back to reading it.

He helped her on with her jacket as they walked outside into the bustling midday Manhattan crowd.

She could see he already needed a shave and probably a drink. She could tell from the way he walked and held his head, today was not a good day for him.

Chapter Thirteen

11:38 A.M.

The clock on the wall reminded Nate that it was nearly eleven-forty-five, time to call his client. He did not like to be late. Inmates developed a daily pattern and did not like it interrupted, and Walker was no exception.

He stood up and stretched his arms and back, still stiff from sitting too long. His researcher was sending over more documents and the proper forms for him to sign and scan. He would make his one o'clock deadline, but it would be tight. It was a strange word—deadline, he thought to himself considering the circumstances. But it seemed to fit the occasion.

He picked up the phone and dialed the number. After going through security and proper identification procedures, he was connected to D-Block and minutes later, he heard a familiar voice say, "Hey, what's up?"

"Hey, Tim. I have the paperwork just about finished and should have it ready for our one o'clock deadline for submission. I've been working for the last ten hours on filing an appeal to the United States Supreme Court. It has to be in by one o'clock."

"Then what the hell you doing on the phone with me?"

"Tim, I just wanted to keep you informed, that's all."

"Okay, you did your duty, now go finish that paperwork. When those nut holes say one o'clock they mean one o'clock. Don't be late. Go!"

"Okay. Timmy, one last thing, I…"

"Don't you ever call me Timmy," he shouted his voice sounding like a madman. "You hear me, lawyer? Never!" The words gave Nate a chill.

"Okay, okay, calm down," he replied and waited a few seconds before continuing. "The main reason I called is… I know we hoped I would be there for the final hour, but with the timing on this latest filing, well... I have to be on call with them here in case they need any other documents, so... I won't be there with you when it happens. If it happens," he hastened to add.

There was silence on the other end before he said with a level voice, "It's okay. Just don't forget to get the envelope to him, will you?"

"Sure Tim, anything."

"And one last thing, I appreciate everything you've done for me, Ralph. Goodbye."

After ten years as his attorney, his client didn't even remember his first name.

Chapter Fourteen

11:45 A.M.

Mitch stopped by the newsstand and shoved some cash into the vendor's hand before he opened the newspaper and found what he was looking for under national news. "Six P.M. as usual," is all he said as he threw the paper away into a nearby trash can. "I need a drink. We've never been this close before."

They took a cab to East Fifty-Fourth Street, Midtown East to *Velliggios,* a small little known Italian restaurant, Mitch's favorite. It was just off Park Avenue and not far from Brighton's bookstore, their next stop.

Carol hated being late and succumbed to his request to have any lunch at all just so they would be on time for his next reading. Her usual lunch consisted of a bagel on the run or some yogurt along with a half-mile jaunt. She could tell he was tiring of the book tour. She sensed he wanted to be free from it; it was a long time to be on the road for any author and for someone like Mitch it was an eternity. He never complained, but she sensed he just wanted to go back to his cottage on the beach in Florida.

The outside tables of the quiet Italian restaurant on the small New York side street were empty as a waiter was busy setting the tables with silverware and white tablecloths in anticipation of their late lunch crowd.

Once inside the dimly lit room, a waitress showed them to a booth and brought them a menu and two glasses of ice water. It was just before the lunchtime rush, but for now they had the bistro all to themselves with the smell of fresh basil, the pungent aroma of garlic, and the scent of freshly made sauces tempting all of their senses.

"Welcome to *Velliggios,*" the waitress said, handing them menus to peruse. "Can I get you something to drink?"

"Scotch on the rocks, *GlenDronach* if you still have it in the back. No, on second thought, hold the ice," Mitch blurted out.

"I'll have some of your iced tea please," Carol said as she shoved her briefcase and purse next to her on the bench and began to look through the menu.

"Well?" he asked "I'm anxious to hear your thoughts about the new book. Do you like it."

She smiled inside. He had turned from a tough, hardened cop to an author; it reminded her of what she called "the expectant father syndrome." Waiting to hear her approval or disapproval for his latest work. He was always showing her some of his short stories and once a collection of poetry he wrote, but this time it was different; she could tell this book was special to him. She set down the menu and looked at him. "I know about Timothy Walker, the killer, but tell me about the young Timmy Walker, the best friend."

His fingers drummed impatiently on the table before he responded. "You mean how did he get on death row, and how I did I wind up as the cop who tracks him down when he escapes from death row? Then write a book about it? Hell Carol, I don't know. We played together as kids. Damn, he was my best friend. He lived down the street from me, and we grew up together, but there were over sixty other kids living near us in a four-block radius, and he was the only one who wound up in prison, on death row."

The waiter brought them their drinks and took their luncheon order.

Mitch took a long, slow drink and then set the glass down on the table. They had forgotten and put ice into his drink and now rivulets of condensation dribbled down the side of the glass onto the table. No coaster caught the expanding pool. Lost in thought, Mitch swirled the water on the table with his finger, making drawings and letters before he continued.

He rambled aloud, "Timmy was like a moth drawn to the flame. He could feel the heat and the danger but he kept going closer and closer until it embraced him and finally consumed him."

She sipped her raspberry tea, it needed sweetener. She poured sugar inside and watched the grains trickle down to the bottom of the glass then noticed the mint leaves floating on the top. She sipped again while keeping her eyes on him. He was stalling.

He looked at her, "Do you mean do I think it was it his parents' fault?" He asked before he took another drink. "They were good parents. Hell, his father was a doctor. Don't you think I've agonized about that over the years? Hell, we were best friends. Growin' up we played together every day, me, him, and… Sunny." Her name came out of his mouth, twisted, painful for him to say, as if it were wrapped in barbed wire.

He held the drink in his hand then shoved it aside. "God, do I miss her. Goddamn him. Goddamn him to hell. I hope he rots in that inferno for all time for everything he did."

She reached for his hand and held it in hers. "Mitch, after reading your new book I now begin to understand some things a little bit better. I know this is a tough day for you, but we'll get through it. Together. I promise."

He looked at her, smiled, and patted her hand. "Ironic timing, isn't it?"

She smiled, still holding his hand, but then moved her hand to take another drink of her iced tea. *Where is this going?*

"You're the best, but you know already know that don't you?" he said with a grin.

"Yeah of course I know that. Maybe I should ask you for a raise?"

"Let's not get carried away."

She moved her hand to flag down their waiter. "I'll have another iced tea please."

"Make that two," chimed in Mitch, sliding the half-empty whiskey glass to the side.

Her salad was huge, his pasta steaming as she took in a deep breath. This tour had caused her to eat three or more meals a day, not good at her age. Her clothes were shrinking; she could feel it. *Maybe I have time for the gym at the hotel before the news conference?*

"Tell me about Brighton's." He asked her over lunch changing the subject.

"It's a small but influential bookstore. If we're lucky, their readers can create a nice buzz for the book, to help propel sales and keep people talking about it. Today is a long day for you." She looked up to make sure he was listening. "For your type of book, after the reading they will normally have a steady stream of customers coming into the store. They will usually keep you signing for a couple of hours, so eat up." She glanced at her watch. "We'll have to get going soon."

"Thanks, Cal," he said and smiled at her as he finished his lunch then touched her hand. "Thanks for everything."

She smiled, "Time to go, slowpoke. Hey, I thought people from big families were fast eaters?"

"There's exceptions to every rule, remember? Maybe I'm just not that hungry." Then he grinned, and she knew he was okay.

"Come on, we're late. We have to be there by one o'clock." she said extending her hand to him. He shoved the remaining pieces of Italian bread into his jacket pocket. "For later," he said with a sly grin.

Chapter Fifteen

12:55 P.M.

All the files from Nate's research assistant at his downtown office had arrived earlier that morning, and she called to verify that he had received everything.

"Yep, got it all. Thanks, Linda."

"Let me know if you need anything else. Do you need me to come out to the farm and help organize and box everything up for archiving? Then maybe you can get some rest."

"Naw, thanks, Lin; I'll be okay. Once I get this off my mind, I'll be fine, really. Thanks for everything. I'll talk to you later."

Nate Hutchinson had reread the documents three times and nodded to his wife. Now he was ready. They just made the deadline as Nate pushed the enter button on his computer, sending the paperwork on its way to the Supreme Court for a review of their request. This was his last chance. Unless he could get the governor to change his mind. He had to resist the temptation to call and make sure they had received all 123 pages of his appeal. He always double-checked everything, but he knew how busy they were and he did not want anything to slow the process down. He just wanted it done, and quickly.

"I'm sure they got it, dear," said Agnes stroking his head when she came into his office and saw him studying the phone. "Come on now; let me fix you some lunch. Then later, I need you to take Hero here for a walk, maybe go down the hill to the pond." Hero was their thirteen-year old, golden retriever. Hero still liked to amble down to the pond, trying to relive his younger years. The ever present dried mud between his toes was a testament to those daily sojourns.

"Naw, I'll be okay," Nate said. He knew what she was trying to do. Trying to get him out of the house so he didn't think about it as he waited to hear on the appeal. This was always the worst part, the waiting. He could only imagine what Walker must be thinking at this time, with only five more hours to live.

Agnes saw the age and worry lines once again deepening on his face and knew this constant anxiety was bad for his heart. She made him a hearty lunch of homemade fresh beef noodle soup, something she had just thrown together and then fixed him a ham and cheese on rye—his favorite. She had tried in the past to have him eat healthier, but it never worked. He would just not eat; at least with this food she knew he was eating something.

When he finished the sandwich and the last drop of soup, she stood there with Hero lying by her side. "Okay now, git. Both of you. I got work to do around here and I need you outta here."

"But Agnes…"

"I don't care. I said git. You'll just be in the way of my house cleanin'. Take Hero down to the pond. It'll be good for both of you to get out of the house. Don't worry, I'll call you if anything happens and I need you."

He looked at her and was convinced she meant business. No sense in fighting it. "You wanna go for a walk? Come on boy, you heard the boss." He could tell the nearly deaf dog was straining to hear what he had to say, but when he said the word "walk" Hero was all ears and sat up, mouth open and tail wagging.

"Then come on, let's go," he said. The old dog stood up and waited patiently for his longtime master. Neither one of them moved as fast or easy as they did years earlier.

She watched them both slowly amble down the hill to the bench at the edge of the pond under the weeping willow tree. Hero ran ahead still game enough to chase the ducks back into the pond. Nate sat on a bench near the water's edge, underneath the old tree. The long elegant green branches hung beneath its canopy and nearly touched the ground as they swayed in the gentle breeze off the lake.

Nate looked around the property near him and up the hill to the acres in the back forty and noticed that the grass was higher than ever. *Needs a cutting. Maybe I'll get out the tractor and do the back, just around the lake. Maybe tomorrow? Maybe tomorrow it'll all be over, or maybe it would be just a new beginning.*

After he sat down on the old bench that he had made in his workshop years earlier, his trusted companion made himself comfortable on the ground beside him. Hero laid his head across his master's feet. It was warm and sunny, and within minutes, they were both fast asleep.

12:59 P.M.

"You got company Walker; name is John Henry Taylor." He had heard through the prison grapevine that Taylor was coming to Starke.

He watched him come in, hands and feet shackled together surrounded by five guards. They weren't taking any chances with their new ward. John Henry was a mountain of a man, a big African-American man with broad shoulders, big hands, and a smooth bald head. Walker could tell his biceps were huge.

Taylor bent down low under the doorway to enter his new home but never uttered a word to any of the guards as they unshackled him. He just stood there. He obviously had been through this routine many times before. When they were done and the guards left him, he sat down on his bed and glanced around at his new surroundings then laid back, and stretched out his huge frame. Walker could hear the heavy weight sink against the prison bed under his massive weight.

"Hey neighbor," shouted Walker. No reply.

"John Henry, name is Walker, Timothy Walker," he shouted through the bars.

The new man did not move at first but then simply raised his hand above his head, signifying that he had heard him and then promptly went to sleep. Walker could hear the big man snore, and snore loudly. *Christ this is all I need,* Walker said under his breath.

Chapter Sixteen

1:00 P.M.

"Do you have any messages for me?" she asked Eva, her executive assistant, as she blew into the corporate office of Teanna Tea Corporation, a chain of pricey gourmet tea stores. She had made her rounds visiting some of her other store locations in the area before she made her way back to her office.

"Yes," Eva said, standing quickly as she tried to keep up with the fast-paced walk of her take-charge boss. "I put them all on your desk Sari. But, you may also want to check your emails. Lots going on. The realtor has called at least four times about the space in the Fort Lauderdale and Orlando locations. He said it's a prime retail space, and it'll go fast." She briefed her quickly in bullet points from her list, the way her boss liked it. "And the PR firm wants you to approve the final layout for the grand opening of the new Boca store. I must say, she sounded excited about it. In addition," she said lowering her voice, "you have managers' meeting in the auditorium at three o'clock today. All the managers from across the country are coming in for the meeting. People from the marketing and packaging departments are preparing to brief everybody about the new tea flavors and the expansion of retail sales in other states outside our own marketing area. And…"

They paused at her office door and she turned to her assistant, and placed her hand gently on her shoulder, "Eva, all this really needs to go to Kim from here on, okay. Like we talked about. Remember?"

"Yes, ma'am. I know it's just some habits are hard to break. Sorry."

"Tell you what; just hold the rest of it will you? Okay? And is Kim in?"

"Yes, ma'am."

"Ask her to join me, will you, please."

"Right on it."

Kim McCormick, the new CEO appointed by the Seattle Coffee Company that bought her "baby" walked in with a smile holding two mugs in her hand. "One coffee and one tea. You get the coffee as you begin your new journey in life and me? Well, I'm growing quite fond of your teas, my dear."

Sari smiled at Kim. She liked her, was a quick learner, had lots of good ideas but wasn't sure if she knew how to read people.

"Can we talk?" she asked. "I'm a little nervous," she confided. "You built this company from nothing to the powerhouse it is today. These people love you, and now you're walking away with a big fat paycheck, and I'm left here to uphold your legacy. That's scary. Why did you do it?"

Sari smiled, "Because it's time, it's time for the grey-hairs to let the young ones run things for a while. I don't want to overstay my welcome, and I need somebody else to take it to the next level. Somebody with deep pockets to fund expansion. I was spending most of my time with bankers, designers, real estate brokers, lawyers, and ... well, you know all of that. Your company has departments to handle that kind of stuff. You and your company can do that. I could not, or if I did could not do it as well. That's why."

"What are you going to do with yourself in the sleepy little town of Delray Beach?"

She smiled a wry grin. "I'll figure out something, besides I've learned that there's more to life than just business. I will be teaching entrepreneurship for women at a local college. And I want to spend some time and finish the book I've been writing, and I want to start enjoying life, enjoying…"

"But you really understand your people more then I'll ever be able to do. I understand marketing, brands, retail, and such but you know what people want and how to…"

"Don't sell yourself short Kim. Wait. Eva? Join us, please," she said to her assistant passing by her office door.

Kim sipped her tea as the young assistant entered.

"Yes, ma'am?"

"Eva, let's finish up the bullet points we were talking about earlier, okay?"

"Sure, Sari."

"But Eva, I want you to brief Kim… our new CEO."

She looked at both of them, before turning to Kim saying, "Okay... The last item was, if you remember, you, I mean Ms. Novak, promoted Danielle from Jacksonville store manager to run the Western Region. So we need a new manager to run the Miami store to replace her."

Kim stopped Eva and asked, "If I recall from your personnel records, that's your hometown isn't it?"

"Yes it is. My mom and dad and other family still live there. Why?"

"Wanna go back? I remember you worked as an assistant store manager in the Kansas City store before coming to this job. It would be a nice pay raise and promotion for you." She knew she had surprised the young girl with her quick decision, which was her style. "Think about it if you like."

"Okay... I thought about it. I'll take the job."

"Good. However, I'll need you here during the transition for a while. Okay?"

"Sure," she said with a grin.

"What else?"

"Nothing."

"Thank you, Eva. That'll be all."

She turned to walk away and Sari asked her, "Eva, I didn't get any calls from...?"

"No ma'am. Not a word. Sorry."

"Okay, that'll be all. ... And Eva, don't forget, clear my calendar for the next month or so. I'm taking some time off."

"Off, like vacation? You? But you have meetings with..."

"Not anymore, remember Kim is now in charge." Kim gave her a knowing smile. "Unless you need something critical from me, which I doubt you will, I'm gone after the three o'clock meeting. My official swansong. Then I'm going home. I'm going to make a nice dinner, open a bottle of wine, take a warm bath and listen to the ocean waves. Don't call me unless somebody is bleeding or dying." She was suddenly struck by the irony of her words. *Dying?*

She missed him, now more than ever. She fingered her cell phone, tempted to text him. She knew what they agreed to, he didn't like to be disturbed, maybe later, but she... later.

1:06 P.M.

Brighton's was much smaller than the Megabookstore but was frequented by some of the most influential readers in the greater New York metropolitan area. They were patiently waiting for him when he walked through the door. The reading room would also function as the book-signing area after the reading. Stacks of his books were piled high on a nearby table. His chair was already waiting for him, accompanied by a glass and a pitcher of water on the podium next to the table.

"Showtime," he muttered, under his breath to her. Over the last few weeks it had become his favorite term, he said it helped relieve the pressure. *Maybe it was a worthwhile lunch after all?* It felt good to say the words he had been thinking all these years. He had kept it bottled up inside for so long telling no one. Maybe it was for closure, he thought to himself.

Carol heard him cough as he began to read. She stood at the back of the room, looked at him, and watched the audience. She watched him settle into his rhythm, and began to read. He was good, no, he was very good.

Mitch looked up once, and she shot him an approving glance. He would be fine. His voice found its strength as he continued to read.

...they said he was a bad seed, a bad influence, something evil, but at one time I knew him as a friend, a good friend... no... he was my best friend. Timothy Walker was the only person in the world who had ever stuck up for me.

Chapter 1

The glowing full faced moon was high in the night sky above them as the two fugitives ran down the gravel back road. He turned around, nervous, to look behind them. Houses set off the road surrounded by sugarcane fields were dark as they made their way North towards the Florida highway. They needed to make it to I-95, and then they would be home free. Once on the highway he could make his way back to Boston. In Boston, he knew he would be safe and he could just disappear into the night.

The younger, shorter man had trouble keeping pace with his long-legged companion. "Tim, we need a car or truck or something," he said nearly out of breath. "We're gonna get caught just as sure as shit if we don't get the hell outta here."

"Shut up, Leroy. Don't you think I know that?" Tim glared at him, moving the pistol around to the back of his jeans after taking a swig from the half-empty liquor bottle. "I'm thinkin'." They kept walking, only now at a faster pace. The smaller man continued to mutter under his breath but not loud enough for Walker to hear him.

Earlier that night they had pulled the truck into a gas station. They needed gas and money, because they had driven away from the pier empty-handed. No money and the cops were there waiting for them at the pier and the offshore boat to arrive that was carrying their drugs. Somebody had told the cops they were meeting the boat and about the cocaine on board. Somebody he trusted had ratted on him.

The old man at the gas station was a pushover, but he only had eighty-five dollars in the cash register, and then their damn truck broke down five miles later. The two had been walking ever since.

"Did you hafta to shoot that old geezer, Timmy?"

Walker bristled at the sound of being called by that name.

The Florida native kept talking, "He's dead, dude, and you know a murder like that is the death penalty in this state. Do you want to land on death row? They don't screw around here in Florida."

"Shuddup, I told you... or you'll be next. And don't ever call me Timmy again, you hear me?"

The younger thug looked at the gun stuck inside Walker's jeans then looked at Walker, whom he had only met days before at a methadone clinic, and even though he only knew him for a couple days, he believed him. He knew Tim would not hesitate to pull the trigger if he had to and leave him dead in some ditch or back road. This one had a strange silence about him. He had seen that in the joint before from other inmates, and it always gave him the willies. Walker was just like that, a breed apart. Quiet but always thinking. He was dangerous. Very dangerous.

Headlights glared at the end of the dusty road racing towards them with flashing red and blue lights. Cops! They jumped into a nearby roadside ditch to hide as the police car raced by them.

"Damn," Leroy cried in pain. "I think I just screwed up my leg."

"Shut up, Leroy. All you do is complain." For this trip, all he asked his contacts for was somebody who knew the local roads, docks, and somebody who could stay straight and sober, and this is who they sent him. Shit, just my luck.

"No shit, Tim, I think I broke it or somethin' on that concrete block over there."

Tim looked down in the moonlight and could make out a pool of blood on Leroy's torn jeans. Another cop car went by, slowed, and began shining the patrol car's broad spotlight to the left and right before speeding up again. They ducked down deep into the ditch.

"Goddamn, it hurts, Tim. Give me some of that whiskey."

"Wait." He leaned forward and looked up and down the road. Deserted. He stood up.

Tim felt for the bottle, his hand paused for the briefest of moments on the .45 tucked in his jeans before moving on to the liquor bottle. He stopped again, thinking. "Here," he finally said. Leroy promptly drained the rest of the liquor from the bottle.

Tim took a long look at his traveling companion, his eyes narrowed, twitching, fixed on his target. If Leroy knew him better he would have known what that look meant, and he would have kept his mouth shut.

"Can you walk?" Walker finally asked impatiently.

"Let me see." Leroy stood in obvious agony and let out a painful squeal. "Ah! Damn!" He turned to Tim, "No, I can't. I'll need to lean on you."

Walker turned; something down the dirt road caught his attention. A porch light went on outside a nearby house. A small group of people crowded onto the porch as their voices floated in the night air, as two of the younger ones walked to a car parked on the gravel driveway.

Seeing that Timmy said, "Come on, let's go. There's our ride out of here."

Walker dragged his companion behind him. They walked faster as they neared the old house and saw the car. As they neared the small farmhouse, they heard the admonishment from the older couple on the porch to their departing guests, "Now you two drive careful and call me when you get home, you hear?"

"Yeah, Grandma, I will," came a young, sweet voice in reply.

"I don't know what the sirens are all about, best lock your doors until you get home— okay, Jerry?"

"Yes sir, Mr. Simpson," said the tall clean-cut young man, "but I'm sure it's nothing to be alarmed about," as he moved the packages into the trunk and then opened the front car door for his fiancée.

"Congratulations again. We're so excited for you. Let us know the wedding date as soon as you know, okay?"

She waved goodbye, "Will do, Grandma. I love you and—"

They stood in disbelief looking as the two fugitives approached them on their front lawn pointing a gun at them. The two interlopers surprised the small group in the driveway, and Tim shouted, "Everybody back inside the house… now!" He meant business as he pointed his silver-plated pistol squarely at the younger man's head.

"Move!" he shouted. The four were hustled inside the small farmhouse at the end of the gun brandished by the tall, skinny, fugitive.

Inside the old farmhouse, the smell of rhubarb and fresh-baked pie from the evening's dinner still lingered in the air. Their aging hound dog sniffed the newcomers before lying back down on his favorite tattered rug and fell asleep.

The old man eyed Timmy then the shotgun hanging over the sofa.

"Don't even think about it, old man. Everybody sit…on the sofa where I can keep an eye on ya'," Tim commanded, waving the gun in their direction. The four of them sat bunched together on the old goldenrod-colored sofa while the television blared in the corner. The old sofa was covered in clear plastic and still looked new. They all looked scared except the old man, whose gaze returned to the shotgun. The television blared in the background.

"Shut that thing off," Timmy told the old woman. Her husband grabbed the TV remote and after numerous nervous attempts finally silenced the squawk box.

"Now, if you all follow my instructions nobody'll get hurt. I need your car keys for the Ford out front and I need money, food, and whiskey… and fast before those cops come back and decide to check in on you. Put all your cash and wallets on the table. All of it! And make it quick."

He pointed the gun at the young woman who was in her early twenties, blonde with a good figure wearing pink shorts and a tight white t-shirt. He pointed the gun at her and said, "You… get the food…sandwiches—whatever and be quick about it. And see if there's any whiskey or scotch or anything in the old man's kitchen."

She began to shake and cry as he waved the gun around.

"Now!" he yelled. He didn't have time for drama.

"Bobbi, it'll be okay, just do what he says," said her boyfriend as he handed over the car keys. Tim eyed the privileged college boy in his Florida State t-shirt. Yeah, you tell her college boy, he thought to himself.

She stood and stumbled to the kitchen.

Tim watched her walk away. He liked her long, athletic legs, and the way her leg muscles moved and stretched when she walked. Tight. Nice chest too. He heard the refrigerator door open, and saw her quickly pulling out food and putting it on the kitchen table.

He smiled at the young kid. "That's it college boy, you tell her," he said. He looked back at her being busy in the other room. "God, you know how to pick 'em. She has a body that won't quit. Whoa!" His eyes were transfixed on her in the kitchen, but his mind was busy working on another nagging problem as they all emptied their pockets and wallets onto the table.

"You better listen to him, boy," said Leroy, "or else you're liable to wind up dead like the gas n' go fella down the road." Walker cringed at his comment.

"Shut up, Leroy. Tell the whole world, why don't you?" This trip was becoming more and more complicated as time went on Tim said to himself. He needed time to think.

Flashing red and blue lights bounced off the living room wall as another police car sped by the front of the house. Tim made his way to the front window. Cop cars rolled by, churning up dust from the old country road and stopped. He stood looking outside, thinking about the last couple of days. Then the cops were finally gone. God, what a mess.

This was supposed to be a quick two-day jaunt from Boston to Florida to meet the offshore boat at an inlet north of Delray Beach. He was to oversee them unloading the cocaine, deliver it to his connection in Miami, and make a cool two hundred thousand dollars for the Brotherhood for his efforts. The Brotherhood desperately needed the money to support their paramilitary training efforts and buy more guns. As their leader and founder, it was Walker's responsibility to raise the money and keep them well funded. How the hell did the cops know he was going to pick up the drugs at the pier? He had told no one...

He shoved the gun into the front of his jeans. He heard her bring in the food and turned away from the window as she set it down on the cocktail table. She was nice, real nice lookin'. He eyed her up and down and the luscious curves that filled out her snug-fitting clothes. No time, he thought. She reached for her fiancé's hand, sat down and moved closer to him. Humph! They must be in love. Love. Who the hell did they think they were?

Leroy sat in the large side chair with white lace doilies hanging on the arms. He was already eating one of the sandwiches she had brought in from the kitchen. Tim knew Leroy wasn't going to be able to keep up with him. The two seniors, two lovebirds, and... Leroy. Five witnesses. Now they would all be witnesses. He knew he could land on death row and get the "juice" for killing the old man at the filling station. Then hell, what did five killings more mean?

Tim grabbed the brown paper bag with the food and picked up the cash and car keys from the table. "All right, everybody listen up, I need time on the road to make it back to Boston. So..." He turned away from them then pulled out his pistol and turning back leveled it at the people on the sofa.

Get the strongest one first.

He shot the young lover in the right eye, then the old man and his wife as they clung to each other in surprise. He stopped for a moment before placing a slug into the young blonde's forehead. Damn, that hurt. Then he turned to a surprised Leroy, pulled the trigger, catching him laughing with a mouthful of a bologna sandwich. Dumb hick never saw it coming. The living room was filled with the foul smell of gunpowder and the sound still echoed in the farmhouse. Now his gun was empty. I'll reload later.

"So long, suckers," he said leaving the bodies where he found them, chomping down on a sandwich and opening the front door. He was still lost in thought. Who turned him in? Damn, he had told nobody...nobody except his oldest buddy. There was only one person who knew he was coming into town for the drug shipment, his old friend from the neighborhood; it had to be Davey. He had called him to tell him he was coming. Now he would make him pay for his betrayal if it was the last thing he ever did. He would make Davey regret that he betrayed his best friend and...

"Hands up, Walker! Don't move. You're surrounded," said a loud voice holding the megaphone. Six cop cars encircled the house. The state troopers all had their guns drawn and pointed at him.

Walker then remembered his gun was empty. He froze.

The big cop nearest him bellowed, "Drop the bag and the weapon and get down on the ground and put your hands behind you on your back. Now!" Tim stood still frozen, thinking. "Do it you piece of shit. Do it now or I'll blow your head off!" said the sheriff with the shotgun pointed at his head. Timmy could tell he meant it.

He dropped to the ground and was soon swarmed by police officers who cuffed and disarmed him. He had been caught red-handed with five dead bodies mere feet from him. How was he going to talk his way out of this one?

It took two years to bring Timothy Elroy Walker to trial in the Fifteenth Judicial Circuit Court of Florida. A jury of his peers found him guilty. After that he went through the entire appeals process, including the DNA testing, retesting, Proportionality Review, State Trial Court appeals, Federal District Court appeal, legal review hearing, competency hearing, State Supreme Court hearing, Federal Evidentiary Hearing, Federal Court of Appeals hearing, a cruel and unusual punishment appeal, and finally a petition to U.S. Supreme Court as he waited on Florida's inevitable death row.

He was at the end of the line, and he was next in line to be executed for multiple murders. It was just a matter of time while he plotted his revenge on the traitor who turned him in to the cops. He needed his freedom first. But he could wait, he had nothing but time. Time. He had lots of time, and he was finally transferred to the state prison in Starke, Florida, to await his imminent execution. He had lots of time to plan his revenge and his escape.

Chapter 2

The journey from death row at Florida State Prison outside of the rural town of Starke Florida to Jacksonville Memorial Hospital was...

Carol walked to the upstairs lounge in the bookstore and made herself comfortable in one of the large wing chairs scattered about there. She put back on her reading glasses and retrieved the manuscript from her briefcase—she was excited to read more. It was already beginning to feel like an old friend, the true sign of a good book.

Chapter Seventeen

She opened the now dog-eared manuscript to the page she marked and continued to read his latest efforts.

~

"Davey, take a look in your room. Mr. Jost left something for you," I heard my mother say. I ran to my room and there on my bed was my new radio, the BlauBruin International IR2600K. On top of it was a note from Mr. Jost, brief and to the point as usual.

> *Davey—*
> *I hope you enjoy using this as much as I did.*
> *Pay me the money as you can.*
> *—Charles Jost*

Standing there, I looked at it, amazed it was mine, but all I could think of was Sun Lei, and Timmy's bloodstained Smith & Wesson snub nose .38 pistol. I knew there was no talking to him, and I knew he would not get rid of it. If I said anything to my dad he would call the police, and there would be hell to pay I thought to myself. Just shut up and don't say anything. Maybe Timmy will just get tired of it. Or his brother Dutch will want him to give it to somebody else.

The next day I hooked up a wire through my bedroom window and down the side of our house, across the short way to Mr. Jost's massive radio antenna hookup, which hovered over the roof of his house. I connected my wire to the base of his antenna. Now, I could use his antenna with no worries.

My new radio was on every night from that day on, and I found new friends all over the world. A man in Brazil played me some new music, "Bossa Nova" by Antonio Carlos Jobim. I loved it, even though the music was filled with static. I loved my radio and all the new friends I made. Now all I had to do was to figure out a way to pay for my newfound treasure.

I had to make twenty dollars, and I only had until the end of August before summer was over to earn it! Because once I went back to school after Labor Day, I would not be able to work and earn it. How was I going to accomplish that feat? It was a lot of money. I decided I would do whatever I had to do so that I didn't have to wash Mr. Jost's car. Anything but that.

I also decided to keep track of my summer and start writing. That night I wrote an entry into my journal for Mrs. Corcoran about my new radio. I wrote every night after that. I enjoyed putting my thoughts on paper, but I wasn't sure if this is what she wanted. It was more fun than I originally thought it would be. I knew I had to return some books to the library soon and thought I would show her what I had written and see if I was doing it right.

I leafed through the pages I already wrote and after closing the door to my room, I read some of them aloud to myself. I hope Mrs. Corcoran liked them as I shoved the journal into my bag and walked to the library.

Mrs. Corcoran smiled as I came in and handed her the journal of stories. I smiled a nervous smile. *I hope she likes my stories*, I thought to myself as I walked away to look for any new books that may have come in and saw her begin to read.

My Family

My family consists of me and my mom and dad and my brothers and sisters. I have two brothers and three sisters. My oldest brother Josh is in the Marine Corps. I miss him a lot, but he writes me all the time. I'm glad we are not at war anymore. I wouldn't want anything to happen to him. I love my brother.

Just about everybody in the family has a name that begins with the letter J. — Josh, whose real name is Joshua Jeremy Mallory, is the oldest (I always call him JJ), then my brother Jack, my older sister Jane (named after my mom), then me, Joanie, and the two-year-old baby, Janet. My mom says if the next one is a girl, they will name her Jessica or if it's a boy then we'll name him Jess after a family member. I asked my mom one day why I don't have a name that began with a J. My mom hugged me and said, "We almost lost you at childbirth, and your father and I want to always remember that you are very, very special." She pointed to the red heart-shaped birthmark that I have on my neck and said, "See, you were kissed by an angel here." I felt very special from that moment on.

My Mom & Dad

My dad works for an architectural & engineering company that designs and builds retail stores in and around Overland. He is always very busy and works hard. Business is very good. He gets up real early every day and has breakfast with my mom. Then he kisses her three times before he leaves the house. He told me he kisses her once for him, once for her, and once for the family.

My mom is also very busy and every couple of years or so she goes into the hospital for a ten-day vacation to have a baby. She always says she deserves the rest. When she had baby Janet, Joanie and I went to stay at my Aunt Ginny's house in the ritzy area called Saint Louis Hills. It's where all of the doctors and dentists live in Saint Louis. All the baseball players live there too. My aunt calls Joanie and me "precious." I don't know why she calls us that but she does.

She doesn't have any kids of her own but has a big white Chevy convertible with a red leather interior. She reminds me of Loretta Young, very pretty, sophisticated, and glamorous-looking. Aunt Ginny is married to my Uncle Jerry, a real nice doctor, who is always asking us if we want candy or a Coke. They once took us to lunch at their country club; we have to be real polite when we go there. They make sure we eat slow, and to always say please and thank you. The ten days went by real fast when we stayed there. Then it was home to greet the latest member of the Malloy family, baby Janet.

Everybody says that all mom and dads fight all the time, but I've never, ever heard my mom and dad argue, much less fight about anything. They must really love each other.

Neighborhood—

We live on a street called Lackland, which is one of the main streets in Overland. It is a long tree-lined street with lots of houses and businesses up and down but mainly houses. One street over is Charlack and at the bottom of the hill is Baroda and then beyond that is Midland where Sunny lives. She lives across the street from Irv and his son Barry who live next door to police chief Gestridge. The chief is real nice.

The mayor of Overland lives down the street from us right next to Clarks Pharmacy and Lackland Office Supplies. The lady inside the store always buys boxes and boxes of my peanut brittle that I sell for the Boy Scouts. Across the street from Clarks is the Sycamore Inn restaurant. I never ate in there. It cost too much money. My dad told me once that a lunch there cost like five dollars. Wow! Five dollars just for lunch? Are they crazy? That's a lot of money. Only rich people can afford to eat there.

Next to the Sycamore Inn Restaurant is Irv's liquor store and then Weis Brothers Market. I get all my baseball cards with the pink sheets of chewing gum *there and that's where I go grocery shopping there for my mom when she needs something in a hurry for dinner.*

The post office is down at the other end of the block next to the Overland Diner, which is next to Nielson's confectionary and across from Barclay's Bakery. They make the best cookies and cakes. I had a crush on their daughter Roberta for centuries until she had to move away for college. My sister Jane works there and always brings home really delicious leftover pastries and cake that they don't sell.

Next to that is some church with a real tall steeple then the YMCA and then the camera store, which always has great pictures hanging in the window. It is across the street from the City Hall building and next to the police station.

The Drancys live down from City Hall on a little driveway behind the police station. Timmy told me that Mr. Drancy is always taking pictures in his basement of his new, pretty young wife without any of her clothes on. He says you can see everything from the bushes outside their window. I mean everything. I saw her in church one Sunday, and he was right, she was as pretty as an angel.

Our Backyard

My mom and dad love flowers. One of the things I always looked forward to was springtime; it is warmer than winter, and the days are longer. I also know it soon would be time for all the flowers my mom and dad had planted around our house to bloom. The first to appear, sometimes through a late snow, and announce the arrival of spring was the crocus, with green, and purple flowers in little clumps around the front of the house where my mom had planted them years ago. Then the tulips pop up tracing the sidewalk from the front street down the steps before they stop around the side of the house. They have such a vibrant color and an exotic fragrance.

Soon the forsythias in our back yard would shout their arrival in bright trumpets of yellow bouquets. They had no smell but they were a remarkable sight. Next to them stood a mock orange bush and the beautiful pink and white dogwood trees. They bloom for the longest time and my father would cut some of them and scatter them around our home in large vases. My sister always said it smelled like a funeral home but I loved it. The spiraea blossomed out in front of the house with so many small clusters of white blooms that smelled as sweet as the honeysuckle in our back yard. But they were a mess when the petals fell off.

As summer began, it was time for the deep purple and yellow bearded irises to sprout. They grow near the front of the house on the dividing line of our house and our neighbors, the Josts. They grow wild, and every year my mom and dad and all my brothers and sisters would dig some of them up to give them room to grow and deliver some plants to neighbors.

Then came the queen of them all, the annual arrival of our pink and white peonies that lined the driveway from the very top of the hill to the gate used to fence in our dog named Dizzy. I love peonies and I don't care how you pronounce it, they smelled out of this world. The only sweeter flower was the small patch of the Lilies of the Valley around the backyard near our Saint Francis statue.

Weeks later the tulip poplars in the back yard would open, with their huge yellow and orange blooms making the tree looked like one huge tulip.

Then the lilac trees would begin to open and the whole yard smelled of sweet nectar. My dad went wild cutting, trimming, and placing lilac blossoms around our house. I was in heaven with the delicious aromas filling the house. It smelled even better than my mom cooking bacon on the stove. Sometimes, I would sit in the living room, close my eyes, and pretend I was in France somewhere, lying beside a river or a stream with some nearby slow moving water beckoning me to dip my feet in and feel its cool swirling waters. Yes. I love lilacs and…

Mrs. Corcoran sat and read my journal as I looked through the biography section, piling a number of books onto a small nearby table for me to take home and read. She coughed a little, smiled a little, and then waved me to her desk. It was early and the library was nearly empty.

"Davey, sit with me, please," she said and pointed to one of the nearby research tables. She sat next to me and said, "Your writings are very good Davey. It is a good start, but let me ask you something, do you feel you can do better? I mean do you think you can write better stories?"

I hadn't thought about it until she asked me. *Could I write better stories?*

"Or let me ask you… do you want to write better stories? These are nice writings, but they just give me information like a phonebook. I want you to tell me a story, a good story. Like you did when I gave you the three words to make up a story to write. Do you understand what I'm saying? Do you know the difference?" Her nose and face wrinkled slightly, and she became very intense. Clenching her fist with a passion I had not seen from her before then she relaxed for a second and asked, "Davey, do you think you can do that?"

I knew I could write better stories, and I was going to prove to her that I could. "Yes, I can, Mrs. Corcoran. Yes, I'm sure I can."

"That's the ticket. Now I have something special for you. I have some of my favorite books, both written by the same author, Jack London. I was saving them for you." She went to her desk and pulled out two books from her one of the drawers and handed them to me.

I looked at the cover she showed me. One was the *Call of the Wild* and the second book was titled *White Fang*. "These are stories written by a young adventurer by the name of Jack London. He went to Alaska to find his fortune during the Alaskan gold rush and after spending time there, he wrote some of the most wonderful stories. These are two of his best, and they are my all-time favorite books so... take extra special care of them for me. Okay?"

"Sure Mrs. Corcoran."

I was in heaven—more adventure books to read!

"I have one other book for you, it will help you write. I call it my rule book, but I think it will help you, and I think you'll really like it." She handed me a small book titled *The Elements of Style* by William Strunk and E.B. White. "This book was first published in 1920. It may be a little difficult for you to understand at first, but I want you to read through this a couple of times before you write anything else. It will help you. Inspire you and guide you. It will give you the main rules of writing. From now on, when you write, I want you to pretend you are telling a story to a small group of children and you want to fire their imagination with your stories. Can you do that for me?"

"You bet, Mrs. Corcoran." I shoved the treasured books into my rucksack. "See ya later."

JULY 1959

July in Saint Louis was always hot, very hot, and humid. During the summer, the city of Overland work crews would come down the side streets and spray tar on the old roads and then shovel small bits of shiny golden brown gravel over it. When the summer sun made the streets scorching hot, the tar would rise up with big bubbles, like bubble gum and you could have a great time popping them, but you had to make sure you didn't run over them with your bike. The tar was very messy and never came off your bike tires. My Schwinn still had messy goo on the side of its tires from the previous summer.

It was summertime, the best time of the year, but my mind kept returning to my problem. *How am I going to earn twenty dollars this summer? It's impossible. It's July, and I only have two months to earn all that money to pay Mr. Jost for the radio. It can't be done.*

I got dressed, putting on my tennis shoes, cutoffs, and my Marine t-shirt. My mom was drinking her tea and sitting at the kitchen table relaxing, and suddenly it hit me. "Mom would you like some mint with your iced tea?"

"Why yes, Davey… that would be nice," she said with a surprised look on her face.

I ran to the backyard and cut some mint, which was growing in a large wild patch between some old dead trees by the fence and took some to my mom. I rinsed it off in the sink and stuck some in her tall glass.

She took another drink from her glass of tea. "Thank you, Davey. That was very sweet of you, and it tastes delicious. What made you think of mint in tea?"

"When you were on vacation in the hospital, Aunt Ginny took Joanie and me to some fancy restaurants and they always put mint in our iced tea. Do you think restaurants around here would like mint for their customers?"

"I don't know, but it is a very good question. Why don't you ask them?"

I did just that. Within a six-block area around our house were four different diners and restaurants. They all said they would try my Blue Ribbon Missouri Mint, as I called it, for twenty-five cents a bunch. I cut the mint, trimmed it, washed it, and tied a blue ribbon that my mom gave me around the stalks and delivered it to them. I made one whole dollar. I did the same the next day and made another dollar. My mom said I was making a mint. She thought it was funny, but I didn't understand. I wasn't making it—I was just picking it and selling it, but I was on my way to paying for my radio sooner than I ever expected. Wow!

On the morning of the Fourth of July, I made my next trip to my mint field. I was shocked to see that the mint had turned brown and shriveled to the ground. Tall black earthy looking reeds now replaced my once-dark green leafy mint plants.

Mr. Jost saw me from the back of his house and walked towards me. "You don't have to worry about pulling out any more weeds Davey; I sprayed them all with weed-killer. That should take real good care of them." He smiled; he was serious.

My new business venture was dying right before my eyes. I made two dollars… two whole dollars but that was not going to be enough. *No!* I screamed inside. *This isn't fair! Thanks, Mr. Jost. Thanks a lot.*

My sister shouted from the rear window, "Davey, come out front! The parade's starting."

"Come on or you're going to miss it," my mother shouted from the top of the steps walking out front. The Overland Fourth of July parade was one parade you did not want to miss.

I ran to the front yard and stood on the sidewalk watching the cars, the fire trucks, the ambulances and police cars roll by our house with their lights flashing and sirens blaring. It was spectacular.

Norman Myers, our mayor for what seemed like the last two hundred years came by, smiling, waving while sitting in the back seat of a shiny new red convertible driven by "Stinky" Murdoch. The mayor was throwing candy, suckers, strings of candy beads, and wooden nickels that you could use in any store in Overland. I followed the parade down the street, picking up candy as I went along that they had thrown from the cars in the parade. Heaven! Free candy.

I reached down and grabbed as much candy as I could. My hand reached for a candy necklace at the same time I saw another fist clench a hand around it. It was Barry Rohrbecks, the bully. "Let go of it you little punk. It's mine."

"Sssure, anything you say Bbbarry." I looked far behind him at the parade. "Wow, look at that girl...in a bbbikini!"

"Where?" He turned around in the direction I was pointing.

I grabbed the last of the candy off the ground and ran like the wind.

"You little punk. Wait 'til I get my hands on you. You'll be sorry. Come back here," he yelled trying to chase me but was soon out of breath and stopped. It was no use: I was too fast, and he was too big.

When I reached home, I ran inside and then looked at my watch. I was already late for the Legion so I grabbed my swim trunks and supporter and wrapped them inside my pool towel. Then I reached for my rucksack and headed for the American Legion Park.

By the time I got to Legion Park, the Fourth of July holiday fair was well underway with all the rides, games, Ferris wheel, and prizes all set up. People were everywhere, all having a grand old time. I walked through the grounds and rides, up the hill to the pool, changed clothes then took the locker key and pinned it to the inside of my swim trunks. I grabbed my rucksack and headed outside.

By the time I reached the pool, I saw that all the chairs and chaises around the pool were already taken. It was jam-packed. I heard a voice as soon as I left the boys' locker room, "Davey! Davey... I saved one for you over there." It was Sunny in the pool pointing to some recliners over by the lifeguard.

My brother Jack wasn't at work yet, and some new guy was sitting in the lifeguard chair usually reserved for him. I waved at Sunny and set my sack on one of the open chaises before heading for the shallow water to join her. As I got nearer to her, I could see the cleavage between her breasts as clear as day in the shallow water. I began to get excited. She looked prettier than ever in her two-piece yellow swimsuit. Wow!

"You're late," she said with a fake scowl.

"Sorry, Mom."

She burst out into a big grin. "Where you been? You don't know what I had to go through to save that chaise for you. Oh and…Timmy's here, but he's acting real strange. What's with him lately?"

"Who knows with Timmy, I sure don't." I looked around and didn't see him before turning my attention back to her. "I'm trying to figure out what to do next to earn some money this summer. I bought a ham radio from my neighbor, and I thought I figured out a way to pay for it but now that won't work."

"What won't work?"

"I was picking a bunch of mint in our backyard. It grows like a weed back there, and I've been selling it to local restaurants for their tea. I made two bucks."

"Wow, that's a great idea. So what's stoppin' you?"

"Well, my neighbor thought the mint was a weed and sprayed it with weed-killer, that's what."

She burst out laughing and could not stop. She finally turned away for a moment to compose herself before she turned to face me.

"What's so funny?"

"I'm sorry, Davey. I just wish I could have been there to see your face when you found out and saw it was all brown and wilted."

Now it was my turn to laugh. "Very funny, but now I have to figure out some way to earn some money to pay for the radio."

"Hey, I got an idea. We have lots of mint growing wild in the back of our yard. You could do my grandmother a big favor if you pulled it out. What do you say?"

"Wow that would be great Sunny. Thanks a lot. You saved my life," I leaned forward to give her a thank you kiss on her cheek, she turned slightly, and it landed on her lips. She brushed against me and I could feel her breasts. When our lips touched, she held the kiss longer than I thought. She stepped back and gave me that smile of hers. I was getting excited again just looking at her.

How can I kiss her again without looking like a jerk? The whole world was watching. She's my best friend. I didn't care... all I wanted to do is to kiss her again and again...

"Hey Davey," I heard a shout from above the pool. It was Timmy, but his voice sounded different. I could only see his outline looking into the sun, but I knew the voice belonged to Timmy. I waved to him. *Had he seen us kiss?* We were all the best of friends. For some reason I was nervous if he had seen us kiss.

"Hey, we been waiting for you, buddy boy. Where you been? And what's this I found in your bag?"

I looked up and shielded my eyes with my hand. He was holding up one of the new books Mrs. Corcoran had lent me. He pretended he was going to throw it to me in the water.

"Timmy, don't!" I shouted. "It's my library book. Don't drop it! That's mine!" I hollered to him struggling to make my way to him in the water.

"Oh... okay... here then why don't you keep it... catch!" he said with a crazy grin. I saw him sail the book into the air. It glided towards me, and I watched it splash into the deep water just beyond my reach on the other side of the floating pool dividers. I lunged for it as it sailed by me. I missed, but paddled furiously towards it.

Grabbing it in from the pool, I held the water soaked book high above my head. Suddenly, I began to sink and drink in gallons of pool water. The raw, harsh taste of chlorine burned my throat as I struggled to breathe. I gasped again but I kept a tight hold onto the book.

My head sank below the surface, then somehow I pushed up and my head came above the water, my arms waving in panic, trying to shout for help but instead swallowing more pool water. My face came up again. I sucked in a deep breath of air and saw people walking around before my head disappeared under the water. I heard Sunny screaming then heard nothing but gurgling sounds. I was drowning. I tried to swim, but nothing happened. I kept sinking, taking in more water.

Everybody was there, watching me sink and struggle. I felt so detached as if I was watching a movie or something as I sank into the water. Nobody helped me. Water filled my mouth instead of air. I could see nothing. I was no longer a swashbuckler, an adventurer, or a cowboy, I was just a young kid sinking to the bottom of a local public swimming pool, and nobody seemed to care. I could still feel the book in my right hand, afraid to let it go. It was my lifeline. As long as I held the book in my hand I was safe, it became my reality. I was sinking further into the deep water as I sat in the chair of life and watched it parade past me as my soul drifted to the bottom of the pool.

Suddenly, a strong arm reached around my neck pulling me upwards towards the light above. I was lifted from the cold water and laid flat on my back onto the rough concrete. I coughed up water, then more and more. My eyes opened to see my brother Jack looking at me pumping my chest.

"What the hell are you doing, you dope? You don't know how to swim. What are you doing in the deep water? You scared the shit out of me."

Timmy and Sunny were standing behind him. "You okay, Davey?" she asked in a terrified tone, holding her hand over her mouth. I could taste nothing but chlorine and then more chlorine.

"Yeah I think so," I finally was able to say, while still coughing up pool water.

"Hey, what the hell were you trying to do, get yourself killed?" asked Timmy. "I thought you'd catch it. Who would've thought you'd go diving for it. I guess I was wrong, but you looked so funny wiggling in the water like that. And then sinking to the bottom, wooo." He laughed.

My brother turned to look at him with angry eyes but said nothing.

I looked up at both of them. "Where's my book?" I demanded.

"You still have it in your hand," said Timmy with a laugh.

"Come on. Sit up over here for a while until you catch your breath. Breathe deep," Jack grabbed me under my armpit and helped me stand.

Standing up I looked down at the ruined book in my hand. *What was I going to tell Mrs. Corcoran? She trusted me with her favorite book. And now…*

I sat down and Sunny snuggled close to me with Tim on the other side watching.

"What book is it?" she asked softly.

"*Call of the Wild* by Jack London. Mrs. Corcoran lent it to me. She said to be extra careful with it, and now look at it."

"You mean Meg?"

"Yeah… Mrs. Corcoran at the library. Meg. She's been helping me choose some books to read. Now she probably won't let me take out any more books." I shot a dagger look at Tim sitting nearby.

"Don't be so sure. Like most librarians, she really likes to help kids get involved in reading. Just tell her what happened and I'm sure she'll understand. She's been helping me with a summer project for school," Sunny said smiling at me with her hand gently resting on my leg. I looked at her.

"You really think so?"

"I'm sure of it. She's the best. Stay here. I'll get us a Coke. Be right back."

Sunny was probably right. Sunny was always right. She looked different in her swimsuit for some reason. It was the same suit she had worn last year, but this summer when she leaned over, I could see things I had never seen before. I could clearly see her well-formed breasts in her swimsuit. The bottom of her suit rode a little higher around the back and the bottom. Oh my God, was she beautiful.

"I'm really sorry, man." Timmy said with his most apologetic voice sitting down next to me. "I got a little carried away. Sorry." He smiled that sheepish smile. He took a long look at Sunny as she walked away, watching her before turning back to me. "Sorry, man. Really I am."

It was no use. I couldn't stay mad at him. "It's okay. I know you didn't mean to do it." I continued to cough up water and my mouth tasted like chlorine.

He grinned and asked, "So what's with you and all of this readin'?"

"My grade-school English teacher called my mom and said I needed to read more now that I was going to high school. Wait until you see the other cool book she gave me." I reached for my bag, searched through it until I found what I was looking for, pulled it out, and handed it to Tim. "Just don't throw this one in the water." I joked. "Look at this. It's cool. It's about an adventurer, you know like the Three Musketeers book I told you about."

The look on his face was blank as he sat there and held the book in his hands, staring at the cover. No recognition registered on his face. He chuckled, but the look remained. "Yeah, I've seen this one. Pretty good, huh?"

Strange. "Yeah, it's Tom Sawyer. The best," I said. I wanted to see if he would correct me.

"Yeah, I read Tom Sawyer in school. It was okay. We had to read it in Miss Wilson's English class. I really liked her... a lot, nice legs. Too bad we don't go to the same school Davey. You should see her. I stayed back in her class for two years I liked her so much." He grinned, handing the book back to me. "See ya. I'm going in for a swim."

I watched him walk away to the diving board. Timmy went to the local public school Ritenour, and I attended parochial school. I had never even seen the legs of my English teacher, Mrs. Hammacher. She always wore long black dresses that went down to her ankles. Everybody in school thought she was secretly a nun.

Soon a voice behind me made me turn around. "You started another book already?" asked Sunny handing me an ice cold Coke. "You don't waste any time." She looked at the book in my hand. "Oh, *White Fang*. Another Jack London book," she said paging through the book. I looked at her, then at Tim as he dove into the pool.

I never said a word to anyone… not even to Sunny. Timmy didn't know how to read. I never told him that I knew.

~

I was sleeping in my room that night and heard a noise outside by the trees. I heard it again, then I heard the steps creak as someone walked up the old wooden stairs outside our house and quietly pulled open the screen door. I heard footsteps.

I could just make out her slim figure in the dark as she slowly took off her t-shirt and slid off her jeans. "Hi ya, Davey," her sweet voice said. She wore only her bra and panties. They tumbled onto the floor as she slid into bed next to me. She felt so warm and soft. I thought I was going to explode when she touched me. It was a night I had only dreamed of, being with the girl of my dreams. Things were happening to me that had never happened before.

I had kidded her many times about marrying me, but now I was serious. I was in love with her. "Marry me? Marry me, Sunny. Marry me today?" She was beautiful and I loved her.

"Yes Davey, whatever you say."

"Then you'll marry me?" I asked, panting.

Muffled voices came from the other room. "Davey, are you talkin' in your sleep again?" I heard my sisters shout from the other bedroom. "Shut up and go to sleep."

She was a dream, only a dream—my dream girl and now she was gone. *Sunny. Come back to me.*

Chapter Eighteen

"This book is ruined," she said holding the cherished novel in her hands. "Davey, I trusted you with this book. You promised me you'd be extra careful with it."

"I'm sorry Mrs. Corcoran. IIII really aaam. IIII was at the ppppool and a friend of mine, Tttttimmy threw it to me and itttt sank into the wwwwwwater. IIIII really didn't mean tttooo…"

She removed her glasses and peered at me. "Davey, is that a reason or an excuse? Either way this book is ruined. Follow me," she said with authority.

She sat down on her chair and slid in closer to her desk. Opening a drawer, she pulled out a pink slip of paper, and began to write. She handed it to me.

"The cost of the book that you ruined will be five dollars. You have two weeks to bring in the money; otherwise it will be treated as an overdue book at an additional cost of two cents per day." Her voice softened. "Davey, I hate to do this, but you must learn when somebody entrust you with something you must take that trust seriously. Do you understand what I'm saying?"

"Yes mmma'am. I uuunderstandddd."

She took in a deep breath, gave me an exasperated look then pointed at a nearby chair. "Davey, sit down for minute, please. We need to talk."

She sat across from me and removed her glasses from the bridge of her nose. They swung back and forth from the beaded chain that hung around her neck. She sat near me and I thought I smelled a sweet scent of perfume, lilac I think. She wore a white starched blouse with an ivory cameo stickpin over the top button.

"Davey, I like you, but there are some things that you must remember. This is a library. It is a place where people come and find books that they want to read or do research on a school project or just pass some time reading, like you did when you first came in here.

However, these books are precious. Think about it, these books contain the words of great people passed down through the ages. Imagine that the greatest people of all time have their voices right here in this library." She looked away for a moment as a mother and daughter entered the library, smiled and went to the other side of the big room.

"Sometimes when I walk through the aisles here," she began again... speaking so gently I could hardly hear her, "I can hear their voices asking... no begging me to read their words inside the book. But when a book is destroyed, you destroy not only a book but everything the author has said in that book. You silence the author's words for anyone else to ever hear. No one can hear what they have to say Davey. Ever again. Do you understand me?"

"Yes ma'am, I do now."

She stood up and smiled then hugged me. "Go read, Davey," and walked away, back to her desk.

I walked outside and I looked at the pink paper in my hand—the book was going to cost me five dollars. *Five whole dollars.* All the money I earned for the radio was now going towards paying off the debt for this book.

I called Sunny and ask her if I could pick some of their mint from their backyard. I needed to make some money and hoped I could sell it again to the local restaurants. *Five dollars plus the twenty dollars for the radio. I was never going to get enough money to pay Mr. Jost.*

I could almost hear Sunny smile over the phone line. "Sure, Davey, anytime," she said. "We have lots of the stuff growing in the backyard," she told me when I called her. When I got to her house, I saw she was right, wild mint was everywhere. I began to cut the stems and piled stacks of the fragrant leafy elixir on some wet newspaper on the ground next to me.

Sunny walked down the hill and stood over me. "Here, try this," Sunny said shoving a spoonful of food into my mouth. It was spicy but very good.

"Hmmm. That's good what is that called?"

"It's called *dukbokkie*. It's a traditional Korean stew. Here's some tea for you. You must also learn how to savor and distinguish the subtle flavors of various teas. There are millions of types of teas from all over the world. What did you think of the *dukbokkie*?"

"Tasty but spicy."

She ran back into the house only to return moments later with more food.

"Here, try this," she said handing me a pancake dripping with syrup. "It's called *hoeddeok*."

It was delicious. "That is really good and very sweet. You got any more?" I asked. She beamed at the compliment. "And some more tea? What are you doing all this cooking for anyway?"

"I'm practicing on you to see what you like to eat and well… my grammy wants me to learn to cook so I can write down all of her recipes from the old country. I'll be right back." I watched her run away and saw her for what she was, a sweet, loving, sensitive girl… who I had fallen in love with from the first moment I saw her.

She was back in a few minutes with a rolled cabbage dish. "This dish is called *kimchi*. It is a traditional dish in Korea."

I tasted the cabbage roll and the sour and spicy taste filled my mouth. Ughh! I wanted to look for a place to hide or spit it out, but I didn't want to hurt Sunny's feelings. I took a huge gulp and swallowed. I didn't like it, but I still smiled at her.

"Good? Did you like it?" she asked.

I was at a loss for words. My mom always said to tell the truth, I fudged a bit. "Yes, but it's just not my favorite," I told her politely. "But everything else was very good," I hastened to add.

"It takes a while to get used to it. You'll learn to love it." She smiled and with that smile, I knew she was right…about everything.

That week I sold three more batches of mint, but the managers of the restaurants all said they were going into their slow season and they weren't sure how much more mint they could use. They told me to keep coming by anyway, just to check with them. They invited me to try their lunch specials. I told them I had errands to run for my mom. They were too expensive for me.

I had to try something else to raise money to pay for the radio and now the book.

Finally, I called Mr. Jost. "Let me know when your car needs washing Mr. Jost and I'll be right over."

"Davey, you can come over now if you like, and I'll review the instructions on how to wash it with you. Okay?"

"Sure Mr. Jost. That sounds great," I said with mock enthusiasm. *Uggh*.

Three hours later, I was done washing his car, all for one whole dollar. Never again, I promised myself, never.

I called Timmy and told him where I spent the last three hours.

"Oh man, I'm really sorry about the book. I'll give you the money if you want since I was the one who threw it to you."

"Are you kidding me? Man that would be great. It's five bucks." My spirits soared until I remembered who it was I was talking to on the phone. Timmy.

"Okay good. In the meantime, let's go down to the lake. Just you and me. No Sunny. She's been acting a little strange lately. Have you noticed?"

"No… not really." He looked at him closely before saying, "See you after lunch."

I met him at the corner. We walked and walked. On Midland Avenue, we stopped by a small stream that ran underneath the four-lane road. He reached inside his rucksack and pulled out a small bag. Timmy took out a firecracker that was nearly as big as my hand with a huge wick sticking out of the middle. He took one for himself, one for me then pulled out some matches.

"What's this?" I asked him.

"They call it an M-80. They use them in the army to simulate hand grenades. Dutch gave 'em to me before he went into the joint. It's so cool. They are really loud. Hold it a minute, while I light 'em."

"Are you crazy, I could blow off my hand off!"

"Chicken?"

"No, I'm nnnnot ccchicken."

"I always thought you were a chickenshit. Just hold it while I light both of 'em. Unless you really are a chickenshit? Just hold it, like this. And we'll see who the real chickenshit is. Hold it. The first one to throw it away is a chicken. Got it?"

He lit both fuses, and they began to burn. I could not take my eyes off mine until I looked up at Timmy, he was grinning some crazy grin. He wasn't even watching the fuse burn. The wick kept burning, lower and lower. Then I could feel the hot flames coming closer and closer to my fingers. Finally, I threw it over the bridge and it sounded like a cannon when it exploded. It echoed underneath the viaduct over and over. It was really loud. Timmy still held onto his, all the while he kept grinning. Holding. Holding. Holding, then he finally threw it. It exploded about five feet in front of us. It was so loud it sounded like a bomb.

"I knew you were a chickenshit. Come on let's go." He was wrong; I just wasn't crazy like him.

We walked down Lackland past Brown Road and past the new church, which was on one side of the street and the new bank on the other side. It was hot, but a slight cool breeze made it bearable. I had my rucksack, my book, my journal, an army canteen filled with water and my new compass in my army surplus shoulder bag. I carried my bag everywhere. Two blocks past the church, we turned onto Sherwood Drive.

It was like a different world there on Sherwood. Tall pine trees stood watch over the shady narrow street with the big homes set off far away from the street. The houses were big and majestic with huge front lawns with pools around the back hidden by fences and landscaping. I loved this street. I knew a couple of kids who lived here and they were normal just like me. Many of the houses were empty because the neighbors went to Cape Cod, Nantucket, Block Island, or elsewhere back east.

We walked down the hill to the end of the tree-shrouded street until we could see Lake Sherwood off in the distance. It was a private lake just for residents. We jumped a fence then cut through a side yard that stretched all the way down to the lake's shore and sat on a hill under an old oak tree overlooking the lake. It was cool and sheltered underneath the tree.

Timmy threw his old carpetbag on the ground and we laid down on the soft bed of pine needles and grass.

We watched lake boats go whizzing by with skiers trailing behind them churning up the frothy water with their skis. We made sure we were back from the tree line so no one could see us as they went by on the lake. It was all private property with no-trespassing signs posted everywhere. It never stopped Timmy.

"So let's see, how much money do you need?" asked Tim as we lay back looking up at the sky.

"Well, I need five dollars for the book and twenty dollars for the radio. I have just enough money for the book and I washed Mr. Jost's car so I only owe him nineteen dollars. And I got three dollars from the mint I sold to the local restaurants."

"Well, then you'll need to wash it another sixteen times and then you'll be set." He laughed.

I knew then he had no intention of paying for the book he destroyed. I was on my own to come up with the money to pay for it.

He reached into his bag and pulled out two plastic cups, a bag of ice, a soda, and something else... a bottle of cherry sloe gin. "You'll like this, Davey boy. Oh and something else," he pulled out a new pack of Newport cigarettes. "These are my mom's cigarettes, but she'll never miss 'em. What I was thinkin', we could always walk into that new bank and ask them for some money. They don't know us there."

I laughed. "Yeah, but first of all, I don't have an account with 'em or any money in their bank and I certainly don't want a loan from them." He kept pulling more stuff from the bag including six long Slim Jim sausage sticks.

I could not believe everything he had in the bag. "Where did you get all of this stuff?" I finally asked him. "We could get in a lot of trouble with all this gin stuff," I said looking around the yard and on the lookout for cops.

"It don't matter where I got it, I just got it, okay? And about the bank, hell we don't need no account, we just walk in, ask them for money, and just show them this withdrawal slip," he said as he pulled out the pistol his brother had given him to keep.

"Whoa!" I slid far away from him. "Ttttimmy are you crazy. You ccccould go to jail with that, Tim."

"Who's going to tell the cops? You?" He waved the gun around in front of me.

"No not me, bbbbut if anyone sees you with it and ccccalls the cops they'll throw us both in the ccclink."

He put the gun back inside his jeans. He just sat there smiling with a grin from ear to ear.

I heard a noise behind us, somewhere underneath the tree, in the tall grass near us. I sat up to look around. Then I saw it. A robin's nest had fallen from the branch above and two late hatchlings were chirping for their parents. Sad. Timmy saw it at the same time and walked closer to it.

"Timmy, leave it," I pleaded never knowing what he may do. "My dad says parents will not come back to them if they smell human scent on it. Leave it."

He turned to look at me for a moment. "It's not right to just leave 'em here. They'll die if we don't do something." Then he cupped his hands together, grabbed a pile of leaves inside his palms, and scooped up the fallen nest. He lifted it and gently returned it to its former location marked by a remnant of twigs and leaves. "There that should do it. Hopefully, the parents won't be able to smell me and will come back to them." Then he smiled. A large feather drifted down from underneath the nest and he picked it up, put it his hair and smiled a big grin. He looked so goofy, but I'll never forget what he did that warm summer afternoon by the lake. I admired him for what he just did.

"Wow man, that was great," I said.

"Ah, forget it. Here have some," he handed me the soda with the cherry sloe gin. It was sweet and harsh at the same time. "This is like cough syrup," I said, as I tasted it.

"Yeah. Good, isn't it? Hey, help yourself to a cigarette, they're real smooth."

I lit one and took in a drag of smoke, and started coughing and could not stop.

"Menthol. My mom smokes menthol, yuck, but what the hell man, they're free. What's better than free? Huh?"

"Where did you get the gin?" I asked taking another drink. It tasted smoother now.

"At Irv's liquor. When he wasn't lookin' I grabbed a bottle off the shelf and shoved it in my pants. Here have some more." He poured more in my cup then he poured some soda. It looked like he had done this many times before. I took a bite out of a Slim Jim, but it tasted funny at first, like cherry.

I drank more from the cup and had another cigarette. My head began to spin, and my stomach was churning.

"There's a lot of things we can do to make some money to pay for the book you screwed up," he said leaning with his back against the tree. "We just start asking around. Pick up soda bottles and take them into Weis's and they'll give you a two cents for each one."

I was no longer listening and put my head between my legs to stop my world from spinning.

"Hey man, don't do that, you'll get sick. Lift your head up and focus on something. Here look at the boat on the lake." The boat stopped and began motoring towards the shoreline. The people in it began to yell about it being private property.

"Aw shit, they've seen us, and I bet they'll call the cops. Come on. Davey, can you stand? Let's go. We need to get outta here and fast." We picked up all our stuff and ran.

I went to bed early that night and slept until eleven the next morning. From that moment on, I got sick if someone even mentioned a menthol cigarette. But I fell asleep still remembering what Timmy did that day and that goofy-looking feather he stuck in his hair. Sometimes, he surprised me.

Chapter Nineteen

Following Timmy's advice, I gathered empty soda bottles all week from around the neighborhood and turned them at the Weis Market store. I sold more mint to the Sycamore Inn Restaurant, but I still needed more money.

Later that week I took the pink slip of paper and five dollars for the book to Mrs. Corcoran. She looked at me and smiled. "Thank you, Davey. Do you have any new stories for me?"

I was a little shocked that she would ask me that question. "No, Mrs. Corcoran, I thought you were mad at me and didn't want to read any more of my stories."

"Davey, sit down. We need to talk again." We walked over to the reading table as she sat down across from me. "I'm not mad at you, Davey," she began. "I was disappointed, yes... because I expected more of you." She stopped for the briefest of moments, not sure of what to say. "Never stop writing, write what you know and when you come to a mental roadblock... just pick up a good book and read. It works wonders. You will be a great writer someday, but you have to keep at it every day. Do you hear me?"

"Yes, ma'am."

"Good. That's my boy. Now, to show you I'm not mad, I have a new book for you to read, *The Adventures of Sherlock Holmes* by Sir Arthur Conan Doyle. I think you will really like it."

"And I'll be real careful with it Mrs. Corcoran, I promise."

"I know you will. Just remember what I said, okay?"

"Yes, ma'am."

I loved to read my latest friend, Sherlock Holmes and I thought about what she had told me. A few days later, I spent all day Saturday with my dad, just him and me. We went for a long drive out to the "country." I loved it. It was a perfect day. Just me and my dad.

When we got back home that day I remembered what Mrs. Corcoran had told me, "*Write what you know Davey. Write a good story about what moves you. Nothing fancy, just put it down on paper.*" I opened my journal and began to write.

Saturdays with My Dad

The days I look forward to the most are the "special" Saturdays I get to spend with my dad. Just him and me. I love the special Saturdays with my dad. Last Saturday was one of those days.

We have a big family, which includes my mom and dad and five kids. One would think that you would get lost in the crowd they always made sure that they spent good quality time with each of us. My time with my dad was usually Saturdays.

I remember sitting on the floor next to my dad's chair as we watched the Gillette Friday Night Fights. This was only one of three TV shows he would watch other than My Little Margie starring Gale Storm and 77 Sunset Strip with Efrem Zimbalist Jr. I liked Margie better, but I sat next to my dad hoping that he would say the magical words, "Want to go to the country tomorrow?"

The "country" was about an hour or two west from where we live. It was filled with tall hills, running streams, lots of trees and very few houses. You could drive for hours and not see anyone on Wild Horse Creek Road, the main road through the valley. It was very different from our home in the suburbs with their lush green manicured lawns and trimmed bushes and long wide driveways.

When he asked the question I looked at him and said, "You bet!"

At six A.M., the next morning I questioned the wisdom of my decision. I heard a voice say, "Davey?" Minutes later, my dad gently nudged me on the shoulder saying, "Davey, come on, time to get up. Come on. Let's go to the country."

I loved to sleep more than anything else in the world. I crawled out of bed and tried to see how far I could walk with my eyes closed without bumping into something. I brushed my teeth, combed my hair, and threw on my old Marine t-shirt, jeans, and sneakers. Dad wore his old blue cotton dress shirt, which was frayed around the collar, along with a beige sweater with the smallest of holes at the seams around his neck and a pair of well-worn khakis and sneakers.

Then I helped my dad load up the car. We filled the trunk with everything we would need; boxes, shovels, gloves, buckets, old newspaper and soon we were on our way. He drove down the still darkened roads with his headlights on as I snuggled next to the front door and went back to sleep.

A short while later, I heard him say, "I guess you're too sleepy for an ice cold glass of milk and some fresh Krispy Kreme donuts? Huh? Well, I'll just have to go inside by myself." But he waited until I sat up and propped open my eyes as we both followed the noise of my now growling stomach.

Once inside, he ordered a cup of coffee for himself and a large frothy glass of milk for me, accompanied by a fresh-from-the-oven chocolate covered crème filled donut. All mine. I savored every morsel. I glanced at him and the server brought me another, then another at which point he ordered another cup of coffee and his favorite, a French glazed donut. After three donuts, not only was I full, but also wide-awake.

We left the donut shop waving goodbye to the manager, old-timer Mr. Marley behind the counter and we began our journey in earnest. Dad drove west, away from the city, away from the suburbs, away from the traffic towards the elusive 'country'. The streets became less congested and narrower as we drove along the main western thoroughfare. He turned off the rural main street onto a two-lane road, which wound through the countryside away from the nearby meandering Missouri river. We drove along the bottomlands. In the springtime, I remember seeing the deep dark black river bottom soil turned over for planting where corn now grew as high as a house in every field.

My dad drove slow and pointed out the different birds we would see along the way. "Look there's a cardinal! Davey, there—an indigo bunting on top of the telephone wires?" he shouted as a fellow explorer. "Watch the kingfisher on top of the tree dive for his meal into the stream!"

The country road narrowed, and we had to move far to the right shoulder to let an oncoming farmer's oversized columbine or tractor pass us by.

The forest was coming alive with activity. He slowed to let a red fox then later a possum pass in front of our car. The possum, stopped, glanced at us and continued on his way. The ever-present railroad tracks kept us company along the left side of the road until the river and we crossed over them as we turned away and headed up the hills high above us. The road seemed to go straight up from the valley floor and soon we saw the mighty Missouri River in all of its majesty down below us slowly winding its way south.

After an hour of driving my dad pulled over near some wild woods, opened the trunk of the car, and pointed to his target. I smiled and nodded in agreement, as I spied the big hickory tree just off the side of the road and admired the treasured bark it was hoarding.

It looked like the bark from the old hickory tree would simply pop off at the slightest tug. But it took much more pulling and yanking then one might expect to make it give up its prize. We gathered nearby hickory nuts from the ground and low-lying branches and loaded them into one of the buckets we brought with us. Later at home, my dad would soak the bark and nuts in a bucket of water. Then, when he was barbecuing chicken or steaks on the grill, he placed them over hot charcoal, which would produce a thick nutty smoke, giving them that special hickory flavor.

When the buckets were full, we loaded up the car and continued our drive and our talk. Dad didn't ask me about school or girls or anything like that but instead asked what I thought about politics and religion and such. He asked about the wars our country fought and if I thought it was just and how I would go about ending it if I was the president.

He continued to drive higher and higher into the hills. It was sunny and warm. We passed some old abandoned houses where we saw wildflowers blooming in the woods. After he stopped the car, I pulled out our hand shovels and then we carefully dug the flowering treasures from their locale before they became dessert for hungry deer. He knelt down and carefully dug around the roots and then reached under the plant with his hands pushing underneath the black, warm cool earth. He always looked like he said a prayer over the plants as if he were apologizing for disturbing them.

We placed the wildflowers inside the cardboard boxes for my mom to plant these treasures in our backyard to join the other wildflowers in our garden at home. In the woods, they didn't last long because of the deer, but in our backyard, they spread like wildfire, big and healthy. When the patches of them would grow too large or unruly we knew it was time to replant them back in the woods to help them spread and prosper.

Eventually, my dad asked me, "Hungry?"

"Always. I'm starvin'."

We drove back down the mountain to the small roadside tavern along the railroad tracks and sat down to order lunch.

"Hi James, hi Davey" the friendly bar owner greeted us as we entered the empty tavern. As always he was wiping down the wooden bar top with an old rag. My dad was always James, never Jim or Jimmy just James. He always said that his name was the first thing his parents gave him and he never wanted to shortchange them or show them any lack of respect by altering his name. I always admired that about my dad.

Dad ordered two huge corned beef sandwiches on rye with mustard, pickles, and potato chips then he got a beer and ordered me a root beer. While we waited for our sandwiches, we played shuffleboard on a long elegant table, which ran the entire length of the bar. The windows above it let in the cool light of day. The shiny wooden table deck was dusted with sawdust to make the surface glide smooth. I beat him, as usual, but I always think he let me win.

After lunch, we walked down the railroad tracks for hours. This was his private time and we never talked until we turned around and were walking back to the car. I respected his time as much as he respected mine. Afterwards in the car, we drove past one of the fast moving creeks and we stopped to go crawfishing.

I grabbed the bucket from the trunk and followed my dad's instructions exactly. I put the bucket on the rocky shore, rolled up my jeans, waded into the cold water without stirring up the sandy bottom, and began my hunt. When I saw a good size crawfish, one the size of my thumb or larger, I curved one hand in the form of a scoop in front of the wily creature and the other hand behind it. As my right hand closed in on him, he would shoot backwards like a bullet into my waiting left hand then I immediately tossed him into the waiting bucket of water on the shore. Sometimes I was not fast enough and felt the sharp pinch of the crawfish claws. I learned quickly not to have the bucket too far away.

Dad said, "If you fill up the bucket halfway with crawfish, I'll have mom make us some wonderful Cajun crawfish chowder." I never got that many; perhaps a dozen or so then we released them back into the creek. Thinking about it, I probably caught the same ones month after month. But I loved it.

Later, came the best part of the day. We played a game we called "Get Lost." Dad would drive the car back up the mountain and I would tell him which way to go.

"Make a left, then a right," I said. "Now another right, now left, go straight for two miles now left, then right, then left and another right." This would go on for hours until we were totally lost.

"You really did it this time Davey," he told me. "Whew. We're really lost and we'll never get home." I knew he was joking. Only once did I ever see a look of concern on his face as he drove the curvy back roads of Missouri, but eventually he drove into a familiar driveway with the mailbox marked, The Saint-Enges Farm. They sold everything including fresh dairy and farm goods. I would smile and he would not look at me at first, then he laughed. "That was a close one there, Davey boy."

A nice, elderly French couple lived there. They were always so nice and they raised chickens, pigs, cows, and turkeys on their farm. I looked forward to taking a drink of fresh ice-cold spring water from their well after I primed the hand pump. The water was always cold and tasted so sweet.

My dad bought dozens of farm fresh eggs, some newly churned butter, fresh cream, homemade sausage and fresh-baked bread. I knew my mom would cook it up the next morning for breakfast before we went to church. Delicious and so fresh! Those Saturdays were always the best.

Looking back, only once were we rained out on a Saturday. A tremendous rainstorm flooded the back roads, and they closed the roads. We turned around and headed for home. But dad didn't give up, he made it an adventure. He set up our old barbecue grill in the garage out behind the house, turned on the radio and we listened to the baseball game while it continued to rain outside.

While he barbecued we listened to Harry Carey give us a play by play from Busch Stadium. My dad would stop what he was doing when Stan Musial, the greatest Cardinal baseball player of all time, came to home plate. You could hear the crack of the bat over the radio and Harry Carey shout: "It might be, it could be, it is—a home run by Stan the Man! Holy cow!"

I would run inside and get him a cold beer to pour over the chicken. When it was done, the chicken was so moist and sweet when you picked up a piece the meat would fall off the bone. It was the best.

I loved those Saturdays.

A couple of days later I took my journal to the library and gave it to Mrs. Corcoran so she could read my latest story. I went to the bookshelves for some more books but looked over at her to see her lost in reading my journal. A few minutes later she sat back in her chair, smiling. She waved for me to join her.

"Wonderful story, David. You're a good writer. Keep writing. But for now I would like you to write something about your mom, and bring it to me as soon as you finish it, okay? Can you do that for me?"

"Sure, Mrs. Corcoran. But what should I write about?"

"Whatever you want. Just have it to me as soon as possible, okay?

"Sure," I said, my mind already thinking about my next story. I nearly ran home. *She liked my story, and thought I was a good writer.* I was walking on air.

Two days later, I handed in my next story.

Camera

My mom loves to take pictures of the family. A few years earlier, my father gave my mom a 35-mm Kodak motion picture camera and a portable screen to show her films. My dad would set up the screen in the living room and make popcorn and we would watch our family antics again and again. Mom would take pictures of us on Fourth of July, Memorial Day, Easter, all the birthdays, Thanksgiving, and of course Christmas.

Every Easter the pictures would be the same. My sisters would dress up in their latest Easter outfits and would walk down the backyard steps carrying their Easter baskets. We would then search the yard for Easter eggs and whoever found the egg covered in aluminum foil got the large chocolate Easter bunny all to themselves.

Thanksgiving at the Malloy house was always about food. My mom took motion pictures of the family eating Thanksgiving dinner, which always included turkey, stuffing, sauerkraut, cranberry, olives, lima beans, mashed potatoes, and gravy. And of course my mother always made two or three deserts. There was always the inevitable picture of someone holding up the largest turkey leg for all to see, it was usually me. Everybody helped with the meal including setting the table, carrying in the serving dishes, breadbaskets, and all the other food. Then we helped with the cleanup with taking out the trash, picking up the dirty plates and silverware, washing and putting away the dishes. It was always a great time. I love Thanksgiving. What was not to like? No school, lots of good food and the family all together. A fire in the fireplace. Perfect.

Then there was Christmas. Everybody in the family had their traditional "spot" year after year where their Christmas presents were piled together waiting for them on Christmas morning. My spot was underneath the front window by the Christmas tree next to my brother Jack's usual spot. My sister Jane had the place underneath the side table next to the sofa. Christmas music played in the background, playing' Little Drummer Boy,' 'Jingle Bells,' and 'We Wish You a Merry Christmas.' I always wanted to be a drummer in a band and admired people who could play a musical instrument. A special talent I always wished I could master. Everybody joined in the singing as we opened our gifts.

My mom loved to take home movies of all of us in the snow but usually it was of me and my sister Joanie and Jane making angels in the fresh powdered snow. Then there was always the inevitable snowball fight with me and my brothers and sister against one another. Jack served as the mediator. Dad always joined in with the fun, taking no sides. Afterwards, Mom would serve up a fresh batch of cocoa and homemade chocolate chip cookies for us to help us warm up.

Every year Dad took me and my brothers to a tree farm in the country and we would fight over which tree would look the best in our front room. Once my father decided, we would then cut it down and carry it back to the car. The whole family would spend the night decorating it accompanied by nonstop Christmas music while drinking cocoa. We got to stay up late on Christmas Eve waiting for the carolers to come by. They would stop in front of our house and sing Christmas carols. My mom handed out mugs of cocoa to keep them warm. I loved it. And my mother loved it. My mom was special.

I never referred to my mother as "she." I once remember saying to my father, "She told me to go outside." Before the words had even left my lips my father stood tall, his face all contorted and red as he stood glaring over me.

"She?" He bellowed in no uncertain terms to let me know he was not to be trifled with and that I should definitely pay attention to what he was about to say. "She," he said again walking towards me, straightening out his six-foot-five frame but looking more like a mountain at that moment. "She? The woman who carried you in her belly for nine months? The unselfish woman who nursed you through *scarlet fever for weeks on end? The one person on God's good earth who makes sure that you eat and drink before she ever does. Is that the SHE you are referring to?"*

"Yes," I managed to whisper, suddenly near tears. "I'm sorry, Dad. I didn't mean it that way."

"Don't apologize to me... apologize to your mother. Then go to your room."

"I'm sorry, Mom," I said, now with tears streaming down my cheeks. I couldn't stop crying.

She pulled me close and held me while she ran her fingers through my hair.

"I'm sorry," I kept saying repeatedly. "I didn't really mean it like that, I'm sorry."

She came into my room later that night and hugged me then I felt her kiss my head, her hand once again running through my hair. "Hmm, I think you need a haircut, Davey boy. Tomorrow. We'll get to it tomorrow. Goodnight, Davey. I love you. "

"I love you too, Mom."

I couldn't be sure but I think Mrs. Corcoran had a tear in her eye when she finished reading and turned to me. "This is a wonderful story, and you should be proud of it."

AUGUST 1959

Two weekends in a row, I washed Mr. Jost's car and earned two dollars. He didn't give me any cash money, just a credit towards what I owed him on my radio. He always said it helped build character. I now owed him fifteen dollars.

My brother Jack asked me to help him out and take care of one of his lawn customers, Miss Viola. He was busy at school. I think he did it just to help me make some money. Once a year she had Jack come to her yard to pull out weeds and cut the lawn.

I spent two days working for the widow, who lived six blocks away from our house. First, I washed her late husband's black Cadillac, which was still parked in the garage the same as it always had been for the last ten years. She never drove it but said she would pay me a dollar to wash it for her. She always said that's the way her Harold would have wanted it. I told her to keep her money, and I washed it for free. She was such a nice lady.

The old woman lived by herself in a big dark brown brick house and had a lawn of lush green zoysia grass. A double lot just like Mr. and Mrs. Jost. It felt like a carpet under my feet when I walked on it but when weeds cropped up throughout the lawn she always said it looked terrible.

She paid me two dollars to pull out the weeds and another two dollars to cut her double lawn, trim, and sweep the sidewalks. At lunchtime, she brought me a sandwich, some apples and poured me some fresh squeezed lemonade. I sat under a huge oak tree to have lunch. It all tasted so good. The next day after doing all of her yard work my back was so sore I could hardly move. I now owed Mr. Jost ten dollars for the radio.

Later, I took more soda bottles to Weis grocery store. I had found them alongside the road while doing my daily search for soda bottles on Midland Avenue. When I was leaving, I saw a neighbor, Mrs. Arnsberg, carrying home two bags of grocery. She lived behind us on Baroda Avenue. "Can I help you with those bags, Mrs. Arnsberg?" I asked.

"Oh that would be lovely, Davey. Thank you so much." When we got to her house, she gave me a quarter for helping her. I stayed at the store all day and made another seventy-five cents. I still needed a lot of money to pay for the radio so every penny helped.

At the end of the day, Mark Weis, the store owner's son, came outside as I was leaving. "I've noticed you around here, and you seem to be a pretty industrious boy there, Davey Malloy. Would you like to earn some money and do some work for me?"

"Sure, Mr. Weis."

"Well, we had a couple thousand of sales circulars printed up for our big annual summer sale, and I need some boys to take them around the neighborhood and put them into mailboxes. It will take the whole day, but I can pay you three dollars. What'd ya' say?"

"Three dollars? Sounds great. Sure."

"Just be here early on Saturday, eight o'clock sharp, and a truck will take you and a couple of other boys around and drop you off in different neighborhoods. If you know anyone else who can help I'll pay them the same amount."

"Gee thanks, Mr. Weis. I'll ask some of my friends."

I called Timmy when I got home. "Yeah man, I can use the three bucks."

That Saturday the truck picked us up at the store and drove us a couple of miles away. They dropped off stacks of circulars along the route and said for us to work our way back to the store and then come in for our money. Timmy took one side of the street, and I took the other. The Murphy brothers stayed on the truck and worked in a different neighborhood.

When I reached each pile, I cut the twine holding them together with my Swiss Army pocketknife and began to deliver the circulars. I saw Timmy on the other side of the street racing me, putting them in doors, mailboxes, and newspaper holders. But as the day wore on I saw him blocks up the road and soon he was out of sight. It was hot that day, one of the hottest days of the summer. I brought my Army canteen and wanted to drink from the cool water. I sat for a while under a big oak tree on Brown Road to cool down for a few minutes. I sure don't know how Timmy finished so fast.

At five o'clock, I was finally done, and I was the last one to show up at the rear of the grocery store. Mr. Weis was there waiting with the two Murphy brothers, Jimmy, Mark sitting with Timmy. Mr. Weis looked angry, but he didn't say a word as I walked up to join the crowd.

"I'm all done," I told the young Mr. Weis. I was covered in sweat and my hands and t-shirt were the color of the flyers—red, black and blue from handling so many circulars. I was tired, but it was worth it—three whole bucks.

"Did you deliver all your circulars, Davey?"

"Yes sir, I did," I said proudly.

"Well somebody didn't. Somebody here tossed piles of our sales circulars down sewer pipes and scattered them around some backyards trying to hide them. I need to know who did it?"

"I don't know, Mr. Weis. It wasn't me. Can I have my three dollars now?" Then looking at my watch said, "I have to go home for dinner."

He glared at me and the others, "We spent a lot of money printing those circulars and now one of you threw them all around neighborhoods. I had to send two of my stock boys to pick them all up. It took them a couple of hours. I'm not paying anybody until somebody comes forward and tells me who did it." I could tell he was angry.

I was hungry, and I wanted my money. "It wasn't me," I told him, almost pleading holding out my hand. I had done my work and now I wanted to be paid.

"It wasn't me," Timmy chimed in. "I don't know these other boys you hired but you know us, Davey and me. We want our money."

"I'm not payin' anybody, any money until I find out who did this. So you boys talk amongst yourselves and let me know who did it, then I'll be happy to pay you what I promised you. But I need to know I can trust you, so I need you to tell me who did this." He turned around and walked away back into the store. Nobody said anything other than blaming somebody else.

"I don't think that creep ever intended to pay any of us," proclaimed Timmy. "I'm goin' home. With that, I saw my three dollars disappear. All that hard work. Timmy and I walked home together, but he didn't say a word. All he said was "See ya," as he walked towards his house. I stopped him at the steps.

"Tim… did you do this? Throw the circulars away? I know you finished faster than me."

"You're just a slowpoke Davey, that's all. See ya later."

I never was paid for delivering the circulars. Later that night, somebody threw a brick through the Weis store's plate glass front window. They never caught who did it, but I think I knew who did it.

Three days later Timmy joined me outside the store as they were putting in the new glass in the front window, and I waited to carry groceries home for some neighbors. The older women usually gave me a quarter for carrying their groceries home.

"Here this is for you, Davey," he told me handing me a Coke and sitting down next to me on the top of the concrete retaining wall. Big deal. The Coke was cold, but I would have rather had my three dollars. He reached inside his jeans and pulled out a pile of crumpled one-dollar bills—three of them and handed them to me.

"What's this for?"

"Ah don't make a big deal about it; it's for the money that jerk Weis didn't pay you."

"How'd you get…?"

"Our lawn needed cutting and my dad's car needed washing. And I promised my mom I'd be home early for supper for a week. I figured what the hell… here, just take it. You can use it more than I can." His eyes narrowed, "And don't go telling anybody about this, okay?"

"Okay," I said with a smile. Three dollars! Wow! I would add it to the pile of money I owed for my new radio- just seven more dollars. I looked up and saw Mrs. Arnsberg leaving the grocery store carrying two large bags.

"Can you help me with my groceries, Davey?" she asked. I jumped up just as Mrs. Schmidt came outside to join her. She lived two houses away from Mrs. Arnsberg. I whispered to Timmy, "If she likes you she'll pay you a quarter to carry her groceries home for her."

"Yeah?" Timmy said in surprise. "To her home?"

"Yeah, just be nice and real polite." He had just given me three dollars he had made for the circulars and now was willing to help a neighborhood widow home with her groceries. He was always surprising me. He grabbed the two bags from the older woman, smiled an engaging smile and walked beside her smiling and laughing. They walked behind Mrs. Arnsberg and me.

When we got to her home, Mr. Arnsberg gave me a quarter for helping her. Then I walked with Timmy and Mrs. Schmidt to her house.

"Boys, why don't you come inside? It's cool there. I have some cold lemonade inside. I just made it before I went to the store," she said with a slight German accent. I liked Mrs. Schmidt because she gave us cookies and some pennies and nickels in our candy bags on Halloween. She had lived in the neighborhood for a long time and had a rooster and some chickens living in a shed at the back of her house. I would hear the rooster crow every morning letting everybody know the sun was about to rise. My mom and dad hated the noise, but they never really complained.

Her house was old and smelled of sauerkraut and sausage. Old frayed curtains hung from the windows. Holy cards clung to her icebox held tightly by faded Saint Joseph and Jesus magnets.

She handed Timmy and me a glass of lemonade and offered him a quarter for helping her with her groceries.

"No thank you Mrs. Schmidt," he said in a most unusual well-mannered refrain. "I was happy to do it for you, for free, anytime. But if I could use your bathroom I would really appreciate it," he asked politely.

"Why of course, Timmy. It's right through here, on the left," she said pointing down a long narrow hallway towards the rear of the house.

As Timmy disappeared into the bathroom, Mrs. Schmidt said aloud, "He's such a nice young man. And he wouldn't take any money from me, so honest." She smiled for me, but I knew that if he was around I could no longer make any money carrying groceries for neighbors to help pay for my radio.

Tim continued hauling groceries for weeks until one day I said to him as he was leaving Mrs. Schmidt's house, "I'm real proud of you helping her out and not taking any money for it. I now sometimes carry them for free, like you, when I'm coming home, but you do it all the time for free."

He made a face at me. "Don't be a chump. I don't do anything free. See." He reached inside his pocket and pulled out a bandana filled with a dozen various-colored pills.

"I don't understand."

"Dummy. I grab a couple of pills from each bottle in their medicine cabinet then I take these pills to the pool hall and sell them for a buck apiece. Wanna try one?"

"No, are you crazy? You don't even know what those pills are used for."

"Doesn't matter. I still get a buck a pill."

"Hey man, you can't do that. She needs her medicines, and they cost her a lot of money. Take them back," I said standing in front of him, grabbing him by the arm and blocking his path. "Tell her you need to use her bathroom again and then put them back. Now!"

"You're really serious about this aren't you?

"You bet I am. Now take 'em back!" I said my voice rising in anger. I had visions of poor Mrs. Schmidt lying on floor one morning without her medicine. But Timmy didn't care.

"Get real man. No way in hell I'm taking these back. They're mine now," he said as he shoved me aside and started to walk home.

I stood there looking at him in disbelief as he walked away. I could not believe it. *Same old Timmy, he'll never change.*

That night after dinner everybody in the neighborhood brought jars with holes poked in the top to catch lightning bugs. My sister Joanie would catch them and then get some of the flashing light stuff on her hands and run home to wash it off. When it got dark, she was always the one elected to count to twenty on a tree while we all hid and we played hide and go seek. I had a special hiding place, in a deep grassy ditch by the road where nobody could see me. I hid in my ditch and watched everybody else running around looking for a place while I waited for her to finish counting. All of a sudden, somebody landed on top of me. It was Sunny.

"What are you doing here?" she asked in surprised. "This is my hiding spot."

"It's mine too."

"I was here first. You've got to find somewhere else to hide. Quick! There's not enough room here for both of us."

"Shhhh, don't move, or she'll see us," she whispered.

My sister shined a flashlight at the bushes then across the shallow ditch where we were hiding and she bent over and looked but she did not see us.

"Shhhh," Sunny repeated. She leaned in and pressed close to me so my sister would not see us. I could feel her heart beating against me as her arms wrapped around me tighter and tighter. *What was she doing? I could feel her breasts pressing into me.*

"Sunny, I don't…" I whispered to her.

"I see you both there." My sister Joanie hollered. "Come on out. I caught you," she said with a squeal at having heard me as she ran and touched the tree according to the rules.

It was hard standing, and I was glad it was dark so nobody could see my embarrassment. Sunny looked at me and smiled.

"Everything okay, Davey?"

"Yeah sure, everything is fine." *What do I do now? She's my best friend.*

Chapter Twenty

Timmy was never home when I called him. His mom always said he would be right back, but I could just come by their house and wait for him or I could use their pool.

"I don't know how to swim Mrs. Walker."

"Oh that's okay Davey, I'll show you how. It's easy. Stop by one day, and I'll teach you."

I called Sunny a lot and stopped by her house, but she was caring for her sick grandmother and couldn't come out and play, so it was just my books and me.

When I sold mint to the two of the restaurants, they thanked me, but they told me it was August and business was slow for them so it was slow for me. Seven dollars left to pay Mr. Jost.

I would work some days, then sit under one of the big oak trees in the Gilson's backyard, and read my next book. I loved to read and to write, but I kept looking for things to do to earn some more money.

I spent the days scouring the neighborhood for soda bottles littered around the main streets and the fields. It seems people loved to throw soda bottles from moving cars into the field by Sunny's house.

Nielsen's Deli and Weis Market each paid two cents a bottle. But I knew if I went into Nielsen's that I would spend it on candy. They sold penny candy including jawbreakers, Bit o' Honey, Mary Jane candy, black licorice in the shape of pipes and others that looked like a records with a red dot in the center. They also sold wax tubes filled with a sweet cherry liquid and Bonomo Turkish Taffy, Mallo Cups, Sweet Tarts, and little bits of multi-colored candy on long sheets of narrow paper. All the good stuff!

My brother Jack knew I was working hard to make money to pay for my radio, and he knew I was doing everything I could. Jack was always doing odd jobs to make money and worked part time as a caddy at the golf course, his paper route, and at the Legion as a lifeguard. He made two dollars carrying two golf bags at the golf course. But they said I was too young and scrawny to work there as a caddy.

"Hey Joe (he always called me Joe for some reason but I liked my nickname), I could use some help delivering my newspapers today and collecting for the month. I'll pay you two bucks."

I knew it didn't take two people to deliver the papers, but I knew he was trying to help me make some money just like he did when he asked me to help the widow Miss Viola.

"Are you interested?"

"You bet. Let's go." I helped him load up the wagon with all of the papers. It was a local paper called *The Wellston Journal* located in Wellston, Missouri, near Ferguson. The paper ran multiple ads for local grocery stores, and everybody loved the coupons they contained in the paper. Jack had to deliver the paper to every house on his route even if the people didn't want the paper or didn't want to pay the monthly .35 cents for it.

We rolled over three hundred newspapers and put rubber bands around them and stacked them into my old red wagon. My hands were black from the newsprint ink. The route was a mile away and took us over twenty minutes to get there, but I liked it since it gave me time with my older brother. He delivered to one side of the street, and I took the other. I threw papers on the lawn near the front door of each house. As we finished each street we walked together taking turns pulling the wagon, talking.

"See those trees there. That big old one there is a sycamore tree like the ones we have out front of our house. That other tree is a chestnut tree. That one is walnut tree, they each have nuts." He told me all about them and how he could tell how much snow we would get during the winter based upon how many nuts fell in September. He said the squirrels knew and they buried more nuts if it was going to be a snowy winter. But every winter in Saint Louis was snowy. I still thought he was so smart.

Once we delivered all of the papers, we went back to each house and knocked on the doors to collect for the month. Our paper route covered the "land streets" as we called it, Hartland, Graceland, Northland, Ashland, and finally Midland.

Collecting for the papers for me was always the best part. Jack would knock and just smile and take whatever money they gave to him. Some customers gave him a tip but most gave only .25 cents, not even the .35 cents it was supposed to be. Some paid nothing at all.

My approach was to hand the ticket to whoever answered the door and hold out my hand while saying thirty-five cents please and then smile at them. The last house I went to belonged to Mrs. Fermi. Many times, she had called the newspaper's main office to say she had not received her newspaper but she never wanted to pay for it. The paper was still lying in her front yard next to her front porch, out of view. I knocked on the door and stepped back.

"Well, well, well, if it isn't little David Malloy. What can I do for you today?"

I handed her the bill and said, "I'm here to collect for this month's paper, Mrs. Fermi. That'll be thirty five cents… please."

"Well, I never… I don't want that paper, never did, and I certainly have no intentions of paying for that rag. So…"

I politely held up my hand. "I understand completely, Mrs. Fermi. I am so sorry for disturbing you." I turned and walked down the steps, stopping only to pick up the paper in her yard. Dusting it off I turned as she held out her hand I said, "I am so sorry about delivering this by mistake. It won't happen again. We aren't supposed to leave it at houses that tell us not to deliver. Good day, Mrs. Fermi."

She had a look of panic on her face. She wanted those store coupons. She was desperate. "Wait! Wait a minute, Davey. Just wait right there. I'll be right back." She turned and ran back inside the house and soon returned with two dollars in her hand. "This is for this month and last month's paper, and the rest is a tip for you and your brother."

I smiled and handed her the paper. "Thank you so much, Mrs. Fermi," I said politely.

"I guess you're not going to be a priest like your brother Jack?" she said with that certain grin.

"No ma'am, I guess not."

"You'll go far Davey Malloy," she said opening the paper mumbling to herself walking back inside.

My brother could not stop laughing as I told him the story. We stopped at a small store on Graceland and went inside. He bought a jar of maraschino cherries. Later we sat outside the store under a big shady walnut tree and between the two of us we ate the whole jar of cherries. "Thank you, Mrs. Fermi," he said holding up the cherry jar as a salute to her tip to us. "Cheers!" Then he gave me the two bucks for helping him.

When all the cherries were all gone, we took turns drinking the sweet juice as we sat at the top of a hill on Graceland Avenue. It was a beautiful street with big brick houses and large dark green lawns. I looked at him and he began to laugh, "You have a big red mark all around your mouth from the cherry juice." I looked at him and started to laugh, so did he. We both laughed so hard, and I could not stop laughing until my sides ached. Then we just sat there, together.

"I love this hill during the winter," Jack said sounding quiet.

"Yeah, this is the hill during snow storms that they close off on both ends for sleigh riding." The hill was too steep to plow and became very icy after dark so the city of Overland just closed it off and everybody used it for sledding. One of the neighbors always brought out an old barrel with holes poked in it and filled it with wood that he would light. Everybody would stand around it and rub their hands together to keep warm.

Jack pointed at the old tree behind us and told me in his own scholarly way, "This walnut tree, in Latin they are called *Juglans regia,* and are late to grow leaves, typically not until more than halfway through the spring. They also secrete chemicals into the ground to prevent competing vegetation from growing up around them. Because of this, flowers or vegetable gardens shouldn't be planted too close to them. The husks of walnut shells contain a juice that will stain everything it touches. It has been used as a dye for cloth for centuries, so be real careful when you handle the nuts, you'll never get the stain out." He had something on his mind, I could tell.

My brother looked at me for a moment with sad eyes and a serious gaze on his face. He took a deep breath, "I'm not going back to the seminary in the fall," he said handing me the last of the cherry juice. "I'm going to Saint John's High School instead."

"What do you mean? You're not going back to the seminary? You're not going to be a priest?" I was devastated.

"No. I'm just not cut out for it I suppose."

"Do Mom and Dad know?"

"Yeah, I told them last night. They were upset but understood when I told them my heart just wasn't into it anymore. I told them I wanted to talk to you about it today. Just you and me. You understand, don't you?"

No, I didn't understand. I felt lost as if he had betrayed the family and me. First, he was going to be a priest and now he was not. Now I wasn't going to be the brother of a priest?

"No, I don't get it. Why aren't you going to be a priest? And why are you going to a different high school? What gives?"

"Davey, listen to me. I decided I was going to the seminary for everybody else, everybody except for me. It just got more difficult every year. I was only fooling myself. And that's not good for anybody. And if you aren't going to be a priest you have to go to a different school. Understand?"

My brother wasn't going to be a priest. I couldn't go to church on Sunday where he was saying Mass and kneel down and pray with my head bowed and hands clasped together. Now nobody would point or nod their heads at me and solemnly whisper about me in church—"his brother is a priest."

I had to think about this, this was something major in my life. Shit! No priest in the family? Whew. I can't believe it. I thought him being a priest and all might give me a preferred pass to heaven or something like that. You know, Saint Peter standing there at the golden gates and saying, "Oh let him in. He's an okay guy, his brother's a priest" Oh well, it just wasn't meant to be I guess. I didn't know what else to say. I didn't know what it all meant until I thought about it and said, "I guess you're right. You need to do it for the right reasons."

Then changing the subject I asked him, "That tree over there is a walnut tree, isn't it Jack?"

"Yeah, it's a walnut tree, Davey." He put his arm around my shoulders and hugged me like a big brother should. We talked for hours that day sitting under that big old walnut tree. It was getting dark as we started walking home, dragging the old red wagon behind us bumping along the sidewalk. It was noisy when it was empty.

"Mom's going to worry. We'd better hurry up," I told him.

"It's okay. I told her we might be late. I said I wanted to tell you myself, and we would talk it out." He put his arm around my shoulder again as we walked home. I smiled. He was a great brother.

We stopped at Roger Hornsby TV shop on the way home. Even though it was closed, we looked at the largest television set in the world that they had in the front store window with a TV show on the screen. It was huge. And it was in color! Jack said it was the new fifteen-inch color television. We watched a show standing out front with an outside speaker giving us the sound. Cars slowed down just so they could see the latest technological invention. Maybe one day we could have one of these color TVs.

"Come on, time to go home. You okay?" he asked me.

"Yeah, I'm okay."

It was late when we came in the back door, and the house was dark. I went to my room and found a note on the bed from my mom.

Boys—
There is chili in the fridge and for desert I made your favorite—homemade
shortcake and with fresh strawberries.
Keep the noise down and lights off. Your father has to be up early for work
tomorrow.
Love,
Mom

I showed the note to Jack when he came into the room, and we hurried off to the kitchen. I loved my mom's chili, but all we both wanted to eat was dessert, the strawberry shortcake. I could taste it already. Standing in the darkened kitchen, we opened the Tupperware containers and put the fresh homemade shortcake into each bowl then poured heaping ladles of strawberries over the top of it finishing it off with whipped cream. We did all of this in the dark so as not to wake anybody.

With the bowl of shortcake in one hand and a cold glass of milk in the other, we made our way into the living room, far away from Mom and Dad's bedroom. My mouth watered. I could hardly wait. It was my favorite dessert. Shortcake, strawberries, and whipped cream! As my spoon plunged toward the mouthwatering dessert, I looked with horror at the bowl. There before me was the shortcake smothered with—chili.

"Ughhh, God! Terrible," I blurted out in horror. I couldn't help myself and started laughing. I couldn't eat it much less look at it.

Jack frowned at me and told me to be quiet until he looked at his bowl and found the same surprise. He began to laugh and soon both of us could not stop laughing.

My mom and dad appeared at the door ready to shout at us but saw the bowls of whipped cream and chili-covered strawberry shortcake and knew immediately what had happened. They too began to laugh with my dad laughing the hardest.

"You boys are going to be the death of me yet. Well, now that we are up, let me see if I have any of that apple pie left over from yesterday," mom said.

Soon the other doors opened, and my sisters began to file in. Now that the whole house was awake and my mother asked, "Who's for brownies? I'll make up a fresh batch."

Chapter Twenty-One

When I told Timmy about my brother making money caddying on the golf course he sounded very interested. I told him they said I was too young and skinny to caddy. His only response was "Bull!"

The next day he called me on the phone and said, "Come on, follow me. I got this all figured out. Meet me at my house—we're going to the golf course. We're going to make some money for your radio fund."

Caddying? I told him I was too young, but I was running out of time and ideas. I still needed more money to pay for the radio. I only needed seven dollars more. I used it every night when the skies were clear. I talked to somebody I met on the radio who lived in Australia and he said it was winter there and very cold. It was hot in Saint Louis. Go figure. I loved my radio.

Timmy was waving for me to hurry up as he stood in front of his house. "Come on, slowpoke. Hurry up if you want to make some money."

I ran to catch up. It was hot, and I was glad I brought my canteen. I took a sip and gave it to Timmy. He drank half of it, but I didn't say anything. We walked down Brown Road towards the golf course and took a shortcut through some woods towards the back of the course. My brother Jack called it the back nine.

It was a long hilly golf course, and as we trampled through the tall weeds through the woods, we could see the fairway over the tall scrub grasses and bushes. Soon we saw golf balls rolling down the hill in front of us. Some golfers had hit golf balls over the hill and they rolled down about fifty feet away. Timmy ran through the woods, over the fence and grabbed one of the golf balls before returning to where I was standing.

"Get down, jerk. Hide or they'll see us," he yelled pulling me to the ground behind the tall grasses. Within minutes, four golfers and four caddies appeared over the hill looking for their golf balls down near the gully.

"I know it's around here somewhere," I heard the heavyset golfer in an argyle shirt say to his friends. He was smoking a smelly cigar and moving the tall grasses with a golf club looking for his golf ball. He came closer.

"Lost ball, Hank. Two-stroke penalty on your scorecard," said the other golfer in bright green pants. He could not stop laughing. "Come on; let's go. Your time's up," he said with a laugh.

The disgruntled golfer muttered some curse words under his breath and leaned into the brush to look for his ball. His eyes squinted through the fence and I could have sworn he saw us there hiding. I held my breath.

"Come on Hank, give it up," the other golfer said to him diverting his attention.

Ten minutes later, four more golf balls came flying over the top of the hill, rolling down to the bottom of the gulch. Again and again golf balls rolled down the hill. Timmy ran out each time until he had more than two dozen golf balls.

"I thought you wanted to earn some money for your damn radio, Davey boy. Aren't you going to get any balls for yourself."

"Not this way. I'd rather wash Mr. Jost's car then steal something that isn't mine."

He grabbed the front of my t-shirt and looked me right in the eye, his face inches from mine, "I didn't steal anything. And don't you be telling anybody that I did. You got it?"

I dropped my head and shrugged off his grip, "I got it."

"Come on. Let's go sell some golf balls," he said with a laugh running ahead of me before stopping at the big red golf building. He stood underneath the sign that said, Sherwood Golf Course- Members Only.

He held all the balls in a pouch he made at the front of his t-shirt. We walked around to the front of the building they called the clubhouse and Timmy hollered to the golfers leaving to go to their cars on the parking lot: "Golf balls for sale!" He shouted to a group of them. "I got golf balls for sale, water golf balls. Used golf balls. Good balls. Twenty five cents each, five for a dollar."

Soon a large group of men surrounded him, picking over the golf balls he had in his t-shirt. One threw a dollar into his shirt after taking five balls.

He kept yelling, "Golf balls for sale." Then a hand reached through the crowd and fingered one of the balls. "Where'd you get this ball kid?"

"I found it, mister. What's it to you?"

"Because I lost one just like it on the eighteenth hole today that's why." The crowd parted revealing the big man wearing the argyle golf shirt.

"Not this one. This one's mine," Timmy said defiantly.

"Then tell me kid, why does it have a green dot and the initials, HS, written on its side? Huh, kid? That stands for Hank Sawyer, that's me—you little thief." He went to grab Timmy.

For a big man he was quick but not as quick as Timmy who dropped the front of his t-shirt and all of the golf balls started bouncing and rolling onto the asphalt parking lot. Timmy began yelling, "Free golf balls. Free golf balls. Big sale!" He screamed at the top of his lungs then took off running, leaving me standing there. I watched the men as they tried to grab the bouncing white golf balls and Timmy ran down the hill back into the woods. He was fast.

The big man turned and reached out to grab me. I ran. He chased me.

"Come 'ere kid," he yelled as tried to grab me again. He missed. I ran quick as I could amongst the cars on the parking lot and dodged his every move. The sound of his metal golf spike on his shoes echoed behind me. Closer.

Run, Davey.

"Stop, you little runt. I'm going to get you and when I do…" I heard him wheezing and coughing but I ran past the clubhouse and past the big trees and jumped over the fence scraping my arm as I made my way back into the safety of the woods. I soon found Timmy waiting in the brush.

"That was close," I said as I caught up with Timmy lying down in a spot in the woods.

"Not even close there, Davey boy." He lit a cigarette and took in a huge drag. It didn't smell like menthols. "That big jerk cost me three bucks. Come on, let's go home. Maybe we can find some money by the railroad tracks."

We walked down by the railroad tracks looking for money or "squished" coins that other kids would put on the rails to be flattened by the heavy locomotives as they raced by. Kids would then either sell them or drill a hole in the top and make a necklace out of it. You could always find some dimes, nickels, and sometimes quarters lying along the tracks swept up by the train. You could sell the squished ones for twice the face value to other kids.

"Got one!" he said loudly. "Another one!" he said stooping over. "Two nickels!"

Then I saw it, a shiny dime, next to a quarter. "Me too! I got a dime and a quarter!"

"Copycat," he retorted redoubling his efforts to find more coins. "How much did you find?"

"Thirty-five cents. And not squished either."

"You're just lucky, that's all."

I beamed, thinking it was a compliment. We didn't find any more coins that hot August afternoon. I really wanted to take a drink from my canteen, but I only had a little water left and I knew Timmy would want some and drink it all… so I left it in my backpack. I was hot and thirsty and just wanted to go home and cool off. I wanted some of my mom's cherry pie leftover from dinner the night before.

Timmy began to walk on the center of one of the railroad tracks, balancing himself so as to not fall off. "This is not easy to do," he said with his hands stretched out to his side to help him balance himself. "Try it."

I stepped onto the other rail, moved my backpack to the center of my back to help my balance, and soon was walking side by side with him. Both of our hands were outstretched to our sides to help us keep our balance.

"Not so tough to do," I said proudly, balancing myself on the center of the shiny metal rail. We walked in silence, both wobbling while concentrating on staying on the tracks.

"Let's see who can stay on the longest," he finally said as a challenge. We continued to walk shifting our weight from one foot to the other. It wasn't easy.

"You know I think Sunny really likes me," he said, a comment coming from nowhere. "I know she likes you, but now with her new boobs, I think she really has the hots for me. Whew! One night, just one night, her and me. Wow!"

I stopped him. "Timmy, Sunny's our best friend; don't forget that, okay? Let her choose who and what she wants."

He turned to look at me and a chill ran down my spine. It was a dark, evil look.

"Yeah, okay," he said. We walked in a strange silence, still balancing ourselves on the rails.

We both heard it at the same time and looked up. The thunder of the locomotive whistle broke the quiet that had surrounded us. Whoooooo. Whoooooooo, it sounded loud, and it was moving fast. I could see huge freight train coming further down the tracks and felt the rumble beneath my feet as the train shook the rails underneath.

Timmy reached out with his right hand and grabbed onto my left hand. He held it tight.

"Stay on the rails, Davey. Let's play chicken," he said with that strange look on his face. "Whoever lets go first is a chicken and loses, loses everything. Okay Ddddavey boy?"

"You're nuts," I told him. "Let go."

"You want Sunny, ddddon't you? Well, show me how badly you want her," he tempted me again with that same evil look on his face. "Whoever let's go first loses Sunny, got it?"

Looking up I saw the enormous dark blue and white Missouri-Pacific train bearing down on us. Coming closer, and closer, its shrill deep-throated blast horn filled the air. I could feel the rolling thunder of the massive diesel train rock under my feet as the earth shook and it got closer. And closer. And closer. The horn blasted the air. I could see the panic on the face of the locomotive driver, I tried to pull my hand from Timmy's grip, but he wouldn't let go. He was strong, and his grip was powerful. He was so strong, he kept holding on.

"Let go of me, Timmy!" I shouted trying to free myself from his hold.

I looked at him and his expression was calm with not a hint of fear on his face. "Chickenshit?" He jeered.

The train was now so close I could feel the heat from the engine before I shoved him away and leaped into the ditch beside the tracks. Just in time. The draft from the passing train nearly pulled me back onto the tracks. I grabbed the trunk of a small nearby tree and held on.

As he passed us, the driver let loose with a gutsy deep-throated whistle again and again to show his disapproval.

That was close I thought—way too close.

Once the long train had gone by, I saw Timmy standing there with a huge grin on his face. "Wow what a rush, huh man?"

I brushed the mud and grass from my jeans and grabbed my backpack and ran to confront him. "You shit, you almost killed me!

What the hell were you thinking?" I shoved him and felt my face turning red with anger.

He stood there looking at me. His face had a black glow to it when he said, "I won, you chickenshit. I won now, didn't I?" His eyes grew wide as he moved his t-shirt aside, and I saw his brother's pistol tucked under his t-shirt. "Come on, man. I won, didn't I?"

"You're crazy, man. I'm goin' home for dinner."

He stopped walking, grabbed me hard by the shoulder and growled, "Don't you ever call me crazy again."

"Go to hell," I told him and walked away. My heart was pounding so fast and hard I thought it was going to explode inside my chest. I couldn't stop my knees and hands from shaking. *What the hell was he thinking? He's my best friend and he tried to kill me. Or is he just trying to kill himself?*

"Wait, you little jerk," he hollered and grabbed my arm, spinning me around. I had never seen his eyes so full of rage as I did on that day. "Listen, you little chickenshit, Sunny is mine. I won her fair and square. You jumped off the rails, so I win and don't you forget it!"

"What the hell are you talking about? Yours? This was not some goddamn contest, and she's not some goddamn baseball card that you just won. She's Sunny, my best friend, and I'll do exactly as I please."

He lowered his voice, looked at me and said, "Careful Davey boy, be very careful."

My legs began to shake again. Maybe he was crazy. Or maybe he had been swallowing some of those drugs he stole from the old ladies medicine cabinets. I was angry and scared after what had just happened. All I wanted to do was to get away from him.

I started to walk home, leaving him there by the railroad tracks. He hollered something to me as I climbed up the hill, but I couldn't hear what he said… the four o'clock train was coming down the railroad tracks blowing its whistle to clear the way. I turned and saw Timmy standing there in the middle of the tracks, watching it as it came closer, and closer. I turned away, I couldn't watch.

Chapter Twenty-Two

I didn't hear anything from Timmy over the next week or so, which was good. Neither did Sunny. I was still mad at him and was doing a lot of thinking. School was looming on the horizon. My mom was already talking about taking me out for clothes shopping. No more school uniforms in high school. Regular clothes but no jeans. I went back to my writing.

It took me a few weeks to write another story for Mrs. Corcoran about my mom or about family or something. I got nervous. This was going to take a lot more time and for once, I was stuck on what I should write about. *Stop thinking about it Davey, let it flow and let it come naturally.* Then, I began to write.

Peach Pie
My mom loves pies. She's from the south, Savannah. I like it when my mom bakes pies because...
This reads terrible, I thought to myself. *Think Davey, think before you write.* The little voice inside was insistent, sounding familiar, like Mrs. Corcoran.

Peach Pie
I love it when my mom bakes her fabulous pies ...
No. That's awful too. I began again.

Peach Pie
My mother loves pies, all kinds of pies, apple, cherry but her favorite is peach pie. I love it too because I love to eat her pies that she...
No, that didn't sound right either.

Peach Pie
My mother, the southern belle always has an appetite for homemade pie. And...

No, no, no. Be yourself Davey. Tell your story. Make people reading your story feel your joy, feel your pain, and feel your feelings. I started again.

Peach Pie

My mother is a fine Southern lady. She loves her big lacy Easter bonnets, her mint juleps, her after-dinner port, and warm peach pie. In fact, there is nothing finer, she would always say, than fresh peach pie covered with homemade vanilla ice cream to bring to mind those warm summer nights of her childhood. Nothing finer, she would say with that glancing smile of hers and that faraway twinkle in her eye. She always liked her sweet desserts every night after dinner. I love the smell of her fresh-baked pie in the summertime, with the lingering aroma of sugar and cinnamon filling our house.

I will never forget, it was a warm day in August when a kindly neighbor telephoned my dad one afternoon, offering fresh peaches from his fruit trees. It seems he did not want to be stepping on them as he walked through his lawn, and he was too infirmed to pick up the luscious fruit and carry them to his basement. He offered them to us. In return, he only asked that we save him a bushel of peaches and set it on his back porch outside his kitchen. The rest were ours to keep. My mother was in heaven anticipating the sweet juicy peach pies that she would bake. Little did I realize what I was in for that day.

That Saturday my father and my brother and I went to pick peaches. The trees were so filled with fruit our neighbor had to use wooden two by four boards to hold them up and keep the branches from breaking. We picked the low dangling fruit from two of the trees and quickly filled a bushel basket for our neighbor. The rest of the treasured peaches were now ours.

Earlier that day my brother Jack had stopped by the market and bought a dozen bushel baskets to hold our precious treasure. We picked the rest of the fruit hanging from the low-lying branches but soon they were bare.

Being the youngest and the most agile, I volunteered to climb the trees and pick the higher fruit giving the peaches to my brother and my dad below. I love to climb trees. We were having a grand old time. I went from one tree to another picking the peaches, inspecting them, and handing them to waiting hands below.

I climbed higher and higher but then saw my hands were covered with black tree sap, and sticky juices from the soft fruit. My fingers stuck to everything I touched. I had cuts on my arms from broken branches and was covered in itchy peach fuzz.

Soon, I had an unscratchable itch everywhere. As the day's sun got warmer and the sweat dripped off my head down my back, the itch spread to my whole body even inside my jeans. How could something that tastes so good make you itch so bad?

Four hours later, we were finally done picking peaches. This is what hell is like, I thought as I ran home leaving the rest of them wondering what was wrong. I took three baths and even used a fresh bar of my mother's Ivory soap, but nothing seemed to help. Finally, the next day after two more baths, the itching at last seemed to stop.

A few nights later, after we finished dinner, my mother asked, "Who wants some peach pie?" I began to itch all over again. I never wanted to see another peach again for the rest of my life. "No, thank you," I whispered shaking my head. My mom looked at me in surprise, but I think she understood. No more peaches. She smiled her knowing smile. "How about some ice cream instead?"

I love my mom.

I read it, reread it until I thought it was perfect, grabbed my journal, and started walking to the library. It was so hot, damn hot. I stopped to cool off in the Post office's air conditioning and as usual leafed through the FBI wanted posters hanging from the wall. I stopped when I reached one near the back of the flip chart. *Could it be? It looked just like... but oh no, the name was different, the hair was different, the glasses were different, bigger. But...*

I took a drink from my canteen as my hands trembled, and my knees shook. Maybe I was mistaken. It couldn't be. It had to be somebody else who was an identical twin. I knew I could ask Ms. Corcoran, she would help me, she had all the answers. Yes that's it.

Mrs. Corcoran smiled when I came in but it turned into a troubled, quizzical look as I handed her the journal and said, "I hope you like it."

By the time Mrs. Corcoran finished reading the story she smiled an ever-expanding grin. She clutched it to her chest and smiled at me. "Wow—very good work, Davey. This story shows me that you are growing in your writing. You are going to make a fine writer someday. Very good... very, very good."

She looked at me and smiled as she sat there holding the story in her lap like a proud mentor. "I'm going to type up this story for you and mail it to your home so you can show your mom. I'm sure she'll be very happy to read this story you wrote." She paused and peered over her glasses at me. She copied the story onto a sheet of paper and returned my journal to me.

"Now, you didn't have any help with this now did you?" she asked me as she finished.

My mind was distracted and my thoughts were a million miles away.

"Davey?"

"Yes, Mrs. Corcoran?"

"You did this story all by yourself, correct?"

"Yes, ma'am."

"Davey… tell me, is everything okay?"

"Mrs. Corcoran, what does the word embezzlement and fraud mean?"

"Well," she moved back then paused for moment pondering her answer. "Fraud can mean a phony as being somebody you are not. Or embezzlement can mean what the dictionary says… taking money that does not belong to you by wrongful or criminal deception intended to result in financial or personal gain. Why do you ask, Davey?"

"Well… they say that everybody has an exact twin on this earth…Right? Don't they?"

"Yes, so they say. Why do you ask?" she chuckled now, but suddenly she seemed more interested.

"Well, I stopped at the post office like I always do to cool off when it's this hot and I was looking through the FBI most wanted posters and…"

I saw her stiffen at the mention of the government agency.

"There was a picture of someone who looked just like you; so much so she could be your identical twin. The name was different underneath the photo, but it looked so much like you… only she had a different hairstyle and different eyeglasses. The name on the wanted poster was Margaret not Meg. Her full name was Margaret Stanch. She was wanted for fraud, but she looked just like you."

Her eyes opened wide with fear, and her hand began to tremble.

She set the journal down on the table and leaned close to talk to me. "Davey, remember I said that people do things that they don't want to do but sometimes they have to in order to help someone they love and care for… perhaps somebody may die if they don't do something drastic to help. Somebody they love dearly. Remember?"

I was confused. "Yes. But what does that have to do with the picture of your twin… sister? Or, maybe…" I swallowed hard looking at her. I looked deep into her eyes for the very first time. A tear began to form in her eye.

"I have to go home, Mrs. Corcoran. I'll see you next week."

I ran home. I was so confused, not knowing what to do or who to talk to about what had just happened. Jack was at work and so was Dad. Mom was in no shape for any more stress, and Timmy would use it as a way to make money… somehow.

The phone rang. It was Sunny.

"Do you want to come down and pick some more mint?" she asked sweetly but her voice sounded strange.

"Yeah great, and I really need to talk to you."

"Okay, sure."

"I'll be right down." I kept going over and over in my mind what I was going to say to her, but I realized more than anything I was looking forward to just being with her again.

Chapter Twenty-Three

"Davey, I'm sure there's an explanation for all of this," Sunny told me as I picked the mint in her backyard and she sat on the lawn nearby. I put the mint into my mom's wicker basket lined with wet newspaper to keep it fresh.

"Yeah, like what?" I asked looking up at her.

"Well…maybe Mrs. Corcoran has an evil twin sister. They say everybody has at least one twin in the world."

"Not me, my mom says they broke the mold when they made me."

She laughed that cute laugh of hers, and I stopped doing what I was doing to watch her. *God she's beautiful.*

"Maybe it's not an evil sister after all; maybe, yeah I got it, maybe it's a cousin who looks just like her and she got into some trouble, that's all. That's what I think it is."

"Yeah, maybe that's it. Maybe that's why she didn't want to talk about it with me. Yeah, that's it. Some cousin that lives out in Texas or something." That was it. That had to be it.

"Wow, what a relief," I shouted. I spun around on the laundry pole and spun off, rolling down the hill into the weeds. Boy was I happy. I really liked Mrs. Corcoran, Meg. I didn't want her to go to prison. She was a friend. I never thought that way about her until that very moment, but it was true. She was a good friend. She had helped me a lot this summer.

"Davey, I have to go in soon. Are you coming for dinner with me and my family next week?"

"Sure, I just have to ask my mom that's all."

"Okay, but don't wait too long. I go back to Chicago to live with my sister soon. Then I go to school until next summer."

She turned to leave, but I held her arm for a moment and whispered, "Wait, I have to tell you something else. Timmy told me he really likes you… and not just as a friend if you know what I mean."

Her smile faded, then returned as she said, "I like Timmy too Davey, but only as a friend. But you, I really like you." She kissed me on the cheek. "Know what I mean?"

"Yes, I think I do." *Should I tell her about the gun? No, it would just scare her.*

I picked up all the mint that I had cut and looked at my treasure. *This will bring me at least three or maybe even four dollars when I sold it to the restaurants. I nearly had all the money for Mr. Jost!*

"Oh, I nearly forgot, now that we settled the FBI mystery, let me see your story before you go." I handed her my journal. She smiled as she read it, her lips, and eyes moving in tandem, before turning pages.

After Sunny finished reading it, she smiled, hugged me, and then kissed me, on the lips, a long slow kiss. A different kind of kiss. "I love it, Davey. Whatever you do, don't ever stop writing." She turned and walked inside her house, but my hand went to my lips where she had kissed me. Now I had two things I would never forget—what Mrs. Corcoran had said about my story and… a kiss from Sunny.

I ran home so as not to be late for dinner.

"Davey," my mom said as I came inside, "Dinner's on the table. Wash your hands; we're going to sit down to eat."

"I'll be right in mom. I gotta go to the bathroom first." When I was done, I washed my hands and sat down with the rest of the family.

When dinner was over, and my mom was cutting the pie she looked with her usual smile, which turned to horror, as if I was bleeding. "Davey!" she screamed. "What on earth do you have all over your face? It's all red and puffy. And your arms?" She came over to examine me more closely. "Davey, it's all over your face, and neck and arms. Oh my God!"

It was poison ivy!

Chapter Twenty-Four

I itched like crazy all over my body. I took two cold baths in soapy water hoping that would relive the itching and wash the poison ivy away. It helped for a little while but then the itching only became worse. Next, my mom put pink calamine lotion everywhere it was red. It didn't help. I never really got to sleep that night, tossing and turning and scratching anyplace I could reach. God, did I itch. Nothing helped.

The next morning my whole body was covered in blisters, and my mom called the doctor to come by and see me.

Doctor Miller, our family physician, said with a solemn face after examining me, "Davey has an acute case of hyper-allergic reaction to poison sumac. Very rare but he will get large blisters and swelling everywhere that he has touched." He wrote prescriptions for some salve and ointments and said he would be back in a few days to check on me. The prescriptions didn't help. I was miserable.

All I could do all day was kneel down on the living room floor with my books on the sofa and read my wonderful library books. I could not walk around because it felt like I had two huge swollen basketballs dangling between my legs, bouncing from side to side. Sunny called me every day to try to cheer me up and brought some homemade soup for me that she and her grandmother had made. She also left me some homemade tea, which tasted like peaches. Delicious. I never heard from Timmy the whole time I was sick. Not once.

Mom wouldn't let me look in the mirror and would break into tears every time she went by me. My eyes hurt and were almost swollen completely shut. My fingers developed huge blisters between them. I could not close my hands.

The next day I made my way into the bathroom and looked in the mirror. My face was all swollen, my eyes were mere slits on my face, and I could hardly hear because my cheeks were so enlarged. I felt terrible.

My mom was constantly baking pies and cakes for me to eat on the sofa. I ate all my meals there on a towel that mom put on the sofa. I even slept there kneeling on the floor with my head resting on the seat.

When Doctor Miller came back to check on me, he gasped. He gave me a prescription for some sleeping tablets and quickly left for an urgent appointment. The pills helped a lot. I slept with my head on the sofa, awkward, and uncomfortable but I slept.

After a couple of more days, I could finally sleep in my own bed, lying down, listening to the owls hooting in the yard and I heard the distant howling of the night freight trains whistle off into the night. The echoing sound it made was different from what I heard that day with Timmy; this sound was calming as I heard it fade into the distance. Like it was saying goodbye.

Mrs. Jost stopped by and left a German chocolate cake she had made just for me. Mr. Jost never asked about the money I owed him even though I was still a few dollars short. I would get the money somehow. I think he felt bad.

Jack had taken the mint to the restaurants and after hearing about what happened to me collecting the mint they gave him double what they normally paid me but they didn't want the mint. Thought it might have poison ivy in it. I made two dollars and never left home. Nice guys. Good brother.

Days later, the swelling was nearly gone. I had just one more day before I could go outside and play. I lay on my bed at the back of the house facing the open window, reading the biography of Benjamin Franklin and heard a noise outside. I looked in the backyard and through the screen, I saw Mr. Jost clearing weeds in his yard and burning them in his trash container. *Darn, if I was well I could have made a few dollars doing that for him.*

I was reading my latest book and fell asleep lying on the bed with a cool breeze blowing through the window, ruffling the new curtains my mother had just hung. It felt delightful just to be able to lie down again and fall asleep.

My mother called me later at suppertime and when I walked into the kitchen, she looked at me in shock. She dropped the mixing bowl with the cake batter and it crashed to the floor. She screamed, "Davey! Oh my God! What's happened to your face?"

Instinctively I touched it and could feel all new tiny bumps all over my face. It began to hurt as the bubbles grew larger and wet ooze came running down my face.

"Don't touch it," my mother said. "Stay right here … no… wash your hands first. I'm calling Dr. Miller to come right over to look at you." He was in my room in less than an hour. My face was itching like crazy. It wouldn't stop itching.

"Poison ivy," was the two-word verdict issued by our longtime family physician. "Yep, that's what it is all right," he mused rubbing his chin. "What I can't figure out is how he got it." He looked at me with a confused look on his face. "You haven't snuck outside have you, Davey? Or even just for a run with Dizzy in the backyard? Or to one of your friend's house? Come on now Davey, level with me."

"No, Doctor Miller I haven't been outside in over a week. Honest."

"Hmmm, I can't figure this one out." He was interrupted by the front door bell. My mom excused herself and went to answer the door.

When my mom left the room, the kindly old doctor leaned in close and whispered, "You can level with me Davey, did you go out anywhere, anywhere at all?"

"No Doc, nowhere. Honest."

"Hmmm," he said. "I'm stumped. I must tell you that…"

"Well, I think I solved the mystery," my mother said as she returned to the room. "That was Mr. Jost. He heard about how sensitive Davey is to poison ivy that he removed it all from his backyard and… burned it."

The doctor looked at the open window, then at my books. "And I guess that Davey was in here, in his room, with the window open, reading and the smoke blew inside. That's how he got it!"

My mother gasped, and then sprang into action. "All right Davey, off the bed. I gotta wash all those sheets and bedspreads. Now!" She stopped, her face full of pain. "Oh my lord," she said. "Who would have thought," she muttered trying to pull of the spread and sheets, clutching her belly.

"Janey, you're just about due with that new baby of yours," said a frightened Dr. Miller. "Here let me get these for you. I'm not allergic to poison ivy," he said as my mother collapsed in the chair beside my bed. I spent another four days quarantined inside.

One day I overhead Mr. Jost at the front door talking and apologizing to my mother. "Janey, I had no idea that the smoke would be toxic to Davey. Who would have thought?"

"Thank God, he didn't get any smoke down his throat or lungs, thank the Lord," my mother said with worry in her voice.

"Yes… yes…yes. I feel so bad. Tell Davey, me and Mrs. Jost leave soon on our cross-country trip with our new Windstream Motor coach and that… he … he doesn't' have to pay for the radio," he said reluctantly. "Tell him it's a gift from me, a belated birthday gift, so to speak. And I hope he feels a lot better soon."

WOW! I screamed inside. *The radio was finally all mine. Free? I forgot all about the itching and the pain. My very own ham radio.*

"We leave soon. Have to go and finish packing, Janey. See you at Christmas time when we get back from Colorado," I heard him say.

"Goodbye, Charles," she said with a wave before joining me in the living room. She sat down heavy on the sofa.

A week later, I was feeling better, however still tired all of the time, but at least I no longer looked like an alien from Neptune, with pockmarks all over my face. My face still had some red spots on it, but I was on the road to recovery and no longer had to put the pink Calamine Lotion everywhere. Yuck!

My mom looked tired. "Not too much more of this," my mother moaned, rubbing her stomach. "I don't know if I can handle much more of this."

"Let me get you some lemonade."

"Thank you, Davey, but I think I'm going in to lie down and take a nap. Why don't you finish your reading?"

I sat down and began to read, wearing the wonderful new Marine Corps. T-shirt Josh had just sent me. He was the greatest. I must have dozed off in the front living room, the house was so quiet. I heard a car door slam out front which woke me up. I saw somebody get out of the car wearing a Marine Corps. uniform. It was Josh! *Holy Shit. My brother Josh! I couldn't believe it. He's home!*

"Mom," I screamed, "Josh is home." She was up with a start and ran to the door right behind me, running and holding her swollen belly. She had the biggest smile on her face, mixed with a little worry as she pushed her hair back away from her face. "My Josh is home," she said, over and over again as we rushed to the front door. "Josh, Josh, oh sweet Jesus, good God, Josh it's so good to …" she yelled.

At the door stood an older Marine, in his Marine dress blue uniform carrying a folded flag under his arm.

"Are you Mrs. Malloy? Mrs. Jane Malloy?"

My mom was in shock and didn't say anything, she could only nod her head. She knew what was coming and had dreaded this day for a long time. Finally, she managed a weak reply, "Yes, I'm Jane Malloy," as tears began to fill her eyes.

"Ma'am. I'm Staff Sergeant Victor Brandt with the United States Marine Corps Bereavement Center. I'm sorry ma'am, but I'm afraid I have some bad news for you. I regret to inform you that your son, Sergeant Joshua Malloy was killed in..."

My mother began to cry and scream and yell, "No, no, not my Josh. No!" it was the last thing she said before she collapsed to the ground. I rushed to her side trying to console her. I held her head in my lap and I began to cry.

I could not stop, the tears just coming and coming. I couldn't believe it. My brother, my best friend Josh, gone. No, this must be a horrible nightmare and soon I would wake up and he would still be alive. Yeah that had to be it. I thought as I continued to cry. My whole body ached at my loss. Josh was gone forever. He was not coming home. Not Josh, not the brother that took me to the ballpark to see the Cardinals. Who taught me how to ride a bike, to read a compass, to to play basketball, and teach me everything? He always had time for me, his kid brother. Oh my God, he was gone. Not Josh!

My mom stirred in my lap and when she opened her eyes and saw me crying she also knew it was not a horrible nightmare, it was horrible but it was real life. She began to cry. And cry and cry.

Chapter Twenty-Five

The funeral was a small ceremony held at the Lakeside Chapel near Lake Saint Louis. This was his favorite place. A calm and peaceful place where Josh and I would sometimes go fishing. I missed him already. For me the whole ceremony was a blur. I cried the entire time. I didn't care who saw me, or what people thought, I missed my brother, I missed him a lot and he was never coming home again.

I thought back to everything Josh and I had done together. I thought of all the pictures he sent me, the letters he wrote me from all over the world. He always had time to listen to me if I had a problem or a question. *Goddamn, why did this have to happen to him? Why Josh? He was the best brother a guy could ever have.*

My father leaned over to me and whispered. "Be strong. Josh would want you to be strong." He held my hand in his. I never realized how large and strong his hand was until that day.

My mom could not stop crying, even though Doctor Miller gave her some sedatives to help her sleep, they just made her drowsy all the time. The chapel was overflowing with people who had come to pay their last respects.

After the service, we waited at the back of the chapel to greet people as they left the church and thanked them for coming. Everybody we knew came to the service.

All of our neighbors came by to say their final goodbyes to my brother, including the Muldoons, the Vitts, the Drancys, the Grafs, the McIntyres, the Volkerts, Brian and Tim and even Mrs. Schmidt came with Mrs. Arnsberg. They both said what a good boy he was and how much they would miss him. Mr. and Mrs. Jost came, and he was all dressed up in a suit and tie, like my dad. She wore a mink around her neck and hugged me, saying how good and sweet Josh always was to her. Her mink stole had a strange smell to it, it smelled old. "You are so much like your older brother," she said, beginning to cry.

My mom started to cry again then pulled me close to her. She hugged me so tight I could hardly breathe.

Mr. Barclay came by with his daughter Roberta. She was so beautiful and smelled so sweet, like lilacs. She kissed me on the cheek and said how sorry she was to hear about Josh's death. Her tall college boyfriend stopped by, looked down at me, shook my hand and said how sorry he was for my loss.

Sunny and Timmy came to the funeral. She was dressed in a long black dress and as we left the church on the way to the cemetery, she kissed my cheek and whispered, "I'm so sorry for your loss, Davey, really I am. I never met him, but I know he will truly be missed. I'm so sorry. I'll call you later today if you feel like talking, okay?" she said patting me on the back. I nodded and said something I don't remember.

Timmy wore an old grey t-shirt with a black tie, untied and draped around his neck. He stuck out his hand to shake mine and said, "Tough luck, Davey boy, but we all got to go sometime now, don't we? See ya later. Gotta go, Sunny's waiting for me." He gave me a sly grin. It was then something hit me about Timmy. He was not a true friend—and never had been.

Mrs. Walker had driven them to the funeral and stopped to give me and my family her condolences. She shook my hand and hugged me close. I could feel her chest pressing tight against my face. "Stop by again sometime, Davey," she whispered in my ear. "I miss seeing you around. Bye for now." I could smell the sweetness of her perfume as she walked away and it was time for us to go home and...

Carol stopped reading and listened to Mitch's voice as he read from his book. His voice was filled with emotion. She had heard him read the story a thousand times before, but this time was different. She moved closer to him as if to give him moral support by her mere presence. She heard him say, *"Chapter 2..."*

Chapter 2

The journey from death row at Florida State Prison outside of the rural town of Starke Florida to Jacksonville Memorial Hospital was to be a short one for Timothy Elroy Walker. It would take no more than thirty-five minutes to drive north on State Route 301 then East onto Highway 8 to the hospital. Once the paperwork was completed, Florida State Trooper Richard Gallante would turn the state's star prisoner over to the prison ward guards at the hospital. Then he was done for the day and looking forward to three days off with his family.

Walker wanted to donate his organs to an ailing family member after his upcoming execution. This request required that he first be tested to ensure the compatibility for a transplant.

Florida Governor John Richards personally approved the transfer to the hospital for the specialized organ transplant testing. He said in an interview, "While Mr. Walker's crimes are heinous, his willingness to donate his organs and tissue could save another life, and the state of Florida should allow it to happen."

Protocol dictated that three cruisers be used to transport a prisoner like Walker but since budget cuts and because it was a weekend only enough staff for one transport was available. It would have to suffice.

His execution was scheduled for the following week. They would return him to death row once they completed his testing. The prison warden strenuously objected to him being moved anywhere. "He's too dangerous," he told his boss but he was ultimately overruled.

The young state trooper driving the sedan looked at his watch. He had told his wife he would be home by nine o'clock. She said she would hold dinner for him.

Albert Simmons, a fellow trooper but a rookie, was texting his new bride as they made the turn onto Highway 8.

Walker complained from the back seat, "I need to take a dump."

"You'll just have to hold it until we get to the hospital," said Gallante.

"I gotta go now."

"Just hold it. That's the rules. No stopping with a capital prisoner…no exceptions."

Simmons looked up sympathetically trying to understand the reasoning but was willing to back his partner in his decision; but he also had to use the facilities.

"I can't hold it," Walker complained, "It must have been something you guys gave me to eat. I'll just have to mess up the back of this nice new police car."

Gallante was taking his young daughter to compete in a soccer match the next morning in the car and did not relish the prospect of spending an hour or more cleaning up after this degenerate. His partner nodded his head towards an upcoming gas station just off the next highway exit.

"Okay. Hold it just a little longer. There's a gas station up ahead. But Walker you try anything, I mean anything at all and I'll ram this shotgun so far up your ass you'll never shit again. You hear me?"

"Got it, Sarge. Hurry up, will you?"

The senior officer parked the state trooper sedan by the restroom door and sent Simmons inside the gas station to retrieve the key. He knew these highway gas stop restrooms were never left open.

Simmons led the way and stood in front of the door watching the convicted killer.

Walker stood up outside the cruiser and hobbled to the men's room, his ankles and hands shackled together. "How the hell am I going to use toilet paper?"

"Forget it Walker. I ain't takin' off the handcuffs. Now be quick about it and leave the door open."

"Hey, give me a minute of privacy will ya' so I can do my duty? Okay?"

Simmons frowned, shook his head, but turned around while his fellow officer stood watching by the car just as a big eighteen-wheeler came in and stopped for gas. The loud noise from the big truck's air brakes muffled the sound of the gunshot to the back of officer Simmons head. The front of his face blown was away and he was dead before he hit the ground.

A shotgun blast from the driver of the eighteen-wheeler blew Gallante off his feet and pushed him backwards landing him eight feet way. His chest was bleeding through his uniform and the sound of air rushing through his lungs could be heard in the still night air. The driver of the truck rummaged through the dying officer's pockets for the keys to the shackles holding Walker.

Gallante made a feeble attempt to search for his service revolver but the second blast of the shotgun snuffed the life from the dying officer. Walker smiled as he stood over him still holding the smoking shotgun. The two men hopped into the truck and disappeared into the cool Florida night. The stolen truck was found abandoned hours later at a rest stop north of Jacksonville off Interstate I-95. Investigators found maps of I-95 and Massachusetts under the seat. He was headed out of state to spread terror elsewhere.

Police issued an alert for the states of Georgia, South Carolina, Maryland, Virginia, New Jersey, New York, Florida, and Alabama. He disappeared with the help of the Brotherhood, and it was as if the earth had swallowed him up and kept him safe.

Chapter 3

The Delray Beach police department annex was housed in a white two-story structure adjacent to the modern courthouse building just off Atlantic Avenue. A grove of tall, ancient banyan trees spread high over the curved brown Spanish-tiled roof of the building, keeping it cool during the hot summer days.

I was working late trying to finish an accumulated pile of backlogged paperwork so I could take my first vacation in ten years with my wife Sandy and family. Not much more to do, I thought as I glanced at the inbox on my desk.

It was nearly midnight, and I was the only one left in the annex other than the cleaning crew. I stood, stretched, and looked first at my watch then the dwindling pile of police folders left to finish. I should be done here in an hour at most I thought as I made my way to the men's room stopping for a cup of coffee on my way back to my overcrowded cubicle.

When I reached my chair, I saw a picture postcard of some distant pink and white sandy beach, shadowed by threatening dark clouds. It was not your typical touristy postcard. I looked around the office. It was deserted. Curious, I turned over the card as I sat down and read the inscription on the back.

Hi ya buddy boy!
Once we were friends, remember old buddy boy? Friends don't do
what you did!
Hhhows the fffamily?
Sorry buddy boy—but somebody's gotta die –
—T

A chill ran through my body as I reached for my phone and dialed my home number and grabbed my coat as I ran out the door. It was busy. Damn. Then no signal.

Then the phone rang, "Hello,"

"Hey buddy boy; you sure know how to pick 'em. Your wife is beautiful man. Come on home and join the party." Immediately I knew the voice even though I had not heard him in years. The line went dead.

I jumped into my police cruiser and floored the gas pedal as I rushed for home. I nearly hit a late-night pedestrian in a crosswalk. I laid on my horn to warn him but kept on driving.

I picked up the radio microphone in the car and made a plea for help—"Officer needs assistance at his Pineapple Grove residence—fugitive Walker may be involved. Address 6524 Southwest 2nd Ave, Delray. Stat! Approach with extreme caution. Armed and dangerous."

A million thoughts clouded my brain as I sped down Atlantic Avenue, and then turned onto Swinton Avenue with the siren wailing breaking the silence of the quiet night air.

I was four blocks from home but heard other police cars in the distance responding to my call for help. Thank God. I prayed everything would be fine. As I approached the house, I saw the lights were on and her car was in the driveway. The car screeched to a stop in the driveway and without closing the door I ran towards home with my weapon drawn. I heard loud music coming from the living room.

Please God let everything be all right—please let nothing happen to her and my son. I promise I…

Suddenly, a huge explosion ripped my home to pieces and sent me sailing across the street some fifty yards away. Instinctively, I raised my hand to cover my face as shards of glass, torn steel, and large chunks of wood, ripped through my body.

The gas line blast explosion destroyed the small suburban home, killing the inhabitants inside. In the rubble, the charred remains of two people were found dead—bound and gagged in a closet. It was my wife Sandy and my son Derek.

An ace of spades, the calling card for the Brotherhood, was later found nailed to the front door of the demolished house.

I woke up four days later in the hospital, filled with rage and thoughts of how I would track down the killer of my family. The house Walker destroyed was my home and those he killed in the explosion were my family. Once released from the hospital, I joined in the hunt for the fugitive Timothy Walker. Now it was personal. He was a wanton killer and now he had nothing to lose. The manhunt was on for the most dangerous man in America and... Mitch quivered for a moment before continuing.

Carol stood there and watched him recover his composure.

He continued. *The manhunt was on for the most...*

She sat down nearby and returned to Mitch's latest book, *Summertime*. She looked and was distressed to see she was nearing the end of the book. She wanted more. She wanted to learn everything about him.

Chapter Twenty-Six

SEPTEMBER 1959

My mom was lying down, and even though her door was closed I heard sobbing coming from her bedroom. She missed Josh a lot, and so did I. I would be back in school soon, just after Labor Day.

I saw her sitting on the floor going through the family photo albums, slowly turning the pages and tracing her finger around the pictures of Josh. She saw pictures of Josh at the prom, Josh in his uniform, Josh throwing snowballs in the backyard, Josh with the family, Josh at Thanksgiving, Josh clowning around at Christmas, Josh…. She continued to turn the pages in the album and crying the whole time, murmuring something under her breath that I could not hear. She would sometimes stop and lift up Josh's favorite sweater and press it to her face and take in a deep breath. Then she began to cry again.

I tiptoed into her room and sat down beside her. She looked at me, smiled and put her arm around me then had me help her turn the pages. When we were done with one album, she picked up another one.

"Mom," I said quietly.

"Yes, David?"

"Maybe we could take all of Josh's photos and put them into one big album. Then we can see all the pictures of him at one time."

She smiled, wiping away the tears, sniffling, "That's a good idea, Davey. I'll have your father get me one big album from the photo store and then you and I can arrange them all together. Would you like that?"

"Yes, ma'am."

She smiled and hugged me before standing up. It was a welcome smile.

"In the meantime Davey, be a good boy and go to the store for me," she said just above a whisper. "The money and the list for the Labor Day cookout are in the kitchen." I took the list off the refrigerator and looked at it. It was a long one, but my mom wrote on the top of the sheet:

Davey—you can get this at Weis Market if you want. Don't forget the mayonnaise. I'll need that to make your father's potato salad.

That's good, I thought since it was only a block away to the corner grocery store. Schnucks was so far away.

I went to the store, but I no longer rode my imaginary horse; instead, I walked thinking of Josh. I was in my own world. I missed him like crazy.

When I walked into Weis Market it was nearly noon, and it was crowded. I looked at the list and started adding things to my cart for my mom. It took over thirty minutes. I found everything except mayonnaise.

"Hi Davey, how you doing today?"

"Fine Mr. Weis. I need some mayonnaise for my mom."

"Aisle two if we have any. Bea can you help young Davey out over here? He needs some mayo for his mom. Is she making potato salad for your dad again?"

"Yeah, it's my dad's favorite, Mr. Weis."

"Sure, Willie," said Bea, his long-time aisle clerk, who had been there forever or for at least as long as we have lived there. "Hi Davey," said the older lady, she had to be at least two hundred years old with her glasses gliding down her nose, being held in place by a multicolored glass-beaded chain, which hung around her neck. She knelt over to reach the bottom shelf and pulled out a jar and lifted it up.

"Here you go, Davey. I am all out of mayonnaise, but I do have Miracle Whip, which is just as good and it doesn't cost as much. I use this in my salads all the time. Your mom will really like it."

"Well, I don't know Miss Beatrice … she said to get mayonnaise, and you know how my mom is."

"Well Davey, I'm sorry but I don't have any mayonnaise. You'll have to go to Schnucks, if you want real mayonnaise," she said returning the jar to the shelf. "They may have it in stock… or they may not."

It was another half hour or more to walk there and back. My mom was probably going to need it sooner than that so I asked, "Are you sure it's the same thing?"

"You bet, Davey. And I'm sure your mom will appreciate you saving her some money."

"Are you sure?"

"Of course I'm sure. I wouldn't steer you wrong now, would I Davey? Just take this to your mom, and she'll be real happy with you."

"Okay," I said and walked to the checkout counter.

It was just my luck; there were three people in front of me waiting to checkout. I wasn't in a rush but I wanted to get home for my mom. When I looked at the line closer, the woman at the front of the line was a Negro lady. I had never seen a Negro in Weis Market before. She was dressed real nice. She wore a hat with some little multicolored flowers around the hatband, just like the one my mom wore to church on Sundays. I could see that her socks were rolled down around her ankles; I guess it was to keep cool. She had a small purse hanging from her arm with white pearls stitched onto the side.

When I looked closer I saw it was Miss Cora, the lady who worked next door for my neighbors. I smiled at her and waved, but she didn't see me. She looked different without her red sweat-stained bandana wrapped around her head. And I had never seen her feet before. She wore nice shoes, but her feet looked like they were stuffed into them. I was afraid they were so tight on her feet it looked like if she went to take them off, she would never get them back on again.

The line finally moved. I daydreamed and thought of The Lone Ranger and all of the good he does. But he never waits around for a thank you and I always wondered why?

"I'm sorry but we don't serve your kind here. No colored in here, ma'am," said Mrs. Weis for all those in line to hear. "You'll have to leave."

"That's not right. I gots my money right here. I gots to get something for my babies. You sees the store near my house is all out. I needs dis powered milk…please."

"I am sorry ma'am, but I told you, we don't serve no colored folk here. Come on now, you're holding up the line. You'll have to leave."

Miss Cora set the three cans of dry milk down on the shelf right in front of me and shuffled out of the store. When she turned around and saw me, her dignity was gone. A sense of shame and embarrassment came over my whole body.

Cora left under the watchful eye of Mrs. Stella Weis, the owner's longtime wife. Then Mrs. Weis turned to me with the sweetest smile. "Hi ya, Davey. How are you doing today?" she asked me. "Are you having a good summer? Doesn't school start for you next week?" She motioned for me to push the cart closer so she could unload the items from my cart.

"Yeah, I guess."

I should grab the three cans of milk and buy it for Cora and her babies and then find her and give her the milk, I thought to myself. She would look down at me and say thanks, but I wouldn't hear her, because like the Ranger, I wouldn't stay around to listen to people giving me their thanks. But I didn't do any of that. I just stood there, frozen in my thoughts, afraid of the looks people would give me. I was afraid of what they might say. I was not able to move as I came face to face with reality. Years of watching the Ranger help all those people in need didn't help me. I was ashamed of myself.

"Davey, move your cart so I can unload all your groceries for you and ring you up. You have milk, eggs, ice cream, and lots of other frozen stuff in there. Don't want them to go bad now do we? "She continued with a smile, "Davey, we just got our fresh shipment of Wonder Bread in today and I know how you mom loves fresh bread," she told me as she handed me a loaf to put into my cart.

I put my Miracle Whip jar onto the stained rubber conveyer belt and watched it move towards the end of the line. I was unable to make eye contact with Mrs. Weis.

Why did it bother me so? I don't remember ever seeing a Negro in this store before or even in the neighborhood for that matter. She should have known she was different, I thought to myself, and she should not have even come into the store. Yeah, why should I feel guilty? This isn't her place to come here. This is my neighborhood not hers. But this was Cora. This tall, proud colored woman who listens to me babble on about my problems, about my brother Josh, and about my writing. She always gave me good advice. And now she can't even buy canned milk from a grocery store for her baby. What would the Lone Ranger do?

"I changed my mind, Mrs. Weis," I blurted out. I couldn't believe I said it. "I'll just have these three cans of dry milk, thank you."

"What? Ahhh…your mother doesn't even use dry milk, Davey. And what about all these groceries you have here? These are eggs! Milk and ice cream. Bread and Miracle Whip." She looked upset, glancing at all the items on the conveyor. It was a big sale. Her eyes squinted, "Well…" she stammered, "Okay then… but you have to put these things back on the shelf, Davey." She spit out my name.

I made up my mind that I was not going to shop in their store anymore. It wasn't fair. I'd have to figure something to tell my mom. Hope she wouldn't be mad at me.

"The name is David, and my mom put mayonnaise on her list for me to buy. You don't have any so I'm going to get everything on her list from Schnucks. I also understand they let colored people shop there," I said sticking out my chest and dropping a dollar on the counter for Miss Cora's dry milk.

She was shocked but could not find the words to say anything as I grabbed my change and the bag containing the cans of milk and rushed out the door. I saw Cora standing at the bus stop, waiting for the bus as it pulled up to the stop.

I started towards her and a hand grabbed my t-shirt from behind. I turned around, it was Barry the bully.

"Where you going so fast smart ass? I told you I'd get you someday and today's the day."

I stood tall, watching the bus open the doors at the bus stop. The line began to move to board the bus. Cora was at the end of the line and Barry was standing in my way. I looked up at the big lout and when I looked at him closer, he wasn't that big after all. *Stand tall Marine*, I heard Josh whisper to me.

"Get your damn hands off me, you big bully," I told him. "If you don't I'll break every bone in that big fat hand of yours and feed them down your throat. You hear me?"

Whew! I couldn't believe I just said that.

He quickly let go of my t-shirt but still had a shocked look on his face as I raced across the street to catch up with Miss Cora. I ran across the street and caught up with her just as she was getting on the bus in front of the new bank.

"Miss Cora, Miss Cora wait." I hollered.

She turned in surprise to look at me, I was standing so tall.

"What's wrong chil'? Are you okay? Is everything all right with your momma?"

"Yes ma'am, she's fine. I got this milk for you…, for your baby."

She stood there looking at me not knowing what to say. She reached down and hugged me. "You a good boy, young Davey Malloy. Bless you, don't you ever change. You hear me?"

"Yes, ma'am."

"There should be a law against them not being able to sell to folks. And the poo…lice should enforce the law. You'd be a good policeman, young Davey. I'll see ya tomorrow. Thank you."

"Bye, Miss Cora." I waved to her as she got on the bus and watched it pulled away. From that moment on I no longer wanted to be a pirate, a cowboy, or anything else. I wanted to be a police officer. I wanted so bad to be a cop. Yes, that's what I wanted to be.

I walked home, and for some reason I felt good, real good as if I had done a fine thing or something else to make life better for someone else. The sidewalks didn't even feel hot on the bottom of my sneakers. Mom would be angry that I didn't get her groceries and spent the money for the milk. Now I would have to walk to Schnucks for the groceries. But I didn't mind, I didn't mind at all.

The mailman was walking up our steps as I reached our house and he waved at me. "Hey Davey it's your lucky day. I have some mail with your name on it." He handed me the mail, and I took it inside before beginning my trek to Schnucks. I took another dollar from the grocery jar. I would have to tell my mom about it sooner or later. I walked on my tiptoes so as not to wake my mom.

"Davey is that you?" my mother called out from the bedroom.

"Yes ma'am. Weis was out of mayonnaise so I'm going to go to Schnucks. I'll be right back."

"Davey, come in here, please," she said just above a whisper.

When I walked into her room, the lights were out and her shoes were on the floor. The room was cool. I saw my mom lying on the bed and saw belly rise and fall, it looked like a basketball on top of her stomach. It was dark inside the room, but I could see her trying to reach for her feet to rub them. I gently massaged them for her, just the way she liked.

"Davey… that snippy Mrs. Weis called, and she was very upset. Something about Miss Cora making a scene and you not buying anything there… or something like that."

"But mom they were out of mayonnaise, and they wanted to sell me …"

She gave me that gentle smile of hers and ran her hand through my hair. "It's okay, Davey. I know what you did and… you did good. That's all I wanted to tell you. I'm so proud of you, and I told her we won't be shopping at Weis Market anymore, ever. You're growing up so fast, but I'm so proud of you, you're just like your brother Josh. He would have done the exact same thing that you just did. Come here and give me a hug."

"You're not mad at me?"

"No Davey… not at all. I'm so proud of you. I love you."

"I love you too, Mom," I said as I hugged her. She gently put my head onto her swollen belly. "We'll be having a new addition to the Malloy family soon. Can I count on you to help out around here when I'm gone?"

"Yes, ma'am." I could have sworn I heard a small heartbeat inside my mom's stomach.

"Okay then. Now go get the groceries. And I'll make up a fresh batch of lemonade when you get home, just for you and me. Is that the mail you're holding?"

"Yes ma'am, the mailman just delivered it."

"Well, let's take a look. Slide up next to me, and we'll see what we have."

She reached for a magazine addressed to her titled, *Southern Ladies*. The cover read- *Summertime—Still time for Mint Juleps!* She laughed at a private joke.

She turned over an envelope and read it, "It's for you Davey, from *Boys Life Magazine*."

I took the letter and said, "They probably want me to subscribe again to their magazine. I'm just not sure if I'll have time what with starting high school and all. But I do love to read all of their… wow!" I began to read the letter inside. "Oh my God! Mom! Look at this! It's a check for $150."

"What? What do they say?"

Dear Mr. David Malloy:

Congratulations! We are pleased to announce that you are our grand prizewinner in our family essay contest. Your story was chosen out of over six thousand entries that were submitted. In addition to the cash prize, we are pleased to invite you to an all-expense paid week of creative writing at our San Francisco headquarters next summer. We will also pay the expenses for one adult chaperone to accompany you during your time here. More details about this writing adventure will be mailed to you shortly. Once again congratulations on your wonderful achievement.

Sincerely,
Robert Griswold
Senior Editor
Boys Life Magazine

"Davey, that's fantastic. You never told me that you entered a writing contest?"

"I didn't mom. It must have been Mrs. Corcoran. Isn't it swell?"

"Davey it's more than swell, it's fantastic. When I get up from here, I'm going to bake you the best peach... I mean apple pie that you've ever tasted." She kissed me on the head and hugged me.

"Thanks, Mom. With my newfound money, I'm going to buy you two chocolate Chunky candy bars and a large sixteen-ounce soda."

"Thank you Davey, but that money is going right into your college fund."

"What college fund?"

"The one your father and I are going to open for you tomorrow at the bank up the street. But tell you what, use the change from the groceries to buy us each a Chunky and two sodas and you and I will celebrate when you get home. Okay? Hurry now, your father will be home soon," she told me, clutching her belly.

I walked past Mr. Jost house and saw him wiping down the brand new shining, gleaming Airstream motor home parked out in front of his home.

Wow, was it cool-looking. Mom said they were going to travel across the country and live in it. My dad says they were crazy. Mr. Jost waved from inside the shiny silver oversized closet wearing his now trademark red flannel plaid shirt. His Colorado shirt, he told my dad. Three months living on the road, gee, I didn't know about that.

Mrs. Jost waved to me from her car window. I walked to her car, a brand-new Edsel. She smiled, "Well, we're finally leaving. You take care now, Davey."

"Take care of what, Mrs. Jost?"

"Davey, it's just a manner of speaking. We'll see you around Christmas."

"Have a good time, Mrs. Jost. And don't worry I'll keep an eye on your house for you."

"Which one, Davey?" she said with a gleam in her eye.

"What do you mean?"

"Which eye," she said with a slight smile parting her lips.

"It's just a manner of..." I had to laugh. She got me, and I suddenly realized she had a sense of humor after all.

She kissed me on the forehead and waved goodbye. I was going to miss them, both of them.

On the way to the store, I stopped by the library to tell Mrs. Corcoran the good news about winning the contest and to thank her for all her help. I was so happy, $150! She was wonderful. I was so excited. I couldn't wait to tell her and see the look on her face when I told her that I had won. I know she had to have sent in my story to *Boys Life*. It had to be her. I had learned a lot from her this summer and I knew she would be proud of me.

There was a new woman sitting at Meg's desk when I came inside the library. Must be her day off I thought. "Is Mrs. Corcoran here?"

The nice lady with a sweet smile looked up from her filing and studied me. "No son, I'm sorry, Mrs. Corcoran doesn't work here anymore. She left a couple of weeks ago. I'm her replacement and my name is Mrs. Gibson. Perhaps I can help you find what you need."

I wanted Mrs. Corcoran and wasn't about to be swatted away like a fly. *Where was she? I really needed to talk to her, to thank her for everything she did for me. School was going to be starting and now I may never see her again. I had to tell her about winning the contest.*

"Excuse me, but did she leave a forwarding address? I need to send her a letter. Or a phone number where I can call her? You see, she entered me in this writing contest and I won, and I wanted to tell her all about it."

"Well, that's wonderful! But I'm afraid I have no idea how to reach her. She was gone before I came here. What was the story about?"

I smiled and said proudly, "It is a story about my mom. Meg, I mean Mrs. Corcoran helped me pick out books to read and encouraged me to write."

"Well, I think I have just the book for you. Have your read *Sea Hawk*?

"Yes ma'am, I have," I said proudly.

"What about Sherlock Holmes?"

"I read that to," I told her proudly.

"Follow me," she said. "How about, Tom Sawyer?"

"Yes."

"And Huckleberry Finn."

"No."

She spun around with a smile as she searched the shelf and pulled it out for me to see. "You'll enjoy this one. How about *Treasure Island*? Have your read that one?"

"No, I haven't read that one either."

"Here," she said. "It's an adventure story about pirates and a young man who joins them."

"Wow, I love books like that. I love to read and to write. Mrs. Corcoran used to read all of my stories." I looked at the books she gave me. I could not believe it, more new stories, and adventures to read about.

"I would be happy to read anything you write and talk to you about it. In the meantime, I'll just need your library card young man. Mr….?

"David, David Malloy."

"Do you go by David or Dave or Davey or…?"

I thought for a minute before saying, "David will be fine thank you." Yes, that sounds better, David.

"I think we are going to be very good friends… David." She smiled and then I looked at the clock on the wall.

Now I had someone else to read my stories. I smiled at my new friend. But still no Meg. I missed her.

"I better be going. I have to get groceries for my mom."

I nearly ran to Schnucks happy as could be, feeling ten feet of the ground, but it still took me twenty minutes to get there. *I won the contest. What contest? The one that pays one hundred and fifty dollars—that contest. I can't believe there is that much money in the whole wide world. Wow.*

I got everything from my mother's list and then stopped and bought us both a large chocolate nut Chunky candy bar, mom's favorite and two large sodas. I never had a large soda all to myself before. Usually if I got a soda, took a sip, and put it back inside the icebox. Then it was fair game for anybody to come by and just take a "sip." But now it was going to be all mine.

When I got back from the store, the house was empty, and my mom was gone. I panicked until I found a note my dad left for me and the rest of the kids:

Jack & Davey –
Mom went into early labor.
Gone to the hospital. Make sandwiches for dinner.
Watch out for your sisters.
Girls – help out.
Will call later.
Love, Dad

Later that night my father called and told my older brother Jack that we had a new addition to the Malloy family, Jeremy Joshua Malloy.

My mom and dad had always said they were going to name the next baby, Jess or Jessie after my fraternal grandmother. But Jeremy Joshua Malloy, now that was a good old-fashioned Irish name if I ever heard one. I smiled; it was like having Josh back in the family. *Thanks, Mom.*

Chapter Twenty-Seven

Joanie and baby Janet went to stay with Aunt Ginny in her fancy home while my mom was in the hospital on her "vacation." Jack and Janey were working while dad spent most of his time off at the hospital. For once, I was home alone. Dad said I was old enough to take care of myself; at least that's what my mom told him to say. I didn't tell anybody, but I was lonely there by myself; the house was so quiet during the day and the television wasn't working again. School was scheduled to start on Monday. I couldn't believe it, but I was actually looking forward to going back to school. The phone rang. It was Sunny.

"Hey David, I leave for school next week in Chicago, and I just wanted to see you to say goodbye. Can you come down and visit?"

"Yeah sure. Besides, my mom has been bugging me to bring your plates and bowls back to you. I can't thank you enough for making all of that food for me when I had poison ivy. It was really good, especially the desserts. And I really love all of the different teas you brought."

She giggled, "I'm glad you liked it. See you later tonight?"

"Sure."

My mom called from the hospital to talk and tell me about my new little brother. She said he looked just like Josh looked when he was born and he also had a heart-shaped strawberry birthmark on his neck just like me and Josh. Then she told me that he said his first word...and she told me it sounded like he said–David. I laughed.

"I love you, Davey," mom whispered. "See ya soon."

"I love you too, Mom. Good night."

I believed everything she said except about him saying my name, David. He probably said Davey instead, but it did make me smile. Mom said I could come to the hospital tomorrow with dad and see for myself. I missed my mom and thought about her as I walked to Sunny's house.

When I reached Sunny's home, it appeared dark as if no one was home. Only one light was on in the front window. I knocked on her front door and she opened it with a smile. I had missed her.

"Am I early?" I asked seeing her wearing her kimono.

"No. My family called and I was on the phone with my grandmother." She kissed me hello on the cheek. When she leaned forward, her kimono parted ever so slightly and I could see her skin underneath. She was not wearing a bra and her hair was still wet from the shower. I saw her breasts, the ones I had only imagined. She was more beautiful than ever before. I took a deep breath.

"I thought you were coming later so I just took a shower."

"I can come back later if you want," I told her.

"No, that's okay as long as you don't mind wet hair." She laughed shaking her head getting me wet, laughing her wonderful laugh. "Want some tea?" she asked, wrapping her kimono tighter around her.

"Yes, please."

I heard some of her favorite Korean music playing in the background. But I did not hear her grandmother coughing or her two brothers playing or laughing like I usually did when I came to visit. However, I did smell the sweetness of jasmine incense in the air.

"It's so quiet," I whispered. "Is everybody sleeping?"

"No, they went to Chicago to visit my older sister," I heard her say from the kitchen. "I wasn't feeling well so I stayed home. They'll be back tomorrow," she said with a smile as she came back into the small room off the living room.

"Make yourself comfortable. Let's sit here, on the pillows." She set the tray down on a low wooden table and lit more incense sticks. I loved the smell of them. It smelled of burnt flowers, good but bad at the same time.

We ate and laughed about the summer and both of us became sad when we talked about school.

"I'm going to miss you David, a lot," she said, her voice quivering. "Stay here, I'm going to get some dessert and more tea."

She came back with a tray filled with jars and plates of things. On the tray, she had a teapot, two cups, some sugar, cream, a couple of spoons, a plate of my favorite homemade powdered sugar Korean cookies and a square blue jar with a small glass container of yellowish-green liquid off to the side. A small blue box with blue ribbon was also on the tray. I stood to help her.

"Sit please," she said with a smile. She stopped and looked at me, "I'm going to miss you when I go back to school, you know that don't you?" I watched her as she poured some tea, it was very hot. I loved her tea.

"Of course you will, Sunny. We're best friends. We're the three musketeers, remember?"

She threw her head back and laughed but soon became serious. "Well, that was the other thing I wanted to tell you about. Timmy has been calling me every day wanting to come here and see me before I leave for school. He's acting very strange, even stranger than usual."

"Yes, I know," I said sipping the tea she poured. It was delicious.

"Well he showed up here today, grabbing me and tried to force himself on me... if you know what I mean?" her voiced choked slightly as she spoke.

My skin began to tighten around my neck.

"I pushed him away and I said I never wanted to see him again. Friends don't do that to friends. He got angry and hit me when I said it," she turned her head and pulled back her hair to reveal a large bruise beneath her ear.

I was so angry. My blood was boiling, my eyes saw Irish red. *What the hell was he thinking, trying to hurt Sunny like that? Goddamn him.* I went to leave. "Who the hell does he think he is? I'm going to..."

She stopped me, "Wait—please," she said calmly. "I have more to tell you. He showed me his gun and said he was going to kill us both."

"What?" I yelled in anger. "He's gone too far."

"I think he was drunk or on pills or something. I don't know, but I want you to promise me something."

"What?"

"That you'll stay away from him, at least for the next few days. Promise?"

"Okay."

"Say promise." Her face was firm.

"I promise."

The look on her face eased and then she said with a smile, "I leave for school on Wednesday and may not see you for a long while but in the meantime... I have something for you." She picked up the small blue box and handed it to me. "Here this is for you. Something to remember me by."

I looked at it in awe. A present? For me? I unwrapped it quickly and found a small gold coin with a square hole cut out in the center. A strand of black leather went through the hole, making it a necklace.

"It's … amazing!" I said. "But Sunny, I don't have a gift for you."

"That's okay David. Consider it a belated birthday gift. Here have some more tea."

She looked at me strange, very close. She was quiet, then leaned closer to me as she whispered, "Do you still want to marry me, David?" she asked putting her hand on my leg. Her kimono opened slightly and I could see all of her female charms inside her robe. I was becoming excited.

"I've always wanted to marry you, Sunny. From the first time I met you… remember?"

"How can I forget? My grandmother loves to tell that story of you opening your eyes, trying to kiss me, and then proposing." She paused for a moment; her silk robe came open from the waist up. "Do you want to kiss me?"

"More than anything else in the world." I was excited beyond control. She kissed me softly on the lips, her mouth melding to mine, her lips caressing mine, her body so close, so warm, so inviting, so wanting. I could smell the sweetness of her jasmine perfume all over her body. I kissed her neck, her ear. I wanted all of her.

"Wait, we need to do this the right way," she said. "First drink some tea with the magical Korean elixir I have made for you." She poured the green and yellowish liquid into my teacup. "Drink, slowly, my love. Then, we say our marriage vows, we hold each other close and never let go."

I drank the sweet liquid as she asked and set down the teacup on the tray. She smiled then pulled two sheets of pink paper from her kimono pocket and handed one to me. Mine was in English and hers was in Korean and English.

"Read after me." She began to read the verse in Korean then nodded for me to read.

"First we were two streams," I recited, "flowing side by side. Now we become one river, only stronger, never to be divided again."

She smiled and read some more before motioning to me.

"Now it is impossible to see the stream as two, for we shall always be one and never be separate again because we will remain one river. We will always be together and will never again be divided."

I looked at the pink sheet. The words on the paper began to flow, to move about like children playing. All I could see now was Sunny kneeling before me. The lights dimmed then brightened. I saw a white tiger cross behind her but I wasn't afraid. He kept running. Then a goat smiled at me who had one blue and one green eye. Then a two-headed sheep ran by. Next, a cat of many colors stopped and smiled at me. Beautiful blue herons flew behind her in the sky, flying higher and higher. I rubbed my eyes as I said the final words after Sunny.

"I trust the one I love, I love the one I trust, now and forever," were the last words.

She gently took the sheet from my hand, and leaned forward to put the necklace around my neck. Her breasts were inches away. I kissed them and felt her shiver. She ran her hand through my hair and my body came alive at her touch. Her tall white wings stretched out full behind her. I always thought she was an angel.

She lifted her head and leaned back still kneeling over me as she removed her robe. Oh my god, was her body beautiful. So well formed, so soft to the touch, so wonderful. Her breasts were like that of an angel. She was naked and suddenly, so was I. A dragonfly appeared on her left breast until it fluttered, making a small kissing sound and flew away. A hawk flew by to chase it but it was not fast enough to catch her.

She moved her leg over my stomach and sat there above me, looking at me. Her smile came closer and closer. Then I heard the music as if it were the psalms from heaven. I felt her hand and then something else, warm, tender. She began to move. I had feelings, deep feelings, strange feelings as she moaned aloud. I lay there looking up at her and suddenly was on the deck of a flying ship, hurtling through space, rocking back and forth, higher and higher until I thought the ship would fly but instead it exploded in a sense of wonderment. Oh my God! Help me, save me, no—leave me to my world. I was in a deep red and blue world filled with lights and stars and moons. The galaxies unfolded before me. I was in...

"Davey?" I heard her whisper, my eyes were still closed. "Davey?" she asked gently. "Are you okay?"

I opened my eyes, I was still lying there on the pillow, fully clothed, and so was Sunny.

She whispered, "I should not have given you so much *Akada*, your first time and all. I'm sorry. Do you forgive me?"

I touched my head and arm, everything was still there. *It must have been a dream. Such a fine and amazing dream.* "I'm fine but I had such a wonderful dream. About you, me and us. We got married. And then we..."

She smiled then laughed. "I know. Come on now get up. You fell asleep. Time for you to go home." She kissed me on the cheek and walked me to the door. She put her arms around me and kissed me, a long familiar kiss until she said sadly, "Bye, David. I love you. I've always loved you." Then she closed the door behind her and I thought I heard her cry. I stopped and ...

Carol was jolted by the sound of his voice. "Carol? Carol come on we have to get to Reeds Bookstore," said Mitch trying to hurry her along, grabbing her briefcase and helping her with her things.

"We'll grab a taxi," he said once outside hailing a cab from the curb.

Chapter Twenty-Eight

2:38 P.M.

"Nate," she hollered. "Nate!" Agnes ran down the lawn and saw he was still asleep on the bench under the weeping willow tree. "Fine watchdog you turned out to be," she scolded the now bleary-eyed golden retriever. Her husband was still asleep. "Nate, wake up."

He opened his eyes from a sound sleep. He rubbed his eyes, "You had to wake me before I could pull the damn fish onto the boat, didn't you? It was a big one." He saw the look on her face, "What the blazes is wrong, girl?"

"Linda just called from the office. She called the Supreme Court Appeals office, and for some reason they didn't get all of the paperwork that we sent them."

"What? How the hell did that happen? The one time I don't follow up and this happens. Damn. I didn't want to bug them and now look at..." He was on his feet, pulling his suspenders up over his shoulders as he walked. Hero followed behind them as they quickly made their way back to his office.

"Darlin', get me Lin on the phone while I look through what we sent them. Quickly." He looked at his watch. They had lost almost two hours. *Damn.*

"She's on the line," she hollered as soon as he sat down in his office chair.

"Lin, did you check through everything..."

"Yes sir, I checked," came her familiar voice as he listened to her on the speakerphone on his desk as he paged through the volumes of documents they had sent to the appeals office.

"They told me they were missing the two concurrent documents from the lower court of appeals that we did six years ago. It was the COA-1999, a two-page document. I checked, and I don't have it here. Do you have it handy or do you want me to continue to research it?"

He found it! "No, I have it here. I'll send it off right away."

"They want it faxed to them at the number I sent you. And they need it now."

"Got it." His heart was pounding and he felt his face turning red. *How the hell did this happen? He was sure they had sent it to them but they probably misplaced it.* After writing up the fax cover sheet, he put a note on the bottom: URGENT! PLEASE CALL ME WHEN YOU RECEIVE THIS. Then he faxed it.

Within minutes, the phone rang and a squeaky young voice was on the other end. "Mr. Hutchinson, you asked that we call you when we got your documents."

"Yes, thank you so much. I don't know how this happened. We sent everything to you and double-checked that this document was included in the appeals package. I don't understand it. Can you tell me how this..."

"Sir, this is Heather Johnson at the USSC Emergency Appeals Division. I have your paperwork and I will hand carry it to the justice who has been randomly assigned to your appeal. Sorry sir, but I must run to get it to him. Thank you for your quick response. If we need anything else from you we will be in touch." The phone line went dead.

He had to sit down; his heart was beating so fast, it felt like it was going to ...

2:45 P.M.

"John Henry, can you hear me?" Silence.

"John Henry?" he called again

"Whatd'chu want Walker? Can't you see I'm trying to sleep?"

"Just lookin' for somebody to talk to. They don't usually put anybody down here by me, that's all."

The big man swung his feet over the side of the bunk and he sat up. The bed made a loud noise under the shifting weight of the giant man. He sniffed then coughed, adjusting to his new surroundings. "Well, they don't take kindly to somebody killin' one of their own here, Mr. Walker. And you were responsible for killin' two of theirs."

"Call me, Tim, everybody does. We're not real formal here on D-Block."

"Well, no offense, Mr. Walker, but usually I don't make a habit of getting to know no dead man. And you sure look like a dead man to me. You got that air about you, you know what I mean? So if it's all the same to you, I'll keep it at Mr. Walker."

"Suit yourself, big man." He looked at him sitting perfectly still almost as if he were meditating. "So tell me John Henry, what's your story?"

He sniffed and coughed again, stood and turned to face the jail cell door and looked at Walker while stretching out his huge arms to his sides. "Well, you see there Mr. Walker, about twenty years ago I was minding my own business when the police come to my home in Moultrie, just south of Tifton, Georgia. Well sir, they said I killed a man during a holdup. It was a little liquor store owned by some foreigner from Pakistan. Well, they said I shot and killed the man. I was at home all night with my wife and family but they didn't care. They arrested me anyway. Some young feller name of Christian Brown swore on a Bible that I was the one who done it. They sent me to jail; I wound up on their death row. I waited and waited while my attorney filed appeal after appeal. No luck." He grabbed hold of the bars on the cell door and gripped them tight, so tight that Walker could see his black knuckles turning white.

"I was on death row for over twenty-two years Walker. Twenty-two years out of my life, away from my family, away from my children and my grandkids. Near broke my heart." His voice rose and one of the guards looked down at them from his desk in the hallway, then looked away.

"What happened?" I asked John Henry.

"Well, you see Mr. Walker, couple years ago this young feller confessed that he made it all up and that the cops made him testify or else he was goin' to jail for some other crime. They reopened my case and then set me free with an apology and some money in my pocket. But the damage was already done. My wife divorced me and got remarried. My kids won't talk to me; they didn't believe I was innocent. So to them I was guilty."

"So how did you wind up here?"

"Well, that Mr. Christian Brown fella was real sorry for what he done, so some church group arranged for him and me to meet. He wanted to apologize to me and to the world …on TV, so he said anyway."

Walker waited for him to continue.

The big man was silent.

"And?" Walker finally asked.

"So the church set up the meeting at the Holy Pentecostal Baptist Church outside of Tallahassee where he lived and went to church. It was a bright sunny Sunday morning when I drove down there by myself from Georgia, and there he was, the man who put me into a jail cell for over twenty years. Standin' there, all apologizin' and all. Sayin' how sorry he was. He came up and hugged me and asked for me to forgive him."

"And did you?"

"He stood there all small like, mumbling about how wrong he was and all, watching the television cameras filming it all. Smiling for the cameras. Well sir, I just picked him off the ground and snapped his neck clean through. Yes, I did. Well, it was all on film, so the next thing I know I'm right back on D-Block, but this time in the great state of Florida with the likes of folk like you. Yesiree Bob."

"Whew, lordy John Henry. What a story. Well, I got my lawyer who's goin' to make sure nothing happens to me. Just filed the latest appeal and… "

"Okay Walker, on your feet. Turn around, hands through the bars, behind your back." It was his final meal and four guards stood outside his cell. "Time for your last meal," bellowed Shiminek. "Steak, done rare and bloody, grits, French fries and mashed potatoes with parsnips everything just the way you like it. And your raspberry ice cream."

Walker turned and put his hands behind him as they put on the cuffs. They weren't taking any chances with somebody who had nothing to lose.

When they were done, the senior guard ordered, "Step to the back of the cell. Don't turn around. Then you can eat your meal."

He looked down at his clipboard. "I understand you chose lethal injection. Well then, we'll be back after you finish eating and get you all cleaned up for the show." He leaned over, closer to the jail cell door as he whispered to the cop killer, "First, we'll strap you onto the gurney and tighten everything down, nice and snug like. Then give you something nice and warm to help make you sleep, halfway, before giving you the hot shot." He straightened up, "You got thirty-five minutes to eat Walker, starting now. You just behave yourself in the meantime and it'll go real smooth for all of us. Got it Walker?"

"Got it," he said as they uncuffed his hands through the bars. He grabbed the flimsy foam plastic tray with the plastic utensils and ate in silence. This was as close as he had ever got to an execution. He smiled, *I got faith in that old fart of an attorney. He always comes through; it's his job.*

Chapter Twenty-Nine

2:55 P.M.

The meeting room was overflowing as Sari took her seat at the head of the table. Sitting next to her was her Chief Operating Officer, Kim McCormick.

Sari had had done a great job of moving the company forward and coming up with great ideas for expansion of the rapidly growing *Teanna Tea Company.* The business currently had ninety stores, in sixteen states and were expanding their distribution under private labels undertaking a major push into retail distribution. They were poised and ready for huge growth opportunities and Sari knew it would take a company with deep pockets and the desire to do it. That's why she sold the company to the coffee giant in Seattle. It was the right thing to do.

She stood and looked around the room. She hired everybody that was in the room, she had trained them, groomed them and let them grow. She had laid out the growth plan for the next five years. They were ready. Now was the time to launch only this time around she was not going to be at the helm. She looked at Kim and smiled.

"As I look around this room I see a lot of familiar faces. I see growth, I see enthusiasm and I see myself in all of you. I could not have done this without your help." She paused for moment, and took in a deep breath. The room broke into applause.

"I'm counting on you to fulfill the destiny of the Teanna Tea Company.

She held her stomach as she tilted to her side. It hurt. "I leave this company, to take care of ..." She looked at Kim and managed a weak smile. "You all will be in good hands and I want to hear your great success stories. I want growth and I want this company and you all to move it forward over the years ahead. Do your job, be good to everybody and... drink lots of tea. I now would like to turn this meeting over to Ms. Kim McCormick, the new CEO of Teanna Tea Company. Kim…"

When the meeting and handshaking and tears were done she returned to her office. It was Kim's turn now. Back at her office, her big leather chair felt huge that day for some reason. She sat down at her chair in her office and looked around. She was going to miss it but some things you just had to do. She looked at her phone. No messages. The hell with it—she typed: COME HOME SOON, I MISS YOU. – S

Time to go home. Maybe write some more. It was soothing. Maybe she would do just that, or open a bottle of wine and sit on her porch and watch the ocean waves roll in. *Yeah, why not.*

2:58 P.M.

Reeds Bookstore was a midtown tradition for all *Times* bestselling authors to go for a book reading and signing. Mitch Patterson was no exception. He liked this small independent bookstore more than any of the others. Most bookstores functioned to please readers and customers but Reed's was different, it was the one place a writer could go and feel at home. Authors weren't treated as a draw, meant to bring in customers, but rather they were looked upon as members of their long-lost family.

The inquiries from the staff began as soon as you walked into the store. "Welcome to Reeds. Are you hungry? Thirsty? Like a snack or a sweet? Is the chair comfortable? Is it too hot for you? Too cold? Anything we can get you?" Small things Mitch thought, but they meant a lot. This was a great place to end his book tour.

"Good afternoon, Mitch. Welcome," said the smiling bookstore manager, the very tall, English bestselling author Sir Malcolm Reed. "Welcome back to Reeds, Mr. Patterson. Everything is ready for you and of course, if there is anything we can get you or do for you, please do not hesitate to ask. Would you like water, tea, coffee, crumpets?

"Water is fine, thank you."

Reed snapped his fingers, and two cold bottles of water were placed on the shelf by the podium.

"After the reading, there will be a short break and then we will bring in books for you to sign," he said. "Whenever you're ready."

Mitch nodded his head.

"Shall we begin?"

"Of course," said Mitch as he made his way to the front of the now packed room. It was quiet as Mitch took his seat and began to read.

Carol again pulled the manuscript from her briefcase and turned to the page with the bent corner where she had left off.

~

The next day I went with my dad to the hospital to visit my mom and see my new baby brother. Mom was right; he looked just like the pictures of Josh as a baby. Same tiny nose, same dimple on his chin and same soft blond hair. I loved him from the moment I first saw him. Jeremy Joshua Malloy, it had a very nice ring to it. Josh would have liked him; no, he would have loved him.

"When are you coming home from your vacation, Mom?" I asked, already getting tired of pizza for dinner.

"Soon, real soon," she told me and beckoned me closer. "To be truthful with you, I'm getting tired of this place. I'll be home in a couple of days. Be a good boy and help around the house. Okay?"

"Yes, ma'am."

"I love you, David. And, when I get home we'll have that Chunky chocolate candy bar and a soda, just like I promised. Just you and me. Whattta ya say?"

My eyes lit up. "Great. But what about J.J.?"

"J.J.?"

"Jeremy, the new kid over there," I said motioning to the bassinette with my new brother sleeping soundly.

She chuckled at the reference. "Oh him. I'll put him to sleep. This is just for you and me. Okay?"

"Sure Mom. That'll be great," I said with a wide grin. I could tell she was excited but also anxious to get home. I missed her a lot.

As we left the hospital and walked to the car, my dad held my hand, something he had not done in years. Then he said, "When we get home, wash up, change clothes and then get the newspaper before they sell out. Then we'll go out to eat for a real dinner. Just you and me. What do you say?"

"Great!"

We walked hand in hand to the car as if we owned the world, just me and my dad.

As we drove towards home he said, "Your mother comes home from the hospital in a few days, and it will be a whirlwind, believe you me. You go change for dinner and then run up and get my paper. I'm going to get some gas for the car and buy your mother some flowers. Daisies, her favorite. Hurry up now," he said as he pulled the car in front of our house.

He always went to Phillips 66 gas station at the corner and had them fill it up the car with ethyl premium gasoline. He liked it there because they cleaned the windshield, filled the gas tank, checked the air in the tires, and checked the oil.

I knew he wouldn't be long so I ran inside the house, took a quick bath, changed clothes, and ran to the drugstore for the latest three-star edition of the *Saint Louis Post Dispatch*. I passed by Timmy's house and saw him go into our "castle." Walking home, I remembered my promise to Sunny to stay away from him. I promised her I would. I kept saying remember your promise. I kept walking, but I had to say something. It wasn't right, him hitting Sunny like that. Not right at all.

I turned around, ran back to his house, and pounded on the door to our makeshift clubhouse. Bang, bang, bang. The hell with the secret knock. No response. I opened the door and saw him sprawled out on the floor on the mattress with a brown paper bag crumpled to his face. Other bags were strewn about the small wooden clubhouse. The room reeked of airplane glue.

"Hey Davey," he said, moving the bag away from his face, slurring his words still lying on the floor. "What's up, dude?" He had glue dribbling down his face, hands, and large splotches stuck to his spiked hair.

I reached in my pocket and pulled out two small keys. One was to the padlock on the castle door and the other was to the lockbox that contained his hidden horde of girlie magazines.

"Here," I said tossing him the keys. "I won't need this anymore. I start school soon and will be very busy, and I won't be coming around anymore. So long, Timmy." I turned to walk away.

In a daze, he felt around the mattress for what I had thrown and soon it all began to sink in. "What the hell is this, Davey?" His eyes glared at me and he began to come out of his fog. "You been talking to Sunny? Is that it?" he shouted, staggering to his feet. "Yeah goddamn right you been talking to her. I should've known I couldn't trust you. You turned her against me, didn't you? You son of a bitch. Godamn you."

His face was just inches from mine.

His breath reeked of alcohol and cigarettes. "She was fine with me until I mentioned your name and then she got all goo-goo on me and… that's it. You! Sunny! You and Sunny, you did it behind my back, didn't you. Now she won't even talk to me, thanks to you. Goddamn you." He reached around the back of his jeans looking for his gun. He saw it lying on the mattress and turned to reach for it. I shoved him away and as he fell backwards onto the old stained mattress, I ran outside, shutting the door and locking the padlock. So long, Timmy," I said through the door.

I saw the door shaking violently as I walked away. "Come back here, Davey. You can't just walk away from me. You'll regret this, you son of a bitch. Come back here Davey Malloy. I'll get you for this if it's the last goddamn thing I do."

When I got home, my dad was waiting impatiently in the kitchen looking at his watch. "Come on, Davey, let's go. I have reservations at Sea Isle restaurant."

I never saw Timmy that angry before that day. I needed to talk to Sunny to warn her. Warn her about Timmy, that he'd turned into a madman. "In a minute dad, I have to call Sunny first. It'll just take a minute."

"Call her when you get home, son. We have to go or we'll miss our reservation."

I eyed the phone hanging in the hallway. "It'll only take a minute, Dad, please." I pleaded.

He saw from the look on my face that I was serious. "Okay, but hurry up," he said glancing at his watch.

I dialed the number, Harrison 7- 2418. It rang. Then rang again. No answer. Sunny wasn't home. I hung up the phone and redialed the number, still no answer.

"Come on, David. Let's go. You can call her when we get home."

"Okay," I reluctantly agreed.

We had a great dinner, me and my dad, as we ate and talked about the new addition to our family. It was over too quickly and was raining hard as we left the restaurant and soon became a deluge when we neared home and turned off Midland Avenue onto Sunny's street. The street was blocked off with only one lane open. Black and white police cars with their lights flashing blocked the street. Red flares in the road were everywhere. Cops in rain gear with high-powered flashlights directed traffic and kept away curious onlookers.

"Isn't that Sunny's house?" My dad asked as we inched closer to home. I could tell he was starting to feel guilty for not letting me call her again from the restaurant.

The car stopped and he rolled down the window when he saw Officer Reiner waving him on. "Hey Jerry," my dad asked the officer, "what's happened? My son Davey knows the girl who lives here."

He nodded at the ambulance and said leaning over, whispering so I couldn't hear. I tried to lean closer to hear what he was saying.

"They're taking her to the hospital. Bad shape but she'll make it, young girl. She got beat up pretty bad, pistol whipped by some young punk kid and then... he attacked her. God it was brutal. Crazy out of his mind even after we slapped the cuffs on him. Neighbors called us after they heard her screamin'."

I looked up and saw a patrol car drive by with Timmy in the back seat, his eyes straight ahead. *Damn him, damn him to hell.* I was filled with rage and hate. I could have killed him with my bare hands. *Scum.* They drove away towards back to the police station. I saw them bringing someone out of Sunny's house on a stretcher.

"Sunny!" I shouted, opened the car door and ran towards her. "Sunny!" I screamed. I didn't get far before two big cops grabbed me and held me back.

"Where the hell you think you're going, son?" The big one asked. It was pouring down rain, with thunder and lightning every few moments. It was hard to see because of the rain but then I saw them put her in the back of the ambulance.

I yelled at the cops as they held me tight, "I gotta see her, go to her. She's my best friend. She's my Sunny. Let me go! Please! You gotta let me see her. She needs me." I struggled with them to let me go to her. They only held my arm tighter.

"Nothin' you can do for her now son, and besides she'll be in good hands at the hospital."

An ambulance with its siren blasting and lights blinking left the driveway traveling fast to the hospital. I tried to see inside but the curtain was drawn. I finally broke free from their grip and ran after the red and white ambulance. "Sunny," I screamed. She was alone with no one. "Sunny, it's me Davey! Sunny," I screamed again. The ambulance didn't stop but kept driving in the rain and turned onto Midland with me running in hot pursuit behind it. I slipped in the rain and fell in the street scraping my arm. It began to bleed with the blood mixing with the rain as it trickled down my jeans.

"Sunny," I cried. When I sat up my head began to spin and my stomach began to convulse. Suddenly, I felt sick to my stomach thinking of what had happened to Sunny. I threw up all over my shoes, jeans, and shirt. Then I did it again and again until I had nothing left inside of me but hurt. "Sunny," I moaned. "Sunny." She was gone. I sat there in the pouring rain damning his name. Timmy I hate you.

I heard a voice beside me say, "David, come on son," I heard my father say. He helped me up and hugged me for what seemed forever. "Let's go home. We'll find out where they took her, and I'll see how she's doing for you, okay?"

I looked up at him and he managed a weak smile.

"Come on now," he said.

I walked and cried with him as I saw him begin to cry. At home, we talked in whispers as he cleaned up my bleeding arm and knees. He told me he would find Sunny if it was the last thing he did. He kept his promise and took me to County General Hospital in Saint Ann two days later. I think he felt guilty.

The hospital was a big building and new for a hospital. At the reception desk, I stopped and asked for her room. I stood taller to make myself look older.

The rotund nurse at the reception desk looked down over her eyeglasses and asked, "Yes young man, how can I help you?"

"I'm here to visit Sun-Lei Mai Ran. Can you tell what room she's in?"

"How old are you son?"

"Twelve."

"Are you a family member?"

"Yes." I lied and she knew it. She removed her glasses from her nose and said with a tired voice. "Son, I know you must mean well but…"

"Nurse, ma'am, please I must see her. I'm her best friend, just like family. Please I gotta make sure she's okay. Please?"

She looked me up and down then took in a deep breath before saying, "Listen son, I can't just let anyone upstairs to the intensive care unit on the sixth floor unless they are family, law enforcement, or part of the medical staff. I'm sorry, son."

Sixth floor. Intensive care. Got it.

"I understand nurse, thank you very much." I bought some flowers and a card from the gift store and made my way up the stairs. I was determined to see her. I opened the door on the sixth floor and saw the large initials ICU over another reception desk. I approached the woman sitting there with a certain look of nonchalance.

"Yesssss, can I help you young man?" she asked annoyed at having to turn away from her paperwork

"Yeah, got a flower delivery for one of your patients," I started, trying to sound like a flowered deliveryman. I then pretended I was looking at the name on card. "Yeah, this is for a patient, named Sun-Lei Mai Ran. What room is she in?"

"Okay, wait just a minute." She looked down at her sheet, "Ah yes, room #656. Down this hallway, third door on the left. Shhh, be quiet though, okay?"

"Yes ma'am. Thank you," I said and started walking towards her room. My eyes searched the doors and the outside wall. Then I saw room 654, 655, 656, bingo. The name on the door said S. Mai Ran. This was it. A nurse hurried away from her room. I stepped inside and saw a figure lying in the far bed near the window. Sunny! I looked outside and saw it was still raining. The other bed in the darkened room was vacant.

"Sunny," I whispered. No movement. "Sunny," I said again, slowly walking closer to her bed. There was a small light over her bed shining down on her. I could make out her bandaged face in the shadows and heard a slight moan coming from her bed. She had a tube in her arm and a machine keeping time beside her with a tiny light bouncing up and down on a small green screen. "Sunny? It's me, Davey."

Suddenly, a hand on my shoulder jerked me back. "Nice try, son," came a stern voice behind me. I turned and it was a security guard with the ICU nurse standing beside him. "Family only kid. And if I catch you here again, I'll call the cops. Got it?"

"I got it. I just wanted to leave her some flowers. We're friends, close friends."

"I appreciate that son but we can't have people running around the hospital mucking things up. I'm sorry but I'm afraid I'm going to ask you to leave. And quietly," he said.

I turned to look at Sunny and heard her moan again. "Bye Sunny." I handed the flowers to the nurse and said, "Can you see she gets these, please."

She started to shake her head, but I guess she saw how desperate I was and finally relented, taking the daisies from me. She smelled them and asked, "Who should I say they're from?"

"There's a card in there but she'll know they're from me. Tell her they're from Davey."

"Okay. I'll make sure she gets them."

"Thanks."

My dad took me to the hospital for the next three nights but a security guard sitting by her door blocked my way each time I tried to get to her room. I waited in the waiting room for hours, but it was no use. I could not get in. I thought I had seen one of her brothers go into the room but I wasn't sure. I tried to call her but there was no phone in her room. I missed her so much.

Two weeks later I saw a for sale sign on her front lawn, then a moving van moved out all their furniture. The mover told me the stuff was going into storage, and he didn't know where they were moving. I mailed letters to Sunny but they all came back to me. She was gone from my life forever.

Chapter Thirty

Summer of 1959 was over. It was a different time, a quieter and gentler time. America was at peace or rather it was a time between wars at least that's what the newspapers said. For me it was the end of summertime and while my life had changed over the summer, it remained the same. Now I was back at school, a new school with new friends, new teachers. But I still missed Sunny.

While waiting in the checkout line at Schnucks one Saturday, a lanky kid wearing goofy-looking glasses, with short black hair kept looking at me. As I grabbed both grocery bags and began my trek home, he stopped me, "Excuse me, but don't you live on Lackland, right near Charlack? In the Malloy house?"

"Yeah… I'm David Malloy. Do I know you?"

"No. We just moved in from Georgia. I'm Ralph McIntyre. We live down the street from you. We moved into the Murdoch house."

"You moved into Stinky's house? So you're our new neighbors?"

"Yeah. We just moved in, and I start school next week at Saint Ignatius."

"Hey, that's where I go to school."

"Great! My kid sister will go there next year. She's a year younger than me." He stopped and turned, "Wait here she comes now. Hey sis, come here and meet one of our new neighbors."

She was pretty, a petite blonde with tiny brown freckles around her nose and face and wore tight white shorts.

"Hi, I'm Mary Lee." she said and I saw something wonderful in her eyes and felt weak in my knees. Her smile could warm a winter frost.

"What's your name?" he asked.

"My name is David, David Malloy."

"Do you have a cute sister named Joanie?" her brother asked.

"Yeah, why do you ask?"

"She's really cute. I met her yesterday walking up to Clarks to get the paper for my dad. She said she also gets the paper for your dad every night. What a coincidence."

"Yeah, really. What a coincidence." I said with a smile.

The three of us stood talking for over an hour. He liked hiking, biking, baseball swimming, and exploring. He also thought that Stan Musial was the best baseball player ever. I looked at my watch and saw it was getting late. I knew right then and there we would be the best of friends, the very best.

"I hate to leave you, but I have to get these groceries home or my mom will kill me."

"It's okay. My dad is supposed to pick us up here and then he's taking us furniture shopping for our new rooms."

"Well hey, when you get situated at home come on over one day and we can talk about the neighborhood and about school and stuff." She shook my hand and it felt so warm, so soft, it reminded me of Sunny's soft hands. She brought back too many memories. Suddenly I missed Sunny so much.

One Saturday at home, weeks later, and the house was empty and quiet. My mom laid the baby down for her nap and whispered in my ear, "Follow me," she said and took me by the hand. We went into her room carrying a flashlight and she had set up a tent just large enough for the two of us. We sat together cross-legged on the floor in our tent and ate Chunky candy bars and drank sodas but not too loud so as to wake the baby. My mom had me read the *Boys Life* peach pie story to her three times. Wow. It was the best afternoon I ever had, just my Mom and me.

When I was finally finished reading the story, she moved a strand of blond hair from my face and said, "It's very good David. Very good. It's a pity Mrs. Corcoran isn't here to see you win it." She smiled at me and then suddenly pulled back, "Oh, I nearly forgot, I have something for you. It came in the mail for you today." She retrieved it from the pocket in her cotton apron and handed it to me.

It was a postcard with a picture of the Eiffel Tower on it addressed to me. It came from France—from Sunny. I turned it around to read her finely handwritten note.

David—

I can't tell you how much I miss you. You will always be in my heart, my mind, and my soul. I will cherish our friendship and hope I have caused you no pain but my heart breaks every time I think of you and the time we had together. Life is short, and perhaps our paths will cross again someday. Please don't ever forget me, for I will never forget you.

Sunny

"Nice postcard. From Sunny?"

"Yes."

"What did she have to say?"

"She said goodbye."

"Really? I always liked her. Maybe you should send her a…"

"She doesn't want to hear from me, Mom."

"How do you know?"

"There was no return address on the card."

My mom stroked the hair on my head and I heard her whisper what sounded like a prayer. "Please Lord; don't let him grow up any faster than he already is." I didn't want to be twelve forever, I just wanted the pain to go away. We sat in silence for a long time, just being together. That was all that mattered. My mom gave me a new blue leather-bound journal book for me to write stories inside.

That night I thought about the past summer. It was sad. Over the last few weeks, I had lost all of my best friends.

I lost a brother but gained a brother, a baby brother.

Timmy was going to reform school; my father said his brother Dutch was back in court and now going to stay in prison for a very long time. Apparently, the police found the missing gun Dutch had used in the robbery he committed—thanks to Timmy. Now even his own brother hated him. They found the gun on Timmy when he was arrested at Sunny's house.

Mrs. Corcoran had quit her job at the library, and nobody knew where she went. She was the one who guided me in my reading, encouraged me and shared with me her love of books and writing. She taught me how to express myself in my stories. She was the best librarian in the whole world. How could I ever thank her for everything she did for me?

All my friends were gone. Even Cora, my confidant, had found a new job. She was going back home to Mississippi to be with her family. She said she missed them. I looked fondly at the darkened basement window where she would stand for hours ironing, sweating but I remember she always had a smile on her face. She was so wise; somehow, she knew that Timmy was evil, something I didn't see until it was almost too late. And Mr. and Mrs. Jost's house was still dark at night when I walked home from the grocery store. I waved at their house when I went by it. I even missed them.

I never saw Sunny, Timmy, or Mrs. Corcoran ever again, but I never expected that I would. But now, I had a new kid brother, somebody who I could teach all about exploring, how to identify trees, the best places to hide in hide and go seek, go hiking, and fishing at Lake Saint Louis and he could be the one to climb up the peach trees and pick the peaches for mom's wonderful pies. I was going to teach him everything important, just like my brother Josh and my brother Jack had taught me. I was now the older brother.

Our new neighbors seemed real nice, and Mary Lee, well, she was beautiful, friendly, smart and… thinking about it, I guess my life was getting better. And it was only nine more months until next summer—nine whole months until summertime. I could hardly wait.

And Sunny? Sunny had moved away but taught me so many things about people and about myself. She was tender, kind, smart, giving, and loving. I missed her a lot. I missed her laugh, her touch, her wit and her sense of humor. I even missed some of the awful-tasting foods she would shove in my mouth to see how I liked it. Even though it tasted like boiled socks, I always smiled and told her how great it was but in fact, she was becoming a very good cook.

But I was saddened by the fact I would never be able to spend my life with her or for that matter even another summer day and lay in a field of flowers on a blanket, drinking a bottle of wine with some cheese and make love to her until dawn. I would never be able to touch her skin, caress her body, kiss her breasts, or hold her in my arms and have lots and lots of children. She was gone and I had no idea where she was. Some people you meet in life are hard to forget, hard not to love and impossible to let go of. I never liked goodbyes.

For many years afterwards, I would look to the stars and whisper her name. I hurt. But if I looked real close in the galaxy of stars I was sure I saw one twinkle and smile at me. It had to be Sunny. Late at night, we would talk and laugh with one another. Or rather, I talked and she listened, as always. She was my guiding star, she was my sun, she was my Sunny. I missed her terribly. So long my sweet. I love you.

–The End

Carol had to choke back a tear when she finished reading the book, she was miserable because it was over but now she wanted more of him to drink up and quench her thirst. She did not want to share the book—or him—with anyone. She cared too deeply.

She knew he would ask what changes she would want to make because it was her job as an agent to package it up to market it to publishers, but she didn't want to change anything, not even a comma or a word. She saw his soul in this book.

The publishers will kill this book with their changes. They will want to cut it back to fit into a genre or target an audience. Change characters, delete a line or kill somebody off. I can't let that happen.

Mitchell was her twisted genius, like Ayn Rand's *Howard Roark,* and she would fight for him every step of the way. She would accept no changes to this heartfelt story even though her job was to represent him and get the damn thing published. She leaned over and put her head in her hands and wanted to cry. *What am I going to do now?* She heard a sound behind her.

"Carol?" He asked in his tender tone, sober.

"Don't look up, Carol… your eyes will betray you. Not to him, never again to him. Whatever you do, don't look up. He'll know how much you care if you look him in the eyes. Goddamn him.

She coughed to clear her throat. "I'll be there in a minute. Go ahead without me Mitch." Then she saw his shoes standing on the ground before her, not moving.

"Carol, are you okay? Ready to go?" he asked. She saw his outstretched hand reaching to her.

"Yep," she said still afraid to look at him.

"Carol? Did you finish the story? Did you like it? Cal … look at me."

She looked up, into his eyes, then looked away but it was too late, he delved deep into her soul. Her eyes had betrayed her. *This hurts,* she cried to herself. She could feel the pain in her heart. She finally said, "It was wonderful, different…but wonderful. Sorry if I'm so emotional, but it's your best work. I didn't want to put it down, I couldn't stop reading it." She took in a deep breath and tried to break away from the hold he had on her. A tear rolled down her cheek.

Carol looked at him again, he knew. *Damn him and damn his eyes. Damn him to hell, sweet hell.* She knew then she could never have him, nobody could. He was a man with a lost soul.

"Ready?" he finally asked handing her his handkerchief. "Time to go face the lions."

"Yes," she said. "I'm ready."

They rode in the elevator to the ground floor without saying another word. He turned and saw him check his phone for messages. Then she heard him sigh and slowly slide it back into his pocket.

"Anything?"

"No. I sent her a message right after the reading to respond to hers. I even called but I couldn't connect with her. I'll try again later."

She watched him, that look in his eye, the sound of his voice, it told her everything she needed to know. She knew at that moment, hope as she may, that this was not ever going to work out. Not with him, not ever. Face it girl, he's in love with somebody else and there's nothing you can do to change it. She's a lucky girl.

He said aloud, "You know, depending on what time we finish, I may try to catch an early flight back home."

"Yeah," she said weakly.

It was time for his press conference back at their hotel. "Showtime," he whispered and clenched her hand in his.

Chapter Thirty-One

5:07 P.M.

Mitch took his seat in front of the microphones that were scattered about the table. The crowd of newspaper and television reporters was larger than usual.

Carol's introduction was simple and to the point, at Mitch's request. "Good afternoon ladies and gentlemen. I would like to introduce you, to those of you who don't know him, to Mr. Mitchell Patterson, author of the bestselling book, *The Search for Timothy Walker*. Mr. Patterson."

"Thank you Carol. I want to thank all of you for coming today. The search for Timothy Walker itself was a trying time for us and for the nation as the country's most wanted killer was on the loose for those months." He took a drink of water from a glass, drinking in more than usual before continuing.

"Those of you who have read the book can see some of the work that went into the most extensive manhunt in police history. This could not have been possible without the support of state, local and federal law enforcement authorities. I wish to thank them for their help as well as to the various courts for providing me with trial and appeals transcripts to help give this book more insight. I'll now open the floor to any questions you may have due to the limited time we have today and your six o'clock news deadlines." The last comment brought laughter from the local television crews.

A man with glasses and wearing a tight fitting jacket raised his hand, "Jim Gallows from WKNY. How is the book tour going Mitch?"

"Very good, thank you. This is only my third book, but the sales have been through the roof and the reception here in New York has been phenomenal. But I can say that I am glad it's over." More laughter.

A petite woman with glasses in the third row raised her hand as she stood. "Roberta Coltart, from the *National Book Review*. Mr. Patterson, I must ask you, are you in favor of the death penalty? It's sometimes hard to tell your opinion from reading your book."

Mitch managed a terse smile, "That was intentional, Ms. Coltart. It is up to everybody to make up their own mind about how they feel about the death penalty. My opinion is inconsequential. Next please." He pointed to a man in a fatigue jacket at the rear of the room.

"Pasquele Lawrence from *HotWire Online Magazine*—I'm a big fan and I must say I enjoyed this book better than your last one. I guess mainly because it was a true story. Will your future books be more nonfiction than fiction?"

Mitch laughed and said, "Well, I guess you'll have to just have to keep watching the bookstores now won't you. But I will say that I have finished another book that leans toward nonfiction."

The persistent reporter from the *National Book Review* again stood without raising her hand asking, "Is there any significance to the fact that Walker is scheduled to be executed on the anniversary of your family's murder in Florida? Is that the reason that your book tour was scheduled to end here on today's date? And to have it happen on the day you are promoting your book in the biggest book market in the country is purely coincidental? Correct?"

His eyes zeroed in on her, but he remained calm and responded, "You are correct, Ms. Coltart, the timing is purely coincidental. Actually, I tried, for personal reasons, to have the book tour wrap up yesterday, so that I could be home in Florida today. However, unfortunately that did not happen. Next question please." Mitch went to point to another woman in the third row.

Carol stood and quickly interjected, "One last question from the audience, please. It's been a long day." Scores of reporters waved their hands in the air to ask the final question but Ms. Coltart stood again and asked the final question "Mr. Patterson, do you believe the appeals process has gone on for too long for Mr. Walker, and do you believe that Timothy Walker should have been put to death years ago?"

Mitch turned square to face her. "Timothy Walker was tried multiple times by a jury of his peers for the murder of five individuals. He was found guilty and sentenced to death by that random group of jurors of his peers. Walker received thirty court and judicial reviews and retrials to make sure it was fair and just. In the meantime, after the sentence was handed down, he escaped from death row and while on the loose he was responsible for the premediated murder of two prison officers," he paused to compose himself before continuing.

"In addition, Walker then blew up a house in Delray Beach Florida... and killed two innocent people who were inside. One of those was my wife Sandy, and my son Derek. He then went on to kill two elderly farmers in a remote Kansas location." He stopped and leveled his gaze directly at her, leaned forward and said, "I will say that, if the execution had taken place when it was originally scheduled, all six of those innocent people would still be alive today. Is that clear enough, Ms. Coltart?"

"Yes, sir," she said quietly while making notes in her notepad and slowly returned to her seat.

Carol quickly stood and said, "Thank you ladies and gentlemen and feel free to pick up your signed complimentary copy of Mr. Patterson's latest book. Thank you for coming."

Mitch grabbed his briefcase and turned to Carol, "We done?"

"Yeah. Go get a shave and some rest. You've had a long day, and we have an important night ahead of us so... just get some rest."

"See you later. I'm goin' to get a shower." He kissed her on the cheek. "See ya."

She watched him walk away, hanging his head down. *I hope he stays sober.*

5:15 P.M.-

That wasn't so bad, Sari thought to herself. She knew now the company was in good hands, capable hands and if truth be told she was ready to move on.

She looked at the box of her cherished belongs, her writing and her pictures. Her books. She saw the picture of her and her daughter Anna together the year before she died. She gently touched the photo, and traced her finger around her dearest. So young to be taken so cruelly. She set the picture on her desk. She would never forget her.

She put the box on the floor and saw that Eva had tied a pink ribbon around her office nameplate, *Sari Novak –CEO Teanna Tea Company.* She saw the attached note—To the best boss ever. Thanks for everything—EVA. *Nice touch girl,* she thought. Yes, it was time for her to move on with her life.

She glanced at her computer and debated about adding a few more pages to her book. Instead, she toyed with the thought of opening the chilled bottle of chianti in the fridge but opted instead to head for the bath. She could not focus and glanced at her watch. Still hours to go. Maybe he'll come home early? Maybe. The sun would be setting soon, and the air would cool and he would be home. She knew he would, she knew him.

5:25 P.M.-

Nate Hutchinson hung up the phone on the cradle and breathed a deep sigh.

"Is it over?" Agnes asked.

"Yes, the Supreme Court declined to intervene. The execution will take place as ordered."

"There's nothing else anybody can do?"

He didn't answer her, his mind still reeling from the response. *This can't be the end. There must be something else I can do.*

"Nate?" She asked gently. No response again. "Nate, darling? Maybe it's time to give it up. You've done more than anybody can rightly expect you to do. Darling, nobody can help that man now. It's over."

He sat in silence, staring out into the back yard, the sun setting and the light growing dim.

She touched him gently on the shoulder. "Nate, it's over. The courts, the governor, and the people have all spoken and they have said…"

"What'd you just say?" he asked as his head snapped around to look at her.

"I said it's over, darling."

"No, after that—the governor. Right?"

"But Nate you have already been down that path and you made your appeals to the governor before… and he turned you down, remember?"

"Yes, but that was on a compassionate ruling for him to go visit his dying mother. That was denied." Panicked he looked around the room. "Where's my damn cell phone?" He stood searching the kitchen until he spied it on the counter, plugged in, recharging. He unplugged it, brought up his contact list, and punched in the governor's private cell phone number. It rang four times before someone answered it.

"Hello," said a female voice. "Governor Richards' office."

"Governor Richards please. This is Nathaniel Hutchinson, attorney for the condemned prisoner, Timothy Walker. It is imperative that I speak with the governor, now, please."

He heard the voice say on the other end of the line, "Hold on. sir. I will forward your call to the governor. Wait just a moment." He heard static on the line and then it went dead.

"Damn, I got cut off," he said with obvious mounting irritation. He went to dial the phone number but his phone rang, "Hello?"

"Yes, I was looking for Nathaniel Hutchinson."

"This is Nate Hutchinson."

"This is Governor Richards; you tried to call me? What can I do for you, counselor?"

"Thank you for calling me back, Governor. I just learned that our appeal to the Supreme Court was denied. I would like to ask, no beg you that the execution be delayed by at least a day for us to re-file with the court."

"Do you have new evidence or can you cite any case law that would have a bearing on this case, Mr. Hutchinson?"

"No, governor I do not. I am just asking that his case be reviewed one final time. I don't need to remind you, sir, that a man's life hangs in the balance."

"Your appeals have been duly heard, sir, by every court in this great state and by the appeals court and now rejected by the highest court in the land. And now you're asking me to intervene in delaying justice for those wronged by Mr. Walker? Under what circumstances?"

Nate took a deep breath. He knew he was reaching, but he would do anything to try to save the life of his client if even only just for a day. One day was a lifetime to some people. "Well sir, today is the anniversary of the killing death of Mitch Patterson's family that my client was tried and convicted for, and I am sure that you do not want this execution to be interpreted as tit-for-tat revenge execution, now do you, Governor?"

There was silence on the other end.

"Governor?"

"Sir, I appreciate your perseverance and persistence in extending the time for your client, but sir, I am not going to delay justice for the families of his victims for one more precious moment. I am sorry that is not what you want to hear, sir, but it is time for justice to be served. Good night." He hung up the phone.

He had lost. There was nothing else to be done.

"Nate?" Agnes asked her husband.

"He said 'no.' Agnes he won't delay the execution."

He picked up the phone and dialed the hotline to D-Block. When he heard Walker's voice he said, "Mr. Walker… Tim, I'm sorry but both the Supreme Court and the governor decline to give you a stay of execution. I'm so sorry." Walker hung up without saying another word.

Agnes joined her husband in the study.

He took in a deep breath and said, "Agnes darlin', pour me a glass of Jim Beam will you dear? Make it a double. Use the good stuff from the china cabinet in the dining room. I guess it's time to say goodbye and put it to rest."

"Sure, dear. Mind if I join you?" she knew then it was over and the relief was obvious in her voice.

"Of course, darlin'," he responded, managing a small grin finally relaxing and stretching out his tall frame, kicking off his shoes while crossing his legs together at his ankles. He undid his suspenders and relaxed. Now all he could is wait, just like everyone else.

Agnes knew their life was finally going to return to normal when he asked for a drink of the "good stuff" stored in the dining room cabinet. She smiled to herself. From the other room she heard the sound of the sofa whoosh as he stood and then heard voices from the television. Newscasts.

She was glad it was over at last as she brought the glasses from the dining room. When she turned the corner, she screamed at what she saw on the floor and dropped both whiskey glasses to the old tile floor and screamed again.

Chapter Thirty-Two

Mitch showered quickly and debated about raiding the mini bar to have a drink, or two. Instead, he lay back onto the bed, his hair still wet and wearing the thick white cotton towel around his waist. He brushed his hair back with his fingers and lit a cigarette. After three puffs the taste was too much too bear. He snuffed out the offender in his water glass and heard the sizzle of the hot cigarette drowning in the liquid. This is a good time to quit he thought. A time for new beginnings. He thought of Sunny. He looked at his watch; the time was 6:30. It was finally over.

He lay there replaying the day in his head when he heard a voice at the foot of his bed, a familiar voice, a sexy voice—it was Sunny.

"Hi ya, baby," she said moving to sit next to him on the bed as she moved a wayward curl from his forehead. "I've missed you," she said softly.

"Me too, baby. More than ever."

Sunny smiled the sweet smile he always remembered. "It's over. Let it go. Get on with your life. Our life. I won't be back to visit you."

"Don't leave me, baby. Don't go."

"I've got to, honey… but if you close your eyes and think of me… I'm always with you, right there next to you. You can always talk to me. I love you."

"Don't go, please."

She kissed him with the lightest of touch on his forehead. "It's better this way. I love you. Always have and always will, but it's time for you to get on with your life. Put this behind you. Promise me you will. Promise."

He nodded his head in agreement.

"Say it, Mitch. I want you to say it, so I know you mean it. I know you've never broken a promise you've made to me. I want to hear you say it."

He breathed deep, "I promise."

The jarring sound from the phone woke him from his sleep. He could still smell the sweetness of her jasmine perfume in the air. He closed his eyes, and said, "Goodbye, baby."

The insistent phone rang again. Then again.

He picked up the receiver from the bedside table and answered it. "Hello?"

It was Carol. "Ready?" she asked.

"Five minutes. Meet you at the restaurant upstairs."

The puzzlement in her voice was obvious to him. "All right. Five minutes…. are you okay?" she queried.

He knew what she was thinking. "Yeah, I'm good. Just resting. See you in five." He hung up the phone and smiled as he dressed.

Chapter Thirty-Three

7:05 P.M.

Mitch glanced at his watch as the elevator made its ascent to the top-floor restaurant called Skylights. Minutes later the door opened on the thirty-eighth floor, and Carol stood there waiting for him. She smiled.

"Hi ya," she whispered in a familiar tone. "You okay?"

"Couldn't be better." He smiled an unfamiliar smile and grabbed her by the arm and said, "Showtime."

The restaurant and the bar were not crowded at this early hour. Carol had reserved a table for them at a table by the window. It was getting dark and the lights from the skyscrapers and traffic below began to sparkle in the early evening light.

The two of them approached the man at the podium. "Good evening, Henri. Reservation for Litchard, party of three."

The maître'd looked up with a smile that broadened when he recognized Carol and Mitch, his longtime patrons. "Good evening, Ms. Litchard and Mr. Patterson. Welcome back to Skylights. A pleasure to have you with us again this evening. And congratulations on your latest book, sir." He said with a genuine smile. "Please follow me to your table."

As they walked behind him, his path wove among the tables. He said, "I reserved your favorite table for you, by the window overlooking the city. The rest of your party is not here yet. Will it be for three or four?"

"We are not sure at this time. Definitely three, possibly four." He moved aside and his hand waved them through to a small table set in the corner away from the other tables. It was quiet.

"Thank you, Henri," Carol said.

"You are very welcome, ma'am. May I suggest ... some chilled champagne to start the evening... to celebrate the new book? And the book tour finale'! Compliments of the house."

"Thank you."

Mitch sat down across from her, admiring the view. He seemed different somehow. She wanted to ask him but waited. They sat in silence watching the city lights below them come alive in the city the never sleeps. Streams of red taillights and bright headlights made their way down the streets punctuated by the faint sounds of sirens and visions of swirling lights of police cars below.

"Here you go," Henri said, setting down two tall champagne flutes in front of them. "Congratulations again to both of you. Your waiter will be Karl tonight. In the meantime, please let me know if there is anything I can get you while you wait for your guest."

"Thank you, Henri," she said. Then raising her glass to her star client she said, "Cheers! Congratulations on another great book tour. Done!" His look told her everything she needed to know—and feared. It said it all. These book tours were tiring and sapped both of them of energy. She was glad it was over.

There was an awkward moment of silence, unusual for the two of them. She took another drink of champagne, cleared her throat and said, "Mitch, I loved the book. I felt it spoke to me in ways I never would have thought. You married your wife and had a son but they're gone and now... I think you still love Sunny and always will. Tell me about Sunny. I just need to know if..."

His gaze returned to the street scene below with two ambulances roaring down the street rushing to some scene of life and death. He did not answer her.

"It's okay if you don't want to talk about it. I'll understand, especially after reading your manuscript," she said.

Silence.

"Here you go," said their waiter Karl setting down two new champagne glasses in front of them. "Would you like to continue to wait for your other party or would you want to order some appetizers?"

"We'll wait, thank you," said Mitch.

"Go ahead," Carol prodded him after taking a sip of champagne from her glass.

"Sandy encouraged me to write my stories, my cop books at night while I was with the Delray police department. An old friend of mine at the Delray PD offered me a job that had flexible hours and shifts. Cheers," he said and toasted with the champagne before continuing.

"She had some success in writing cookbooks and introduced me to her publisher. They liked my detective books that I had written and agreed to publish them. It reinvigorated my writing. I was happy in my marriage and with my new family but I swore I would never quit the police force. It was perfect until… that night."

"What night?"

"The night Timmy called me at home. He was in town and somehow or another had gotten my home phone number. Probably had seen one of my books in a bookstore. Well, he left a message on our answering machine and said he was going to be in town for a day and wanted to come by and see me. He heard my voice on the machine but I never connected with him." He took a big finishing drink from his champagne glass and asked for some ice water.

"There was no way I ever wanted to see him again… especially after everything he had done in the past. Next thing I know his drug and gun buy was broken up in Delray and he blamed me."

"You didn't know he was dealin' drugs? Or where he was going to be, did you?" She knew a lot of this information from other conversations with him but it seemed to help him say the words, to help him heal.

"Hell no. But that didn't matter to Tim. Once he had something in his mind that became his reality. Later, he left another message on our machine that he was going to get me if it was the last thing he ever did. He called it a betrayal." He took in a deep sigh and looked around for Dan Eliot. Then looked at his watch.

He continued to tell her, "Walker had killed five people then he was caught, tried, convicted and sentenced to death by lethal injection. While he was on death row, his attorneys kept appealing the sentence. He managed to escape on a trip to the local hospital and killed two deputies in the process. He left me a cryptic message on a postcard leaving it on my desk about killing my family in revenge. By the time I got home the gas line exploded killing Sandy and Derek. I was in the hospital for six days recovering." He touched the long scar on his arm. Something that he would never forget. "That's when I vowed I would track him down and bring him back to justice. I needed closure since he was still alive so…"

"You wrote a book about it. And then hired me to represent you," she said finishing his sentence.

"Yes. Exactly. So now you …"

A heavy voice interrupted their conversation. "Good evening, Carol. I'm so sorry if I kept you waiting." Dan Eliot. He was a tall man dressed in a dark, three-piece, pinstripe suit. Distinguished looking. He ran his hand through his thick gray hair.

Carol managed a weak grin but said nothing instead raising her hand to shake his.

Mitch stood and introduced himself. "Hi, I'm Mitch Patterson."

"Pleased to meet you Mitch." Dan looked at Mitch, the author. He had worked with hundreds of authors in the past but this one he felt was different, just by the way he carried himself. He had done his research on both of them. She was his new agent after his first one had died and she was a three-person shop based in New York. She had a reputation of being fiercely protective of her clients; he liked that in an agent and found her intriguing. She was a fighter and had a good eye for talent. She would be a great asset to a firm like Windham.

He pulled down his vest and he motioned to a nearby server.

"Can I get you something to drink, sir?"

"I'll have a glass of whatever they are having." Eliot said with a genuine smile covering his lips.

"I see you guys have already ordered."

"Yes, and now we were just relaxing, waiting for you."

"Sorry I'm late." he said picking up the menu, glancing at it quickly before setting it back down on the white tablecloth.

"My boss, our publisher, Ms. Kincaid, may join us later, just to say hello, mind you. She leaves all of the author and book contract decisions to her staff. I must admit, she seemed to be particularly interested in this manuscript."

Henri brought Dan his drink and left them alone.

"How was the book tour?" he asked, shifting in his seat, observing the interaction between Mitch and Carol since he sat down.

"Good, just a little too long."

"Hmm, I did see that your book moved up the *Times* sales charts and if you're lucky you may make it to the *Times* top ten. Would have been there by now if you had a stronger, more aggressive publisher to help you. You need to have somebody with marketing muscle like Windham working for you, somebody who's not afraid to spend some marketing bucks especially in the big metro markets."

Carol bristled. "We like our publisher, Fosters & Riggs. They're a good publishing house, and they've been good to us," said Carol in defense of their longtime publisher.

"I understand, however if that's so, then why are you talking to me and the good folks at Windham?"

"We showed it to F&R first," said Mitch now taking control of the conversation, "and they took a pass only because they have another writer who has a similar story and felt it would be a conflict of interest to try to promote two competing books in the same genre. They said they would publish it if we could wait the usual sixteen-month waiting period. Now if Windham is not interested in my book *Summertime*, there are other publishing houses we can talk to about publishing it or we can just wait for F&R to complete their timetable."

Eliot was now all business, and moved his drink aside. "Don't get me wrong, Mitch—it's okay if I call you Mitch isn't it?"

"Yeah, sure."

"Let me get right to the point and don't get me wrong—we love the book and we want to publish it. We think it has great potential." He was all business.

Carol breathed a sigh of relief and looked at Mitch who was sporting a slight grin. Mission accomplished he thought to himself.

Eliot continued, leaning closer to them, drawing them in. "Listen, we believe that the public is getting tired of alternative reality books, dystopian tales and that type of book. Ms. Kincaid read your manuscript and loved the book. She then turned it over to me to polish the rough edges, so to speak and make it more saleable." His lips pursed with a slight smirk of satisfaction.

Carol listened to him with a newfound respect. She smiled. She was starting to like this publisher.

"You see, our hard core readers, the ones who are there for us in thick and thin love literary fiction and we feel a book like this could become a mainstay, delivering new readers year after year. That's what we look for in a book. So to say we are not interested in your book *Summertime* is way off the mark." Now his sales voice was sincere and honest. Carol leaned closer.

"As a matter fact, Mitch," he continued, "we can have contracts prepared for your signature with the usual delivery, royalty and other standard items for your agent and attorneys to look over and for you to sign. We are prepared to offer you an additional five percent bonus royalty for any books sold during a book promotional tour."

Mitch held up his hand to stop him. "That's all well and good, but you really need to be talking with Carol, she handles all of my contract negotiations." Carol sat taller and smiled, in agreement.

Mitch took in a deep breath as he glanced at his watch. He still had not had a confirmation of the execution. Nothing on the news as he glanced at the TV over the nearby bar.

Eliot grinned and reached for his drink while saying, "With some minor editing it could become a classic and…"

"What do you mean, minor editing?" Carol asked.

"I am not sure the book's beginning has the strength that would make publishers clamor for it. And, the story is really a story of two boys coming of age during a trying time in our country's history. Prior to Vietnam just after the Korean War, you know all that stuff. Everything else is unnecessary. I also feel that the inclusion of the librarian, Mrs. Corcoran should be deleted and not even mentioned and…" The voices droned on as Mitch's thoughts drifted away. He glanced at his watch again.

"Excuse me sir, Mr. Patterson?" it was Henri.

"Yes?"

"I have a package for you sir. It was just delivered by courier to the front desk downstairs and they saw you had a reservation with us tonight." He handed him a package, not very heavy at all from the feel of it and returned to his podium.

Mitch's cell phone rang, and he bungled in his pockets to retrieve it.

"Hello?" The caller ID said the call came from Jacksonville, Florida. He turned to answer the call.

"Hello?" said a confused female voice. "I was looking for Mitchell Patterson."

"This is Mitch Patterson." The conversation at the table subsided.

He heard a deep sigh on the other end of the line. "This is Agnes Hutchinson, Nate's wife. We talked a couple times in the past when you interviewed my husband about Timothy Walker's transcripts. Nate wanted me to call you and tell you that – it's over. We just got a call from the prison and Walker was pronounced dead at 6:37 P.M. Nate wanted me to call you and tell you."

Over. The nightmare was finally over. Timothy Walker was dead. Mitch reached for his drink and saw the questioning look on the faces of his two companions.

Carol mouthed the words, "What wrong?"

He covered the headset, "I'll tell you later."

"Thank you so much for calling and telling me that Agnes. I appreciate it."

"Did you get the courier package Nate sent you?"

Mitch looked at the return address and saw it came from N. Hutchinson, Attorney at Law.

"Yes, I did. It was just delivered."

"It's from Walker. He wanted to make sure you got it."

He held the phone to his ear listening to her final words before saying, "Thank you Agnes."

"I have to go now Mitch. Nate made me promise that I would call you."

"Is Nate around anywhere? I'd like to talk with him for a moment."

She paused before responding, her voice trembling, "Nate had some minor chest pains earlier this afternoon and is under observation at the Cardiac Intensive Care Unit here at Jacksonville Memorial Hospital. Mitch, I gotta go, the doctors are coming. Goodbye."

"Good luck Agnes, thanks for callin'. Give Nate my best." He finished the call with a lump settling deep inside his stomach. The other two at the table sat and faced him in silence, not sure what to say.

"Mitch, is everything ..."

"It's over. Walker was pronounced dead at 6:37 pm. That was Agnes Hutchinson calling for Nate." He felt as if a huge weight had been taken from his shoulders. Looking up, he breathed in a deep sigh of relief.

Eliot looked at both of them and rose. "Tell you what, I'll let you two have some time while I go to the restroom. I won't be long."

He's not so bad after all, Mitch thought to himself.

His phone vibrated. He had a text message,

COME HOME SOON.
I MISS YOU.
LOVE YA.
-S

He smiled.

"You okay?" Carol asked Mitch as Eliot walked away from the table.

"Yeah, better now," he said with a smile pocketing his phone before turning over the express delivery package. He opened the end and retrieved an envelope from inside.

"What's that?" she asked

He opened the envelope and took out what appeared to be a handwritten letter.

"It's a letter... from Timmy."

He began to read aloud-

Hi ya Mitch-

I know you probably hate me, and I would too if I were in your shoes. But you know something, I always wanted to be like you, good, honest, and well liked. I wanted people to like me the way they liked you. I wanted people to look up to me, to respect me. I thought if I hung around with you, I would be more like you. I wanted them to call me when they had a problem, like they called you—but that never happened.

Everybody always loved you Mitch, even Sunny. I used to think things could have been different but now I know that you are you and I will always be Timmy Walker, the kid that everybody's' parent said to stay away from. The bad kid. But I admired you and everything about you, I always did.

Sorry about everything, but I couldn't help myself. I tried but I just couldn't do it. I didn't mean to do all of those things to you and to Sunny but somehow they just happened. But I knew I could always count on you, you were always there for me and I was never there for you.

I knew Sunny would want only you. I was jealous of you, but it's strange, I miss her even to this day. I ask that you try to remember the good times we had together exploring, hiking, and fishing—just the three of us. The three musketeers, forever. Well, my forever ends soon, and I wanted to tell you I was sorry before I'm gone.

I gave this letter to my attorney and asked him to get it to you once it looks like my time has run out. I'm sorry for everything that's happened over the years. Hope you can forgive me. I only ask that you think of me kindly, if you ever think of me.

Your best friend
Timmy

Carol was nearly in tears when he finished reading. He folded the letter and returned it back to the envelope. Something fell out and trickled to the ground. Mitch picked it up. It was the bird's feather that Timmy had worn so many years before when he put the nest back into the tree. He was proud of him that day, and he had kept it all this time.

"I hope my timing is appropriate?" asked Dan as he rejoined the group.

"Of course. Please join us."

"Where were we?" he asked raising his hand to order another drink.

"We were talking about some changes to the book."

"Ah yes. Our media division is casting about to see who may play the leads in the movie if it goes the way we think it will. But first things first. I think we need to beef up some of the stories of about his brothers and sisters. I think we need to tighten the relationship with his older brother Jack and lastly… we need to remove the character of Sunny. It clouds the substance of the book and the relationships between the two main characters of Timmy and Davey."

Carol's eyes opened wide in shock. "What? That's like ripping out the heart and soul of the book. Sunny is key to the story. You can't just delete her! She's key," said Carol in horror almost screaming inside the quiet restaurant. "You can't do that. I won't allow it." Mitch placed his hand on her knee to calm her down. She glared at him and moved his hand. "This book does not capture your heart without her in it. No way."

"Well, we can talk about some of possible changes in my office tomorrow, perhaps over lunch? We really want this book and I believe we are uniquely positioned to get it maximum exposure in the marketplace." Dan was now the salesman, and he was selling hard, still wanting to make his point while trying to gauge Carol's determination. "If you just think about it as a nostalgia book set in the fifties then Sunny just gets in the way…"

"No," roared Carol defiantly, like a lioness protecting her cub. She was not going to allow any changes to the book especially not that kind of change.

Mitch's head moved from one to the other watching them disagree. He found it amusing and was about to step in as a mediator when he heard a familiar voice.

"Ahhmm. I vote to go with Carol on this one Dan," said a female voice behind them.

Dan Eliot turned and looked up to see his boss, Mrs. Kincaid standing at the table's edge listening to every word.

It was a familiar voice. Mitch turned around and his eyes stared in disbelief. "Mrs. Corcoran? Meg?"

"Hi ya, Mitch. Do you mind if I sit down?" both men quickly rose to find a chair for her and her things. She tossed her brief case and raincoat over the chair and turned to see her old friend.

"Do you two know each other?" Eliot asked in disbelief.

She ignored his question instead turned to Mitch and said, "Yes, but it's been a long time. I can't stay long, I have other commitments tonight. I make a quick stop on the way to the airport then take the corporate jet to California tonight."

Carol watched the interaction of the two and realized something else was going on between then. She just didn't know what was happening

"I have just enough time for a drink, since it looks like Dan and Carol are just about finished here. Am I right, Dan?" she said as she raised her hand for a waiter.

"Yes Ms. Kinkaid. I was just leaving for dinner. Carol, would you care to join me? And we can discuss the ins and outs of this wonderful book."

"Sure Dan, I think that would be a very interesting dinner unless Mitch needs me for anything else? Were you able to get an earlier flight?"

"Yes, it leaves a little after ten o'clock."

She leaned over, kissed him goodbye on the cheek, and said. "It's been fun, Mitch. Now go home and write another book." Then she whispered in his ear so only he could hear, "Call me tomorrow, with all the juicy details." She smiled and said, "Goodnight, Ms. Kinkaid. It was most interesting to meet you."

As they walked away, Meg touched her arm and said to Carol for all to hear, "There is one change I would like to do to the book, a minor change, if you can. Not a deal breaker but…"

Carol looked at her, not relishing a fight with one of the most powerful women in the publishing industry. "Yes… and what would that be?"

"Can we make the librarian, you know, Mrs. Corcoran, well, be a little less frumpy? You know… get rid of the cat lady eyeglasses, long dresses and all?"

Carol began to understand and smiled a wide grin. "Yes, I think that can be arranged." Both Dan and Carol walked away talking and arranging times to meet to begin the process of converting the manuscript to a finished book.

Mitch and Meg watched them leave and then writer and mentor looked at each other and smiled.

She spoke first, "You've done well, Mitch. Your book is very good. I am very pleased for you."

They toasted to each other when the waiter brought her a glass of champagne. "Who would've thought that I'd be reading about my life in a book, and one written by you," she said.

Mitch set his glass down and asked, "What happened to you? One day you were at the library and the next day gone, without a trace."

She moved in her chair and set down her glass. "Years ago, I stole some money from an employer in New Orleans. A lot of money. My husband needed an operation to save his life and we didn't have insurance or the money to pay for it. Turns out it didn't help anyway. He died two months after the operation. Well, when my employer found out I embezzled the money, he pressed charges. I was sentenced to jail and ordered to pay restitution. I got out on bail and skipped town. I ran as far as I could and I thought I was safe when I landed in the small town of Overland Missouri but..."

Mitch interjected, "Then I came along and spoiled it for you. I'm so sorry Meg."

"No, don't worry about it. If it hadn't been you, it would have been somebody else, eventually. After that day at the library I took off on the run again and got as far as Nebraska and changed my mind. I stopped, turned around, and drove to New Orleans where I turned myself in to the authorities." She paused to look at him, taking a sip from her glass.

"I served thirty days in jail and paid all the money back over the next two years. I was also doing two years of community service for the city. I met a man who was on a business trip in Louisiana from New York City. He owned a small publishing company and I told him all about my past. But it didn't seem to matter to him." Meg leaned back in her chair.

He smiled at her. It was great to see her.

Meg continued, "We got married later that year, and he taught me the business and I worked by his side every day until he died of cancer some years later. Then I stepped in to take his place and transformed it into what it is today. Jeff would have been proud. He was a good man, like you Mitch." She smiled and tilted her drink back to finish it then glanced at her watch. She grabbed her coat and briefcase and stood.

"Grandkid bedtimes then off to the airport. Gotta go." She paused. The silence was awkward as the two of them stood saying their goodbyes.

"Wait, I have something for you." She reached inside her handbag, pulled out a gift-wrapped package, and handed it to him. "Go ahead open it."

He tore the off wrapping and saw it was a hardback copy of the book, *Call of the Wild*, by Jack London. He was at a loss for words. It was the book Timmy had thrown into the pool in what seemed like so many centuries earlier.

"It's yours, you paid for it remember? I don't think you ever got a chance to read it, so enjoy it Mitch. So long for now. And now that you know where I am, don't be such a stranger, okay?"

"Sure Meg. It's been great seeing you."

"You too, Mitch." He shook her hand, and then hugged her. She started to leave before turning back said, "About Carol, that one cares Mitch and is a fighter for you. Better hold on to her or I'll steal her away from you and have her come to work for me. I've been looking for a fighter like her to work for me as liaison with other agents."

"She's very good Meg. One of the best."

"So long. Mitch. Have a safe flight back to Florida. Who knows, I may run into you there one day, you know warm days, cool nights, and nice beaches."

"Would love it. Good to see you again, Meg. You take care."

Chapter Thirty-Four

As the plane pulled away from the terminal, he called her. She answered on the first ring.

"Hey baby, I'm coming home, early. I missed you. And not being able to talk today was... terrible. I know we promised no calls, but that was a dumb idea."

"Yeah, you're right." She said, sitting down, slowly rubbing the inside of her legs as she sipped her tea. "I don't think I like these book tours. I miss you, a lot. I mean I really miss you, if you know what I mean."

"Yes, I do," he said, smiling in anticipation. "But hey, I decided this is the last book tour I'm doing. We may do one or two cities for the new book but only if we can do it together and that's it."

"Good," she said firmly. "I'll chill some champagne."

He could sense her telling smile over the phone; it was so sweet, like roses.

"We need to talk when I get home," he said.

"Yes, ... yes we do," she said. "But later."

"Yeah, later. Hey, gotta go now, the steward is motioning for me to stow the phone. I love you."

"I love you too."

The plane lifted from the runway with a forceful but gentle thrush of the powerful jet engines and Mitch settled back in his seat for the two-hour flight back home.

His eyes drooped, it had been a long day but he was finally on his way home. His thoughts drifted back to a quieter and simpler time. He remembered the times with Sunny and her grandmother. He remembered the family dinners, Easter, Christmas, Thanksgiving, all the birthdays, and his mother's homemade pies. His times with his brothers, sisters, and mom and dad. He drifted off to the good times and began to dream.

He was awakened by the lights coming on in the cabin and a voice over the intercom saying:

"Ladies and gentlemen, we are now making our final approach to West Palm Beach International airport. Please fasten your seatbelts and bring your seats and tray tables into their full and upright position. Thank you for flying with us today and welcome to the Palm Beaches."

He bought some daisies for her at an airport kiosk and texted her he had landed then hailed a taxi. He texted her—

ON MY WAY.
SEE YA SOON.
-M

He was getting closer to home, and his heart was racing in anticipation as the taxi headed down I-95 towards Delray. It was late but Delrays' Atlantic Avenue was going strong. The restaurants were still full of patrons and well-tanned tourists who strolled along the streets window-shopping in front of the multiple art galleries. Stuck in slow moving traffic, he drifted off as the car's rhythm on the road lulled him to sleep.

He dreamed of the times when he and Sunny would sit together on the swing on her front porch, both of them reading in the warm summer afternoons with the hint of honeysuckle floating through the air sipping ice-cold lemonade. He would lie with his head in her lap as she read and absentmindedly ever so gently ran her fingers through his hair.

"Okay buddy, you're home. That'll be $36.50, plus tip of course." He threw him a bunch of twenties, grabbed his bags and briefcase.

"Keep the change," he said closing the door and bounded up the steps. He could hear the ocean waves and felt the salt spray on his face. He was so close. His heart was pounding. He would never be away from her again. As he reached the porch that overlooked the ocean he saw her standing there, waiting, watching the waves roll in and roll out.

"Hey baby, I missed you," he said quickly dropping his bags and flowers to the sandy-covered ground.

She turned and saw him, running to him, kissing him trying to take him all in with her kisses. "Oh my God, have I missed you."

"I've missed you too baby." He stepped away. "It's over, finally over. Timmy's gone." She buried her face inside his chest. "I know; I heard on the news" She held him tight, "Don't ever leave me again like that. I've missed you so." Her arms were around him.

"I won't," he managed to say between kisses.

Upstairs in the bedroom with the windows open on the cool night air they heard the ocean waves crash in the background. They made passionate love that night, and then they made gentle caring love, the kind that lasts forever. It was good to be home.

Laying in his arms, she held him close, their legs intertwined amongst each other like honeysuckle vines. He smelled her hair, it smelled of jasmine, sweet jasmine. They lay like that, together for an eternity.

"Did they like the book?" she finally whispered, breaking the silence of the afterglow while her hand traced imaginary figures on his chest.

"They loved the book. They want to publish it so I'll let them iron out the details."

He pulled her closer, "How did the company sale go and the transition with Kim?"

"Good, it went very well. I start teaching at the university in a few weeks. Kim will be good for the company and with her company's backing and marketing support. They'll be able to take the company much further then I could ever have done."

"Are you okay? I'm just sorry I couldn't be here for you."

"You're here now Mitch, that's all that matters but it was time to sell, way beyond time. Strange word—time…" she said her voice drifting off. "The best part is I got a call from their corporate office in Seattle that they will donate $2 million dollars a year for the next five years to the Anna Novak Fund."

He pulled her close, "Wow, baby that's great. Sari, I'm so proud of you. Anna would be too." He kissed her again.

"Thanks, but enough about business. Now I'm all yours, if you'll have me?" she said, tickling his side. "I missed you."

"I missed you too." His hand went to the round coin, which hung about his neck for so many years. He had lost her, now he had found her and was not going to ever let her go. She was his world. She was his sun, she was his Sunny.

"Sunny," he started. It had been years since he had called her by that name. So many years ago. She knew something was about to happen. "You had once said that in your country a woman needed to be asked three times before it was acceptable to be married. Well, I'm asking you again… will you marry me?"

She turned to look at him. "Mitch, we're too old to get married. Marriage is for the young. Besides, we are already married my sweet. Remember so many years ago, we pledged our vows at my home?"

"Marry me," he asked again firmly.

Her eyes opened wide. "You're serious, aren't you?"

"Of course I'm serious. I have never been more serious in my entire life."

She held his hand, "My sweet, we have both lost those we have loved. I lost my Vilari and my dearest Anne. You had your Sandy and Derek taken from you by that monster Timmy. We don't need to marry, we have each other."

"I know that and I am happy just to be with you, but Sunny it was more than an accidental meeting that brought you into that bookstore three years ago where I was doing a book signing. It was kismet. It was meant to be, that's all I'm saying. Meant for us to be together. Marry me; I love you more than anything in the whole world. Now, I have asked you three times to marry me and according to your tradition…" He stood before her as he had done once before as a twelve-year-old boy still so deeply in love. "Unless you don't love me?" he said in horror.

She smiled her wonderful smile. "I love you more than life itself you fool… and you know that. I have always loved you from the very first time I saw you so many years ago."

"Sunny, I want to spend the rest of my life with you."

"Oh Mitch." She stopped for a moment, taking in a deep breath, "Before I say yes, I have something to tell you first. While you were away, I learned that I have …"

He gently placed his finger on her lips, "I know baby, I know. Will you marry me?"

Her hand trembled and her voice quivered, "Yes, I'll marry you. Yes of course, I'll marry you," she shouted.

They were married a month later on the beach at sunrise—to signify the beginning of a new day for both of them. Their closest friends and family were in attendance as they said their vows to one another, including, Kim McCormick, Dan Eliot and Carol and of course Meg Kinkaid, her maid of honor. Her brother Mang and his wife were also there as were his sisters Joanie, Jane, Janet, his brother Jack and Jeremy along with his friends, who all came to witness the long delayed union.

Sunny was dressed in a pink silk kimono with baby's breath sprinkled in her hair and traditional pink pearls strung about her neck.

She smiled then pulled two sheets of paper from her kimono pocket and handed one to him.

He held her hand, looking into each other's eyes and repeated the vows they had made to one another so many years before-

"First we were two streams," she said, "flowing side by side. Now we become one river, only stronger, never to be divided again."

She smiled and read more before she paused for him to say,

"Now it is impossible to see the stream as two, for we shall always be one and never be separate again because we will remain one river. We will always be together and will never again be divided."

Then together they said, "I trust the one I love, I love the one I trust, now and forever," were the last words of their vows. Life was good again and they were friends. They would always be friends, the best of friends.

-The End

Now a special excerpt from Bryan Mooney's bestselling novel-
Love Letters
By
Bryan Mooney

"My Dearest Darling," the love letters began. Try as she might, she could not stop reading the letters she found in the old books. After reading one, she was compelled to reach for another. Her curiosity urged her on. She could not stop…

If *you* found a love letter in an old book, would you read it?

Suppose you purchased some books from a bookseller at a flea market and upon returning home, discovered love letters inside. What would you do? Would you read the letters? Would you try to return them? Would you destroy them?

That is the dilemma in which Katie Kosgrove finds herself when she discovers love letters written by the man she knows only as Jack. Curious but unable to locate him to return the love letters, she begins to read.

The letters all begin with the same greeting, "My Dearest Darling," and they each end with, "Forever, Jack". The letters start to transform her life in ways that she never would have imagined. She is thankful to the handsome stranger she met only once.

Katie knows exactly what she would say to him if she were to ever see him again, until one day he reappears in her life. Their world begins to change once more, but the letters have an awesome power over both of them, until...

Chapter One

Katherine Kosgrove locked the front door of her secondhand bookstore and pushed the large boxes of books to the sofa in front of the fireplace. She made herself comfortable on the old green couch, sitting back with a large glass of wine, soft Latin music playing in the background and her cat Felix snuggling beside her. Katie had saved Felix from certain death at an animal shelter in Boca Raton. Apparently, nobody else wanted a one-eyed cat, but he was her buddy. Independent as hell, like her, but her buddy nonetheless.

Even though it was late, she began to search through the boxes of books she had purchased at the flea market that day. She needed to catalog her new purchases for tomorrow. Felix purred for more food but soon dozed off to sleep. Katie had to be ready for her regular, early Monday morning customers, who would be eager to search through any new books she placed on her "Just Arrived" rack.

While sorting through the first box, she could not help but be reminded of the ruggedly handsome doctor at the flea market who sold them to her. He said his name was Jack and that he was downsizing to a smaller house because his wife had recently passed away. He told her the books belonged to his wife.

The used bookstore, aptly named Secondhand Rose, was housed in a former two-story general store. The main floor downstairs was her bookstore, and the second floor was her apartment. The place had tons of space and the rent was cheap—perfect for her needs. At the rear of the store was an old, rustic stone fireplace. Katie made this area cozy and inviting for her customers. Bookshelves lined the walls, and a sofa faced the working fireplace. It wasn't just pretty, it was functional as well.

Katie's customers could peruse the books they were considering buying or wait out any of the frequent Florida rainstorms; drinking Katie's freshly brewed Tandian orange tea.

She would sometimes light the fire during the rare, cool Florida winter days, when the air became slightly chilly. Sitting there on the sofa, she could still smell the woodsy smoke from the last time the flames burned the old wood on the steel grate. But most of all, Katie enjoyed the stack of white birch logs she usually left on the open grate. They reminded her of home, and the sofa made an inviting and comfortable place to curl up with a good book.

She sorted through the boxes, taking the books out and arranging them by category, condition, and genre. The first box was mainly romance novels, which were her customers' favorites. She found paperbacks written by authors such as Jackie Steil, Robin Macy, Nicholas Sparks, Maureen Hare, Nora Roberts, and Francesca Delarina, among countless others.

There was poetry by Keats, Browning, Frost, and a hardback book of poetry by an unfamiliar poet named Allison White, a book she found buried in the bottom of the box. She placed it in her own personal "to be read" pile.

Katie started forming other piles and was nearly done with the first box when she found the classic *Rebecca* by Daphne du Maurier, the twisted classic love story her mother enjoyed reading. Her mother loved it so much she had wanted to name her daughter either Rebecca or Daphne, but Katie's father would have none of it. Instead, she was named Katherine, after her paternal grandmother.

Her mother, the ballet dancer Roberta Casina, grew up outside the town of Big Sky, Wyoming, on a large cattle ranch, and spent most of her idle time reading. Katie went back to the ranch many times with her mother when her parents fought. She loved its wide-open spaces and undisturbed view of the heavenly stars. The ranch was sold at her father's insistence when he ran into financial troubles. Her mother never said a word about it, but Katie always knew she resented the loss. The last time Katie was there was to scatter her mother's ashes across the wildflower fields.

Next, she came across her favorite, *Wuthering Heights*, by Emily Brontë . "Heathcliff," she murmured out loud, her voice emulating the tone of the novel. "Heathcliff," she sighed again, the sound of an impassioned memory, causing Felix to raise his sleepy head and glance at her.

"Go back to sleep," she said to her feline fur ball, caressing his forehead. "Back, back to sleep, back to sleep," she soothed, and he was soon purring again, dreaming whatever it was that cats dreamt.

Her mind wandered back to the man at the flea market who had sold her the books. He reminded her of some Hollywood movie star, rugged good looks, tall, with broad shoulders and an easy smile. He was the type you would recognize in an instant but could not place his name.

She glanced through the classic Brontë novel, and even though she'd read it countless times, she always found the immortal love story mesmerizing. She smiled to herself, holding the cherished book in her hand. *Jack's wife had very good taste,* she thought, tossing it onto her growing "to be read" pile.

The book bounced off the sofa and landed on the floor, and what appeared to be a handwritten note spilled out onto the carpet in front of her. Katie reached for the piece of paper lying on the floor.

She unfolded the blue-lined note paper and read the first line of the handwritten letter:

My Dearest Darling.

Katie's eyes widened. *Whoa. Oh, my God, this is a treat and a treasure. Most women don't get to read love letters, and far fewer have love letters written to them. What do we have here? Most men have trouble writing and remembering a grocery list.*

She clutched the letter tightly to her chest, looking around to see if anyone saw her reading someone else's love letter. It was a reflex. *Of course there's no one here. It's one A.M. Just Felix and me.*

Katie had to know more. She glanced at the blue paper. This could be a private, personal letter, but she could not resist reading on. Her curiosity got the better of her. Felix yawned in his sleep. "I know, I know what curiosity has done to cats," she whispered, then began to read.

March 2007
My Dearest Darling,

I saw a sunset today, a beautiful sunset. It reminded me of you and of us. Do you recall how we would measure our days by the sunsets we saw? We would always take the time to stop and watch them, no matter where we were.

Remember the orange and red sunset over the plains of the Serengeti—we held hands like school kids and drew each other close, hearing the lions roar just beyond our fires. Remember the awe-inspiring sunset on the Greek island of Petros? Do you recall the marvelous sunset from the top of the hills overlooking

Molokai? Oh, that magical Hawaiian island, shrouded in rainbows every day, from the wondrous mornings until the cool nightfall. And remember the sunrises on the beach in Panama? But the ones I recall most fondly were the morning sunrises on the beach of Islamorada in the Keys. It was always enough to take my breath away, as long as I was there with you, my love.

Breathtaking! The simple, silent beauty. There is nothing on earth like it, and to spend it with you was gold.

My favorite sunset of all time was on our cruise. We were dining on board, sailing the blue-green waters of the Caribbean. From our table, we could faintly see the soft, yellow rays of the setting sun. Together, we grabbed our champagne glasses and left our dinner to be alone. We watched the most gorgeous sunset of all. I cherish times such as those, my love.

Every time I see a sunset, I think of you and remember your beauty and what you mean to me. Each sunrise and sunset brings us closer together. Which sunsets do you recall as your favorite? Which sunrises do you cherish? I count the sunsets until we are together again.

I love you and miss you.

Forever,
Jack

"Wow, how romantic can you get?" Katie took a large, loud gulp of wine. The letter was signed simply, *Jack*. No last name. It had to be the same good-looking Jack she bought the books from. He must have written these letters to his wife.

That was some letter. Jack and his Dearest Darling really cared for one another. Then Katie remembered he'd told her his wife died a while back.

This fellow, Jack, he really loved her. He knew what his wife wanted. She wanted what every woman wants. Simple, really, Katie thought, *we want love and happiness coupled with trust and respect. Everything else is just fluff. Nothing else matters.*

She gazed at the hand-written letter she held. Why didn't he keep the letter? Maybe he didn't know it was in the book? He would most likely want it back if he knew. That she was sure of. Sort of.

I should read the letter again to see if there are any clues, like his last name or contact information, then I could return it. Yes, that's what I'll do. She reread the letter—twice. Nothing. It was a letter he wrote to someone else, and Katie had no right to read it. She refolded it and set it on the sofa next to her.

Somehow, this letter made her think about her ex-husband, Richard. He could never have written anything like this. He was incapable of that kind of passion, that kind of tenderness. Richard could never be that open or vulnerable. There was raw emotion pouring from this man's heart. Jack's wife had been a very lucky woman. The letter gave her hope that there were still some good men out there.

Reluctantly, she pushed it farther away from her. She still had two more large boxes to sort through and it was getting late. She pulled out the last book from the first box. It was a very large medical surgery book. Would any of her customers buy a medical book? She tossed it into her "miscellaneous" pile.

The large book hit the pile with a thud, rolling over on its side. Something stuck out from the bottom of the book. A bookmark? Or another love note? She retrieved the book from the pile, opened it to the marked page, and found a one hundred dollar bill.

Her mouth fell open in shock. What was going on here? Didn't people check these things before they brought them to a flea market? She scrambled to her knees, now determined to go through every book she had purchased at the flea market. Katie was on a mission.

She searched through all the books from the first box, examining each book, turning them upside down and shaking them to see if anything came out before moving on to the next box of books. The second and third boxes yielded more money and other letters, each written on different colored paper.

When she opened the other ones she noticed each one had the same handwriting and signature, *Forever, Jack,* and the same opening, *My Dearest Darling.*

By the time she was finished, Katie had found in excess of three hundred dollars in cash and over thirty love letters. She could not believe all the money she had found, but even so, the letters were more precious than money.

Katie sat there, with her found money in one hand and the love letters in the other. She took the bills and put them into a plain white envelope, and after sealing it, she wrote on the outside of the envelope one word: *Jack.* She tucked it inside her cash register.

She sat down, made herself comfortable, and took a deep breath. She found she was unable to move, holding the treasured stack of correspondence close to her heart. She had read only one completely through, but she felt something happening inside of her, inside her heart. Something good.

Why didn't he just send his wife an email? A handwritten letter was more romantic, she argued with herself, but an email would get there faster.

Katie arranged the letters by date, starting with the first one, dated February 2007. It was then she noticed that they all only included the month and year at the top of the page. Picking up another one, she realized the first letter she had read was actually the second one he wrote.

Should she read them all now or ration them, like she did with chocolates? Or should she just bundle them away? She took another large sip of wine and settled in to read.

Since the first one I read didn't contain any contact information, maybe the next one will help me find out more about him so I can return these letters, she reasoned.

Katie paused for a moment, but try as she might, she could not stop reading. She reached for another, then another. She felt urged on.

> *February 2007*
> *My Dearest Darling,*
>
> *I miss you. Some feelings are expressed so simply. This separation is beyond my control, for you know if it were in my power, I would be there by your side. This journey will take time. Time that I know cannot be replaced. Like the sands of an hourglass, one grain at a time, it drops away, silently but evermore, never to be found again. I will write you. Be comforted by the fact you will always be in my thoughts.*
>
> *Remember, just a short few weeks ago, we celebrated New Year's Eve at the Grand Gala at the Club. You looked breathtaking in your shimmering evening gown, and I know you loved me in my tux as we moved around the dance floor. I love dancing with you. We both agreed those dance lessons certainly paid off, as we spiraled the waltz together, moved to the beat of the samba and the cha cha, and set the dance floor afire with the closeness of our tango. The thunderous applause was always for you, your beauty and grace.*
>
> *Then the band had to play your favorite song, "MacArthur Park," and you looked at me, grabbed my hand and the champagne, and we rushed to the beach to welcome in the New*

Year. Your gown and my shoes were ruined from the choppy waves, but it was a New Year's Eve we will never forget. I hate the beach, but it was still the best way to celebrate the New Year. We always believed that how you spend New Year's Eve is how you spend the rest of the year. Not this year, I am afraid, my love. I love you, my dearest, always remember that. Must go.

Forever,

Jack

She studied the intimate correspondence, which spoke so eloquently to the love he obviously felt for his wife. Katie held it to her chest and took a deep breath, but so far, she was no closer to finding out anything more about him. He had said he belonged to some club. What was the name of that club? She looked again. No luck.

Where was he writing from? Why was he writing? Why didn't he just go to her? Or call her? Was he in the navy? In Africa? Why couldn't he call her or say anything about where he was? Maybe he was on a secret spy mission and was sworn not to speak about it? But he was so handsome and seemed so honest. Maybe he was in jail? He didn't look like a jailbird, though.

His letters sounded as if he could write volumes to this woman he loved. Katie refolded the letter on her lap. She read February and March and now held April in her hands. No, these letters were too private. *They were not written to me. I am returning them tomorrow,* she told herself. *Yes, first thing tomorrow. I will call the people who run the flea market and get his address from them.* She smiled. It would be good to see him again.

April's letter was still in her hand; she caressed it with her fingers. She was surrounded by piles of books on the floor, and the precious letters were piled on top of her as she lay on her sofa. Katie took another sip of wine, stroked the soft hair on Felix's back, and thought about her wonderful day with the letter slipping from her hand. Her dreams swept her away into a land of love. A land she desperately wanted to visit. A place where she could fall in love again.

Chapter Two

Katie was awakened by a loud, metallic tapping sound. *Tap, tap, tap.* She opened her eyes and found herself still lying on the sofa where she had fallen asleep the night before, right in front of the fireplace with the letters piled high on top of her. She had slept through the night—her first night without her horrible nightmare. The tapping began again. She looked at her watch: seven forty-five A.M.

She picked herself up and looked over the sofa. She heard the noise again. It was Donna McIntyre, always her first, and best, Monday morning customer. Donna wanted to be there bright and early so she could be first to peruse any new inventory.

Katie dragged herself from the sofa and unlocked the front door, then opened it, causing the door chime to ring.

"Morning, Kate, did you hear the news? They got him! They got the terrorist, *Numero Uno*! They sent in a SEAL team after locating him in Pakistan. Can you believe it? He was in Pakistan? Just where they thought he was all along. He was living in some big mansion. Go figure."

Kate moaned a sleepy reply to her loquacious customer.

"Got any good stuff? Any new books? Any new Nicholas Sparks or Nora Roberts?" Donna asked changing the conversation. The former school principal loved to thumb through books and would usually buy three to six at a time, sometimes more.

Donna was tall and thin and looked just like the principal, Mrs. Moranski, at Katie's grade school. She always wore a long black dress, even in the hot Florida sun. Her glasses were perched high on her forehead, and she wore a long silk scarf around her neck. She nearly shrieked when she saw the piles of books scattered on the floor around the sofa.

"Very good," Donna said to no one in particular. She grabbed a number of books and plopped down on the comfy sofa, lost to the world.

Katie looked through the large front windows and noticed that for some reason the store seemed particularly dark and dreary, even though the Florida sun shone bright. She tucked all of the letters into the side pocket of her wrinkled sweatshirt, examining the store and her longtime customer.

"Make yourself comfortable, Donna. I think I am going to take down these old drapes in the front, so it may get a little dusty in here. The place looks so dark."

"You know, you are right. I never noticed it before." Donna looked up from her growing stack of books on the floor next to the sofa including her sought after Nicholas Sparks and Nora Roberts novels.

A vision of bright light soon engulfed the shop.

"Wow, what a difference!" Donna said, when the huge green velour drapes came crashing down in a pile of dust.

Katie stood and admired her handiwork but then groaned when it became apparent that the sunlight had exposed smudged, dirty windows. "Time for a bucket of water, some rags, and Windex," she said to herself, as Donna was again engrossed in her own little book world.

When Katie was done, the store was bright and airy. The front of the store shone like never before. She'd need to put some new plants in the front windows, she thought. She stood back by the sofa and breathed a deep sigh.

Her gaze fell on the small pile of medical books from the flea market. She picked them up and placed them on a shelf near the front of the store. She was not going to buy them, but at the last moment figured, what the heck? Her customers were always surprising her as to what they would and would not buy. On top of the shelf, she prominently displayed the largest and thickest book, titled *The Surgeon's Guide to Thoracic and Cardiovascular Surgery*.

"There you go, Jack," she said to the black-and-green book. "See, even if you are not here, I can still talk to you. You can be my Wilson," she said, thinking of the movie *Cast Away* with Tom Hanks. The book became her inanimate friend and confidant.

"I'm sorry, Katie, did you say something to me?"

"No, I was just thinking out loud. I do that a lot. Donna, I'm going upstairs to take a shower and will be back down soon. If you find anything you like, you know the drill; just leave the money on the register."

"Sure. Take your time. I'll keep an eye on things for you here."

"Hey, Donna, I have a question for you."

"Sure," she said, without even looking up from her new hoard of books. "Fire away."

"If you found a love letter in an old book, would you read it?"

"Of course! But I wouldn't know it was a love letter until I started reading it, you see. And besides, maybe it would have the person's address inside. Then I would know where to return it. But I would also be curious as hell. Why? Are there any love letters in here?" she asked expectantly, finally looking up from her books.

"No. No, there weren't any."

The door chimes sounded again as the front door opened, and they both looked up to see one of Katie's strangest customers, Sidney, walk through the door. He was a fixture in Delray, another one of the quirky things about the small town that always amused Katie.

But looking at him in her shop always gave Katie chills. He wore the same clothes every time she saw him, torn and tattered and with an old baseball cap covering his balding head. He always came in, asked for certain books, and then, not finding them, would turn and leave. *Strange dude with a peculiar homeless smell indeed,* Katie mused to herself. Some customers she could just do without. Once, she was pretty certain he'd followed one of her customers down the street. Katie thought he was just coming into her store to see her. He was definitely a strange dude.

"Morning," he mumbled to both of them. "Get any Raymond Chandler books in, Miss Kate?" His voice was slurred, making it sound more like an accusation than a question.

"No, Sidney. No Raymond Chandler books today. Sorry." If she ever found any at a flea market she would not buy them, fearing it would keep him coming back for more, but he never got the hint and kept coming back anyway.

He glanced at her, his dark, brooding eyes chilling the room. He looked at them both for much too long, not saying a word, before turning and leaving without so much as a goodbye.

Once he was gone, Donna shivered before saying, "Now there goes a mass murderer. But that's just my opinion," she quickly added.

"Yes, but so far he's been harmless," said Katie, trying to calm her down.

"Yeah, they say they are all like that and you never know what they are really thinking until something clicks inside their head and then boom, they explode. By then it's too late. Do you keep a gun in here, Kate?"

"No, I don't. Hey listen, I'll be back in a little while. I am just going upstairs for a bit. If you leave before I get back down, just leave me a note with how many books you left with, okay?"

"Sure, Katie. No problem."

Katie clutched all of the letters and headed upstairs. With a sigh, she sat down on her bed, laying the letters down beside her, anxious to read more. Felix came out from his secret space underneath the bed and slid next to her, purring and rubbing against her.

Reading the letters was becoming addictive, but she needed to know what was in them even though it was a one-way conversation. Maybe she could just read one more while the water heated for her shower.

April 2007
My Dearest Darling,
*   I have tried to...*

To read more of **Love Letters** or to order other books by Bryan Mooney they can be found wherever fine books are sold.

Made in the USA
Columbia, SC
14 March 2024

33050523R00128